Gillian White is a journalist and lives in Devon. She has four children.

Critical acclaim for Gillian White:

'A rich and wonderful tale of conspiracy and domestic infamy'   FAY WELDON

'Here is a marvellously exciting new writer. She tingles one's spine. She makes you think about people. She's marvellously literate and the similes really bring the writing to life'

JILLY COOPER

'A gripping read'   *Today*

'A novelist of the highest quality . . . an intense and vividly-written novel which takes you by the throat and won't let go: a splendid book for those who enjoy a psychological thriller with a deep and provocative story'

Sunday Independent

ALSO BY GILLIAN WHITE

The Plague Stone
Nasty Habits
Rich Deceiver
Mothertime
Grandfather's Footsteps

The Crow Biddy

GILLIAN WHITE

PHŒNIX

A PHOENIX PAPERBACK

First published in Great Britain
by Random Century Group in 1990
This paperback edition published in 1994
by Phoenix,
a division of Orion Books Ltd,
Orion House, 5 Upper St Martin's Lane,
London WC2H 9EA

A CIP catalogue record for this book is available from the
British Library.

ISBN: 1 85799 204 0

Printed and bound in Great Britain by
The Guernsey Press Company Ltd,
Vale, Guernsey, Channel Islands.

For
Sarah, Caroline, Sybilla, Martin,
and gothic Seth, the sixth one, who was so
pushy at Bantham. With love.

*'Hush ye, hush ye, little pet ye
Hush ye, hush ye, do not fret ye,
The Crow Biddy shall not get ye.'*

One

Dame Elouise Clough-Ellis touches the autumn leaves with the tip of a bronze boot. A statue to iron endurance. Her eyes, deep in their moulded sockets, look uncannily deader than death and water drips from her nose and her tarnished fingers because Appleyard, a long-stay patient from Underwood Hospital, has just given her her monthly hosing down.

'There,' he says. 'That's done.'

It is Appleyard's last job of the day before he winds up his hose and dumps it along with his earthy rakes and his spade into the wheelbarrow, to be taken back to the shed, tidied and put neatly away before he makes his way home to his ward and the high tea that will be awaiting him. Tuesday – scrambled eggs and chocolate ice cream tonight. Appleyard, puffing moistly on his pipe, is always glad to get out of this bit of garden. Because of his condition it is important that he avoid thoughts and places that might circle him and pull him down. And this bit of garden, especially in autumn, he thinks to himself as the wheel of the wooden barrow squeals up the narrow, box-hedged path towards the vegetable garden, is definitely such a place.

Years and years ago when Appleyard was a young man, in the days when they gave ECT without anaesthetic and used leather straps, years and years ago he had scrubbed Dame Elouise Clough-Ellis with a mixture of turpentine and emery powder given to him by Hunter, Farendon School's head gardener. Got between her folds and undulations with a tough little wire brush used for difficult flowerpots. Oh, he wouldn't have dreamed up the idea on his own, the Founder was far too austere a personage for that, he'd never have dared, he would have thought it desecration. But Hunter insisted and Appleyard put it off and put it off until one day Hunter teased him with, 'What's the matter, Appleyard? Too much of a woman for you, is she?' And gave him the mixture

1

ready prepared and a dreadfully intimate selection of brushes.

And after the experience, after wiping the smooth arms, the waxen buttocks (under the skirts, of course, but he could feel the buttocks there), the spindly ankles and the great, round pigeon breasts, Appleyard found himself apologising. His knuckles and wrists looked huge next to her neat little ones. The hair on the backs of his forearms, compared to all the smooth rotundness of her Queen Victoria jowls, seemed coarse and animal. Now whether he had done something to the eyes – dislodged something, maybe – or whether he hadn't, from that day on (and there is no doubt about it) Dame Elouise Clough-Ellis gives Appleyard the glad eye every time he rounds the corner into the lawned expanse of Farendon's front approaches. Her smile isn't pious, after all. It is fleshily sensual. And Appleyard finds her quite shocking.

It is drizzly. The day has never turned properly on, the sky has never coloured. But now the dusk is full of vaporous autumn, the grass dripping damp round the brick walls of the potting shed as Appleyard shrugs himself into his macintosh. Before he leaves he pokes an old bonfire still smouldering in the corner and stamps the loose soil from his heavy boots. In the distance the bell rings for supper. He is too far away to hear but Appleyard imagines he can hear the chattering of girls as they cross the quad from their various houses, obligatory cloaks thrown over shoulders as they skirt the browning oak with its rustic seat, the kissing bench. No games after supper until the spring term, now. No point in him working overtime in order to observe, scythe in hand down among the lush grass by the side of the hockey pitch, breasts and thighs . . . breasts and thighs and white flesh wrapped in high-pitched squeals. No point in sloping back to the cloakroom where tunics and shirts hang haphazard from pegs and black stockings are strewn across the benches like crazy legs.

And in the summer – tennis. There is always work to be done by the chain-link fences down at the tennis courts. And often Appleyard is called to the swimming pool in order to scoop out some decaying mammal – once it was a fox with a brush sodden and heavy, wringing wet – so that the young ladies can swim in uncontaminated water. But the girls aren't neat like they used to be. No short tunics and black stockings any more. No longer those little cotton shifts, tied tight round the waist for games, that make them look like lime-green nymphettes in a grassy underworld.

The Founder, surely, would not have approved of this new modern look, or would she? She is perched on a plinth on the central sweep of lawn before the Gothic entrance, reading and giving nothing away. Round her, at half-terms and holidays, sweep the powerful, long-nosed conveyances of parents as they negotiate the chain of puddles and swing round the final bend to confront the school after a half-mile approach between lakes and rhododendrons, upwards ever upwards, getting glimpses of the clock-tower above the door which fades and reappears, flickering like a lovingly made home movie.

Farendon is built like a child's greystone fort without the drawbridge or the castellations, as if the Founder had feared that one day her girls might find themselves under attack. You could walk right round the flat rooftop which is, however, strictly out of bounds. The school forms an oblong round a quadrangle and in the middle of the quadrangle, softening the whole rather aggressive effect, is a 250-year-old oak: every autumn Appleyard has to barrow the leaves out through the front door, because it is the only approach wide enough.

The front, downstairs part of the oblong forms the School proper and upstairs is School House. The lefthand, lower ridge of buildings accommodates St Hilda's and opposite, on the right, St Joan's. And on the furthest side of the quad the long, low building that matches the School in length is divided into two houses, St Claire's and St Mary's.

Appleyard hears the regular night-sounds of the School, as familiar to him as the bubbling sounds inside his own body, as he pulls on his bobble hat and starts down the drive. The bass beat of heavy metal music, the occasional hoot of a whistling kettle, chords and arpeggios from the music rooms and the sound of voices in perfect harmony from the choir, practising in the chapel in the woods. Safe sounds. Sounds he is easy with.

Will they let him come here still after they move him?

They say they are closing the Hospital down and that they will find him a home somewhere in the town, but he tries not to think about that. Mr Robbie, Appleyard's psychiatrist, explained this to him last month in that grieving voice he uses to impart bad news.

'Now you will be given an opportunity to speak out, Norman,' he said, folding himself over his chair, finding a comfortable position for his chin, accentuating the over-large cleft in it as he assumed the position of thinker. 'After all, Underwood has always been your home and moving at this stage in your life might well be traumatic for you. But it will be done gently over a period of months so that you get used to the changes . . . nothing sudden will happen, I promise you that.'

Appleyard nodded on a nonexistent neck and pretended he understood. His smile was institutionally ever-ready. He wondered, if this was such a good idea, if it was full of the enormous implications Mr Robbie said it was, why it hadn't been done before. He had lived in Underwood since he was ten years old, most of those years on the same ward, the first five in bed. He couldn't quite understand what Mr Robbie meant by 'moving out'. But Appleyard sensed it would be all right. Someone would look after him. They always had, hadn't they? Appleyard smiled again.

Robert Cohen regarded his patient with baleful eyes. You could stare at Norman Appleyard and find your eyes spiralling for no clear reason. If you stared long enough you virtually experienced trance, as if Appleyard's emptiness was pulling you, sucking you into his own void, drawing you into his own black hole as if he was employing some sort of magnetism, and it then took great effort to draw back again. Poor devil. Poor, brainless, creepy innocent.

In spite of a lifetime of pallid slops, eggy puddings and sticky medication, Norman was remarkably rounded and fit. And not a strand of grey in that coarse brown hair, not a line on his face. But the unblaming eyes were penetrating, and it was the gap between his two front teeth that made his face seem childlike. Norman Appleyard went stone deaf in his

4

teens and nobody noticed until an alert junior doctor decided to syringe his ears. Robert Cohen sighed and felt, again, a deep sense of shame. Norman would never survive outside. Hell, how Cohen hated this role of devil's advocate.

Norman Appleyard walks on rusty leaves down the winding drive towards the main road where he comes out of the myopic safety of Farendon School and feels the world's invasion pressing against his head like rubber pads. Nearly at the railings beside the road where staked and spindly sycamores replace the blighted elms, he thinks he hears a scuffling in the bushes . . . a badger, perhaps, or a pheasant trying to hide . . . stupid birds, pheasants. Appleyard stops and sniffs. Searches in his pocket for his handkerchief. Someone told him once that they guessed where he came from because only Underwood patients still used name-taped handkerchiefs, Underwood patients and boarding-school girls. By the bridge is the usual five-thirty traffic jam and Appleyard hates to walk along beside the cars because you can feel the people inside staring at you and talking about you, especially if you are forced to keep pace with them.

Appleyard loves his work. He glories when his back groans and sweat sheens his face. With his fingers in the soil or the bite of his spade in the earth he is free, for a while, from himself. Work puts the other aches out. Working hard keeps the blackness away. He hates Bank Holidays and Sundays, he especially loathes Christmas. Autumn is a worrying, melancholy time during which he likes to work extra hard and now, as the darkness envelops him, he resents it as anyone else would resent being interrupted during a specially good television play.

But you can't shout at the darkness and tell it to go away.

Three-quarters of a mile to get yourself home. Over the river with your head thrust forward and your scarf across your chest, reflected in the staid, green water you can see the Hospital walls floating in the street lights. Here you join with other, ordinary people making their way home from work with packs on their backs and toolbags. A clutch of head-scarfed women gabble on a corner. Appleyard wants to stop

5

and pick up the litter in the gutters, it offends him. There is never any litter in the Farendon grounds, he sees to that, he and his trolley and his industrial waste bags.

Humble shops only in this part of the city . . . shabby tobacconists selling lighters and floppy birthday cards . . . a tool-hire shop with chainsaws decked with ribbons to give them window appeal . . . a hardware display of galvanised stepladders and gaudy washing baskets. Across the crossing, watching carefully for the little green man, and through the tall gates he goes, joining with the first early visitors who bear white-wrapped bunches of flowers like babies in shawls in their arms. Some bang the bundles loosely against their knees, slouched a little – with shame, that they should be visiting such a hospital at all? Or have their beaten bearings been a factor of breakdown in the first place?

The time on the clock in the entrance hall, so big you can see the hand moving round in surreptitious little jerks, tells Appleyard that his journey has taken him fourteen and a half minutes. He knows because he has timed his departure by the clock on the Farendon tower – and that was at five thirty-two.

Appleyard likes to keep a check on the minutes of his life, to make quite sure that someone, somewhere, isn't trying to take them away from him. Because he doesn't trust them, no he doesn't, he doesn't trust them an inch.

Two

Old girls.

Old girls who don't like to think about their schooldays and who never go back to reunions.

A hundred miles and a world away from Farendon one such old girl sits in the Priest's House, thinks of the Priest's House wryly as her *Innisfree* for recital of which she won, at school, the Bernard Trefold Elocution Prize. The Priest's House at Ashbury is 'of clay and wattles made', quite probably, and in it Molly Tarrent daubs with pen on pad while the night clouds gather. And the slithering plaster within the house's old walls could well be said to sound like linnets' wings.

Molly wrestles with a problem as she sits at the mullioned window with the firelight crackling behind her. And that problem is – how can she turn Jesus into Crispin?

She sucks her pen and brings neat eyebrows together, creates two furrows over a snubbish, freckled nose. Tap tap tap, her teeth are tiny like baby teeth and as pearly white. She hasn't done her 'homework' and it is the writing group tonight. 'Jesus' is the topic but it could be 'Madness', 'Sacrifice', 'In My Mother's Kitchen' – it could be any subject at all but it is all the same to Molly because she will write about Crispin. She will find a way. Shocking them all into appalled silence with her vitriolic pen. This clean, red woman with a face as shiny and scrubbed as any farmer's, with her pony tail and her dungarees, shocks them into silence every week like that.

But Jesus?

Writing for Ourselves is the heading for which the group gets its grant from the WEA. And writing for themselves is precisely what they do, for someone is always going through, heading for or recuperating from a crisis. And what better way to get it safely out . . .

7

Jesus, Jesus, Jesus. Molly taps her teeth with her Bic and is lulled by the sound she makes – a night clock ticking. She calls for help from the sky with wide blue eyes, from her glass with her lips. *Jesus*.

Why does she have to change anything at all? Crispin is goddamn Jesus, after all. Except that with his crinkly black hair and the gold tooth just where his smile starts, he looks more like the Devil. And he does Devil things, like marrying Rose. After eighteen years of marriage to her he ups and offs and marries Rose.

Leaving Molly in the Priest's House which they bought together as a holiday home, leaving Molly in the Priest's House, weeping between the bean rows. And the currant bushes. And the nests in the thatch where the birds twitter happily each morning outside the bedroom that used to be hers and Crispin's.

And now Rose is pregnant. Just when the twins are eighteen and leaving home.

When the telephone rings, Molly jumps for she is out in the Wilderness for forty days and forty nights with a hircine Crispin – a lewd-mouthed Mary Magdalene stalking him among the crags and knowing exactly how she wants to love him in this landscape of biblical browns. Only knowing now, of course, now it is too late . . .

It is Effie Tate from the writing group on the telephone and she says in her usual brisk, busy way, 'Got a problem. Someone here. Wants to come tonight.'

'Who is it?' The new phone, the stupid lightweight new phone has to be held by an elbow to its moorings or it will fall to the floor. How could anyone design such a monster to replace the sturdy old GPO instrument with its friendly dialling face? Things lightweight and simpering, like Rose, seem to be the vogue these days, replacing anything well-tried and familiar. Even the Volvo, she's been told by Charlie at Gant's Garage – she insisted on keeping the Volvo – runs, nowadays, on a Renault engine.

'A client of Roger's . . .'

'A client?'

8

'She's really terribly nice or I wouldn't be asking.'

'But you don't know her?'

'I didn't know her,' says Effie, her voice low and confidential. 'But I know her now. She's been here all day talking money with Roger. She'll fit in. She's okay. Believe me.'

Sometimes Effie doesn't treat the writing group with the reverence it deserves. Effie is not a reverent person and vaguely Molly wonders what she will do with the Jesus theme. But Molly doesn't really care. Let the woman come. Let the stranger come. Let anyone come. What, at the end of the day, does it matter?

She tells Effie, 'You'd better check with everyone else. You know how wounded Jessica can get.'

'I will. See you later.'

'By the way, what's her name?'

'Erica,' says Effie with the phone already half-down. 'Erica Bryant. Poor thing's a widow. It's all terribly sad.'

Don't know that name. Can't be from round here. Must get back to Jesus.

Memories that for years Molly tried to push to her far subconscious, memories too dangerous to deal with, they are always there when she starts to write, they waver round the fuse with all the white-menace of a nursery night-light, vaporous, shadowy, but Molly never lets them in. Farendon memories and the sight of Amy Macey's mother's face . . .

Old girls. Olden days.

If she has to think about it Molly tries her hardest to focus on the good . . . what there was of it. Twenty years, and still she can give 'it' no name.

She has more recent, bolder memories than that to concentrate on at the moment, however, and the blank page meekly calls for her abuse of it. The page is her victim, her pen the weapon with which she will stab and stab and stab . . . poisonous . . . if only she could stab at Rose like that.

Extraordinarily, they were walking on the river bank by the Garden House Hotel (it was Olly and Edward's Speech Day at the Leys School in Cambridge) when he told her. It would have been extraordinary anywhere, the venue had nothing to do with the shockingness of it. She was wearing a hat when he told her, a hat of squashed flowers rather like a bathing cap worn by synchronised swimmers. That's the sort of woman she'd been just three years ago, the sort who wore hats and flimsy two-pieces in lilac. She felt like a synchronised swimmer, too, slow and silly, and would have liked to raise a graceful leg and clock him under his chin. But her leg wasn't graceful. It had a lilac court shoe on the end and it was fat. Honestly, she hadn't known a thing about their affair. That was almost the worst part of all – feeling a fool. She'd even been making plans in her head about how it would be with an empty nest . . . four straight 'A's and the twins were parting, Olly to Oxford, and Edward staying in Cambridge. And Crispin had told her. His face shadowed by weeping willow, flickering greenly with willow and water and his eyes as fathomless as the dark pools disturbed by the wandering punts.

'It seemed to me to be the appropriate time . . .'

That phrase stood out. So did, 'I wanted to wait to see the boys through . . .' and 'while you still have a chance for a separate life of your own'.

Jesus wept . . . the shortest verse . . . Crispin had wept . . . but had she? She saw then that life seemed always to have carried her along, always just carried her along and in this same way she was always 'told' things and then had to cope with them. Molly had got in the car and driven straight off to the Priest's House. Foolish? She shouldn't have left him with their house Little Court, shouldn't have left the way so clear for Rose just to walk in.

Perhaps it was because she behaved so well at the beginning that Molly, at the end, was behaving so disgracefully.

Eight o'clock at Effie's . . . Molly wanders up the road clutching 'Jesus' to her breast. They take turns to play hostess to the group. Well, it's no trouble, just tea and biscuits, although there have been evenings when the whole thing has sunk into a catastrophic débâcle of heavy drinking in smoke-filled rooms.

Effie is allowed to use Roger's study. It tends to be all rather formal at Effie's house, and dizzying, too, since Roger Tate has taken to plastering his walls with prints of weird perspective by a Dutchman called Escher.

Greeted with a kiss, Molly wanders in mindlessly, following the tile squares over the kitchen floor while she watches Effie's stranger filling the kettle with her back to the room – and that isn't Erica Bryant at all! *That is Erica Chorley!* It is dark outside Effie's kitchen window so Molly can see the face reflected . . . and the sight of Erica Chorley, after all these years, turning up in Effie's house at Ashbury so unexpectedly, nearly stops Molly's heart.

Molly knows she is staring. Erica is tall and dressed in a sophisticated coat-dress of black. Mourning? Erica? Necklaces and bangles seem to hang off her everywhere as if she's just slung them on in order to come out, in the way that Molly would slip on her gardening shoes. Erica jangles expensively. And Effie's kitchen doesn't smell piney any more, it smells richly of Sand. Erica's hair is cunningly cut in the way only London people ever achieve, casual but deliberate in the course it takes past her ears to rest on her high-collared shoulders. Very sophisticated indeed, looks Erica.

Molly's memory, scrolling for anything rather than 'that', conjures up an image of a tall, wide-mouthed girl (she's always wanted a mouth like that, you can do so much more with such less effort with a mouth like that than you can with a prim one), a tall girl with thick brown hair in a plait that started at the top of her head and went nearly to her waist. Now that same brown hair is what Boots' own make calls 'Burgundy', but instead of a violent petroleum, Erica's is the kind of Burgundy you hope for when you buy the packet. And it hasn't gone matt. There are lots of lights in it.

Erica is pale and twitchy. Erica looks ill. She must have taken the recent death of her husband very badly. Erica used to play right-attack wing in the first lacrosse team while Molly, if picked at all, was despairingly put in as a back. But mostly she was put in the little crowd at the edge, watching and getting cold.

'Tea or coffee?'

Molly has to think hard to answer Effie's question because a vision of Erica comes back to her so clearly it is too much to deal with. She has to stay with this vision. It is safe, it will keep the other ones out.

Square-necked gymslips with box pleats, Erica's tied so low her bottom used to stick out over the top and she rolled her sleeves up like a man. White knicker-liners under green bloomers. Erica's elastic was always breaking and she went round with one leg to her knee and the other rolled up. But even in her excitement at recalling such remarkable memories Molly realises with a sudden, piercing pain that she, unlike Erica, is not memorable, that even these memories are not good memories, and that the thrill she feels comes from the achievement of the recall rather than the actuality of it.

Erica will not remember her! Erica, perhaps, does not dwell on 'that'. Erica might even have forgotten all about 'it'.

And then Erica Chorley, her eyes, her amber eyes no less bright but her mouth a touch sadder than Molly remembers it, turns round and says, 'Fatty! Is it you? Oh, thank God! Thank God you turned up at a time like this!'

'A time like this?' and Molly Tarrent turns white. Still suffering from shock, she notes with anxiety that her legs have turned into sausage balloons and she can hardly stand. 'Why, Horse, what's wrong?' And Molly pulls herself together enough to feign surprise.

Together at the table in Roger's study waiting for the others.

The shock of meeting over, they have to first go round and round.

Molly touches the handle of the mug to see if it is cool enough to hold. Erica, the beguiling Other that Molly always wished she could be. Erica the extrovert, the actress and the clown. And now . . . Molly wishes she could achieve just a smattering of Horse's sophistication. For if she looked like Erica, Crispin would never have left her. Instead, here she sits, so obviously stuck in the country she could be trailing cow manure on her shoe. Molly touches the mug, sees her stubby fingers touch the mug topped as they are with those neat, white nails, but she doesn't fiddle nervously with everything around her like Erica does. She stares at the milky blob in the centre.

Molly suddenly says, and she can't think where it comes from, 'There's nothing so cruel in life than to experience childhood as a fat child.' And as she speaks she feels a fierce surge of resentment towards Erica, towards this forty-year-old woman sitting palely across the table. For Erica, capable, popular, has not always been kind to Molly.

'It must have been hell,' says Erica. And there it is again, the eyes cut in half to give that wide, endearing smile that means that no matter how unkind she has been you have to forgive her. 'But I never thought of that. I just used to envy you. There you were, not fretting about being the first to be picked . . .'

'How could anyone have possibly envied me? I was fretting, Erica, I dreaded being last.'

'But you always were last. Surely you knew you'd be last? Did you never give up?'

'No,' and Molly makes a joke of it. 'What do they say – hope never dies?'

Out of the silence they both say together, 'Oh, wasn't it ghastly!' and the silence that follows the laughter of that is the silence that is telling.

'Have you ever been back?' Molly's question is tentative.

'Of course not. How could I? How could any of us go back?'

So Molly knows that Erica has not forgotten. That 'it' is still with her.

'Effie told me you were divorced. How long is it since your divorce?' Molly can't help herself smiling. Effie told Erica . . . a stranger . . . Effie told Erica to warn her what to expect at the group!

'Two years. The twins are grown up now. He's thinking of cutting me off because Rose is pregnant.'

Erica, seeming to relax a little, considers a moment before she says, 'It's a pity you can't do without his money. Being around them, having these feelings can't be good for you. You should have let him go by now.'

Round they go, round and round, touching on anything but

13

'that'. But Erica's mind isn't on what she says. Erica is only being polite. God knows what Erica's mind *is* on because she is jumpy as a cat and when Molly puts out a hand to touch her she flinches away . . .

'Erica – what is it? What's wrong?' Apart from the screamingly obvious things that are wrong . . .

And just as, out of the corner of her eye, Molly sees the others approaching the table, Erica shudders terribly, bursts into tears and covers her face with her hands. 'I suppose it's you! I suppose you are part of it!'

'Part of what?'

'Part of the conspiracy against me!'

Now an awful lot can happen to a person in twenty years. Erica is obviously stark staring mad. Effie, Jessica, Fleur, Claire and Linda see and back straight out. They do not know this person. She is not one of them. She is a smart woman from London whom Molly obviously knows.

They will go and wait in the kitchen until Molly calls them back.

Effie, defending herself, tells them, 'Well, she seemed perfectly normal. She's been perfectly normal all day, or I'd never have asked her to join us, now would I? Molly should have warned us! Should have told us she knew her.' And then, over-eagerly, 'Shall we . . . shall we have a drink while we're waiting? Why not?'

And they all eye Effie's rather messy kitchen table.

Three

Tonight they are bussing Appleyard over to see his new house. They make him have a bath and change his clothes. He has to hurry his tea. They tell him nothing will change, much, but already the changes are swingeing.

When he asked about his job they placated him, said, 'Oh, probably, Norman. But there's time to work that out. Let's just concentrate on getting you settled first. One thing at a time, eh?'

He is to share this house with Harold and Dennis, but that won't be for a long time yet. No, first they have to move into a flat in the Hospital grounds and learn how to cook and clean and go shopping. And for that they are to meet a new person, a special man who knows how to teach people about living and his name is Julian Tenby. Julian Tenby, they are to call him Julian not Mr Tenby, is coming to collect them in half an hour to show them the house so they know where they will be going when he has trained them.

'Norman, you'll love it,' says Nurse MacNelly when he goes to ask her what she thinks about it all. 'It'll take time, of course, but you'll love it. You don't want to spend the rest of your life in here, now, do you? You've still got half your life in front of you. You want to get out and about a bit, don't you?'

Norman wanders away, fiddling with the collar of his clean white shirt. He wanders through the day-room and back to his bed, and there he sits, careful not to crease his counterpane, smoothing it now and then with his hand, looking out of the window while he waits for Julian.

Changes. Changes. Things are already very different. There was a time when this ward was full, when there had been a double row of beds down the middle as well as along the sides. Norman smiles, thinking of those days. He had trundled down the middle rows pushing the washing trolley, doling out the false teeth indiscriminately, saying a cheery

15

good morning to all the patients. Gradually the beds have been taken out, and now there are just twenty, and they have put a table and chairs in the middle with flowers and magazines on, but it doesn't fill the space. It just makes the space look emptier.

This hadn't been his ward to start with, he had started off on Gladstone, downstairs, but had been moved to Pitt, or the pits as they call it, because he kept running away. The corridors seemed long then, like great echoing pipes leading to an underworld, an underwater underworld of bubbly sounds and reedy confusions. The vast wards leading off like body parts, in Pitt, with its rounded ceilings all tiled like public lavatories, he'd thought he was being washed down the throat of Hell itself, the door closed like a gurgling gullet behind him. He'd seemed to live his life then, well, it was like letting the bath water cover your ears. That was the drugs . . . and the place itself, of course. One of the last of the great Victorian asylums.

But himself, like a marble, stayed cool and smooth in there. Tiny as a marble and marvellous, in there where nothing reached. And then gradually he had just come to like it, had no longer noticed, or minded about the blocks on the windows or the keys in the doors. The big hope had turned to a small one, and then gone out long before he'd stopped asking, 'Will my mother be coming to get me today?' And his fears were softened by familiarity. They were pleased with him then, told him he'd 'adjusted', and relaxed his medication. Gradually it hadn't seemed to matter much where he was, and he prefers the patients on Pitt. They are quieter.

No drugs, no treatments, no punishment rooms have ever reached Norman Appleyard's soul. There is only one person in his life, other than his mother, who has been able to touch that.

Appleyard sits up straight as a realisation hits him. As long as he can keep his job it doesn't matter to him where he is. That is what is important – that is what is all-important – his job at Farendon. They are giving him a chance to have his say, Mr

16

Robbie explained to him, and that's what he is going to tell them, that he wants to keep on working.

Appleyard looks about him. His life memories are here, all here. Either here or in the Farendon garden. How many years would that be? He starts counting on his fingers and shouts at Arny who comes up, curled over his zimmer, who shuffles over with his trousers round his ankles and tries to interrupt him.

'Bugger off, Arny. Just you bugger off! Don't you mess me up because I'm going out in a minute. And pull your trousers up, you mucky bugger.' Arny's eyes are round as headlamps and the whole awful conveyance seems to fit together so that Arny, zimmer, slippers, eyes and trailing trousers turn slowly and triumphantly on the spot like a prize exhibit at the motor show. And Norman wonders where they will put wild-eyed Arny when they close the Hospital down. Surely Arny is too old, too doddery and too disgusting to be put in a place of his own.

At least, no matter what they do to Norman, he keeps himself respectable. Clean. Neat and tidy with hair well-combed. Ten when he came here ... five in Gladstone ... and he is forty-five now ... that leaves thirty. Thirty years in Pitt. And twenty-five of those coming and going by day to Farendon.

'Oh, Nor ... man! Oh, Nor ... man!'

There is no need for Nurse MacNelly to call him like that. Appleyard is on his way already. He just has to smooth his counterpane again, make sure he leaves no wrinkles behind. He knows the movements in the day-room without having to see them, or be told, and they've forgotten to turn the television sound up. He knows that somebody has come in because of the scraping of chairs and the quick squeaking footsteps across the linoleum floor, the dull twang of keys and the knocking on the radiator because Mickey-Joe always gets up and agitates against the radiator when anyone comes in. And Appleyard knows it will be Julian Tenby because it isn't the day for visitors to Pitt, a ward not graced with ever more than two or three. No doctor is due until Thursday, nobody is at occupational therapy and it isn't time for the shift change.

Harold and Dennis are there already, anxiously grouped at the door with their big coats on, have been since half past six although they've been told seven o'clock. Harold sunk in pretend timidity and Dennis looking wearily forbearing as usual. Norman hurries across the room and seeing Julian's grin, copies it. Copies the outstretched hand, copies the nod and the slight shake of the head, raises himself up a little to copy the alert stance, picking up energy from the young man in corduroy.

'Hi there, Norman.'

'Hi there, Julian.'

'How are you?'

'Very well thank you, Mr Tenby.'

'Now you don't want me to start calling you Mr Appleyard, do you?'

'I wouldn't know who I was if you did, sir.'

He has made Julian laugh. And it is a very nice laugh, a proper laugh, Norman knows the difference. Julian will probably let him smoke his pipe, a habit Norman is proud of because the Hospital knows nothing about it. And Julian touches him, not hurryingly in order to push him into place but slowly, on his arm, and if he wanted to Norman knows he would be allowed to touch Julian back. If he wanted to.

Nurse MacNelly is crisp with smiles. Her sexuality lights her from within like the blinds of a shop snapping up because at last here is a customer worth opening for instead of all these foul old men. And certainly Julian Tenby would make any woman feel like that, thinks Appleyard. With his half-closed eyes and American drawl. 'Here they all are,' she says brightly. 'Shipshape and Bristol fashion. Be good, boys,' she says to her group of wide-eyed men in a voice low with confidential meaning. 'Don't do anything I wouldn't do!'

'And if you can't be good be careful,' chants Harold, haw-hawing in the donkey way he has of laughing, smirking suddenly and clapping his hand to his mouth after he's said it like a rebuked child. But Norman Appleyard feels embarrassed that they speak this way in front of Julian. He shoves his hands in his pockets and stares hard at his feet.

'And don't let this one sulk! He will, oh he will if he gets the chance.' Nurse MacNelly prods Norman fondly on the back, a gesture of ownership, while winking at Julian Tenby.

'Let's go,' says Julian quickly, winking back not at her but at the red-faced Norman.

And Norman who can't wink, blinks back at him twice, and gasps with the very great fear that he might get to like Julian Tenby very much indeed.

Julian Tenby takes these blinks as a signal, like the double pressure for 'yes' on a hand, given by a human being so desperately afflicted he can communicate in no other way.

Four

Erica Chorley, otherwise known as Horse for reasons best forgotten, is, for all Molly's envy, rich, childless and a widow. And she looks extremely unhappy just now. She refuses to say what is troubling her. 'Not here, not here,' she keeps repeating, looking over her shoulder, her tear-stained face incongruous in this room given to bird's-eye views of Escher's vertiginous architecture and daunting rows of accountancy figures. 'Somewhere else, not here.'

Why is Erica so evidently pleased to see her when all Molly feels is revulsion and terror? The start of a throbbing temple tells Molly she has been foolhardy to bestow her sympathy so readily. A flustered Effie, she can hear, is loitering at the door, no doubt wanting to know when they can all come in and start their writing. It is not good in Effie's kitchen. The vibes, caused no doubt by the marmalade rings and the coffee-crusted teaspoons that litter the table, are wrong in there.

Twenty years, twenty-three to be exact, and a lot can happen to anyone in that time. Molly is cautious. Erica might be neurotic, Erica might have a problem that manifests itself in this way wherever she goes, caused by anything from alcohol, nerves, to drugs . . . after all, she lives in London, she probably snorts cocaine. Pot and smack, if she were younger. Molly suspects she would be tempted for she knows there must be another world, somewhere higher than this one. In Ashbury all the kids aspire to is 'hot kniving', whatever that might be. But in London, well . . .

But whatever is wrong Molly the motherly cannot abandon Erica here. Not in the state she is in.

'I'll take you back to my house,' says Molly. 'We can have a drink . . . talk . . . perhaps you ought to stay . . .' She thinks her voice is fat and squeaky. It isn't. But Molly always imagines it is.

'Don't look at me like that, Molly. Please, not you.'

Molly shakes her head. 'I just wish you'd tell me . . . is it . . . ? But Molly can't remember Erica's husband's name. Of course she can't, she never knew it. She has a feeling he was somebody famous and important, but they lost touch immediately after leaving school.

Horse lifts her face and stares at a place behind Molly's head. Molly is able to watch her deciding on whether or not to clinch the matter. 'I've been getting things . . .' She brings her eyes, those eyes that seem without a pupil, more a dark scar down the middle like a lion's, she brings her eyes to Molly's own when she says, 'things', electrifying the word that flies through the space between them so that Molly, staggering, knows exactly what sort of 'things' Erica means.

Molly Tarrent then makes a desperate attempt to think clearly and logically, and fails. Someone has rammed a white-hot shaft in her back. Aghast, she whispers, 'Not . . . that sort of thing? What? Through the post?'

'Sometimes through the post. Sometimes not.'

Molly is held as if captured with chains. She feels a seeping frost inside as if a cold tap has suddenly been turned on in her throat. She swallows hard, and again. But then her protesting brain tells her that Erica is ill and imagining things. Either that or she is playing some grisly joke. But she says, all resistance gone, all thoughts of Jesus and his rampant crook screwed up in her pocket by a clenching hand, 'I'll go and tell Effie we're leaving . . .'

Erica says nothing but shudders and lets her head droop between her arms as if exhausted.

And somehow Molly manœuvres herself from the room and meets Effie lurking in the hall.

'What on earth's going on?'

'I'm sorry. Erica is ill. I'm going to take her home with me.'

'But we . . . Roger and I, we arranged that she stay the night here.'

'I'm sorry, Effie . . .'

'But what about your 'Jesus'? Leave it here. Someone else can read it for you.'

Molly smiles. 'No, I'll take it back with me. I didn't like it very much anyway.'

21

'Oh?' And is there relief in Effie's rather over-hasty acceptance?

Why is she doing this? Getting involved, Crispin would nastily call it after urging her to be more retrospective. After all, Erica is a stranger, a faded face on a photograph, a tippexed-out name in an address book. But even with the ominous feeling of cold in her chest, even with all that dread inside her there is reluctant pleasure in the knowledge that sometime tonight they are going to talk about 'that' again . . . they will have to talk about 'it'. After all these years, at last, something is going to be said. Molly's heart is beating fast. She is an unnatural pink.

'You realise what's happening, don't you?' cries Erica as Molly closes the door on a wondering Effie. They leave the cosy flood of porch-light behind and set out into the darkness. 'Somebody knows what we did and they're doing the same thing to me!'

Molly's heart feels spicy and hot, like the boiled ones they'd been made to eat at Farendon with all those floppy ventricals and aortas. And if she hadn't seen how nervous and upset Erica has been in the few moments since their unwelcome reunion, she would never have believed what she was hearing with her own ears.

A cruel hoax? No. Erica would never go to so much trouble without a motive.

Flirting with danger! Playing with fire! How can Erica flirt with danger . . . what danger is there worthy of the name, what fire can burn her now that Jasper is dead?

Erica the widow was thinking of Farendon this morning on her way down to Ashbury on the train. She'd picked up her post from home and opened it in the dining car over breakfast. She was still getting sympathy letters from people she'd never heard of. She put them aside, instinctively knowing, and the reunion invitation was the first thing she opened. It landed with a lurch across the scrambled egg. Of course she'd normally send it back with a tick by *Unable to attend*, for how could she return, how could any of them return after what they'd done? But Erica, her fingers toying

22

with her teaspoon while the countryside flashed past her eyes outside the window, felt a yearning so strong, a need so great, that she realised her face was set tense, her eyes were staring and the man opposite was leaning forward, about to ask if she felt sick.

Erica sighed to release her face and dropped the teaspoon. If she could just go back one more time. If they could all go back, just once, and recreate some of what they had before. But it couldn't be done – of course it couldn't. None of the others would agree to go near the place. And nor would she have done, eight weeks ago.

But things were different now. Erica needed to go back. It was the only place she had ever felt truly alive.

So it isn't a joke she is playing on poor Fatty. Oh no, it is far from a joke. It is a way – and Erica spotted it instantly – it is a way of getting everyone back. A reunion after twenty-three years.

Remembering to wring her hands she walks down the street at Ashbury, so dark, no street lights here. No pavements, either. You walk with one foot almost in the cottage gardens, embroidery gardens, you see them on cushions old women make to pass the hours. Erica shudders. The white-washed cottages bulge and some are like Doctor Barnardo's collecting boxes, yellowing with age. The pub which they pass reminds Erica of the sort of tin you buy toffees in. Ashbury is the nursery-rhyme land of Old Mother Hubbard, lots of walls for Humpty Dumpty, and underneath are the little maids all in a row. Or a ghost town pin-pricked with the blue-white light of television sets. There is something dreamily unreal about Ashbury. There is a nip in the air tonight. A mist smokes off the hedges. She is interested to see what sort of house Fatty lives in. She hopes it is properly heated.

'Nearly there,' says Molly, reassuring, but throwing a few nervous glances. 'They put a cross on this very door at the time of the Black Death,' she says. It is what she always says when strangers come to her house, but now she gives a quick smile with the information, fearful in case she sounds as if she's trying to put Erica off. Not that she often says it. She's not that hospitable. 'The priest who lived here died of it.'

Erica stares hard at the door, searching for stains, but thinks about herself. She doesn't notice how Molly steps back to let her through first. Typically, Jasper has left her rolling. Erica had half-hoped she might have been written right out of the will, for penury might have been interesting. She could have tested herself, seen how long it took her and what steps she chose in order to climb out of the gutter. It was not beyond the realms of fantasy that Jasper, always perverse, might have done that, but no. Instead she is the sole beneficiary. Everything is hers . . . the lease on the Cadogan Square flat . . . the Mercedes Benz . . . the investments . . . the collection of jade and all those phallic David Shepherd originals. Power, it is her aphrodisiac . . . and Jasper had power. Hell, Jasper *was* power.

Jasper is dead. Boredom stares Erica Bryant in the face like a spectre dancing on an open grave, calling her to tapestries with awful, beckoning fingers.

And then, in the reflection of the kitchen window in that terrible house where she had been forced to spend the day with Jasper's accountant, Roger Tate, then she had seen a glimmer of hope – luminous, it flooded like full moonlight – the face of Fatty Maguire. Tarrent, apparently, now. The thought of spending the night with Roger and Effie . . . he might be the hottest man with figures, according to Jasper, that he had ever come across, but so pompous . . . so moral. And Effie – Mrs Apple incarnate – she had even served dinner with a pinny on. Yes, Erica saw Molly and memories of that terrible-wonderful time came flooding back, filling her with a wild life-force more powerfully fearful than anything she'd felt in the eight weeks since Jasper, damn him, crashed the prototype of his solar-powered aeroplane somewhere over the wounded jungles of Brazil.

Hearing about her inheritance, trailing through all the figures behind the monotonous voice and the fleshy finger of Roger Tate had tired her, that and the journey, and she hadn't been home at all last night. She'd had no sleep. She'd stayed at Stringfellows with friends in the same way she'd done when Jasper was alive, but when she'd got back to the flat at seven o'clock in the morning, there was no scene, no

24

cruel words or cutting remarks that led to the sort of fiery row she loved to be ended, as these things were always ended with Jasper, in glorious bed with her master in the gold room. No, Horracks had merely taken her coat and enquired, 'Do you require breakfast this morning, madam?' and Erica had cursed and remembered her appointment in Ashbury.

Life seemed suddenly devoid of repercussions. There was nobody in control. No one to smack her and send her to bed for her naughty girly wicked ways. Nobody to play to.

Poor old Maurice Horracks. How appalled he had been on the day that Jasper Bryant died, on the day the whole ghastly mess was revealed, spread over the tree tops like a picnic on a red and white checked cloth, spread across the television news for all to pick at, for all the world to see. From his basement flat he and his sultry Philippino wife had listened, horrified, to the music – not *Così fan tutte* or *Il Trovatore*, oh no – but music by people called Chubby Checker, Ray Charles, Chuck Berry and the Big Bopper. (Horracks had gone up afterwards to check on these disgraceful people, had found the motley collection between tatty seventy-eight record covers.) Crashing, vibrating through the delicate sound system, the noise had flooded the air outside this Christopher Robin London of dressing gowns, nannies and teas, of embassies hardly heard of, so that the tennis players in the square had looked up to the open window askance. The sound, reaching the basement, had assailed the Horracks with all the hair-raising suggestions of voodoo drums. And to think that Lady Docker once lived here . . .

Wild . . . Sweet Jesus, how can Erica, now, go wild?

She had provided all the excitement Jasper could ever have needed and for that, he worshipped her. She never had to fear he would go astray, in spite of the fact that wherever they went women, simpering, came after him. Strained their bosoms when they came towards him, batted their eyelids and swung their hips. For Erica is beautiful, sleekly leopardly beautiful with hot-jungle eyes, and as she aged her beauty grew more remarkable, and so did the acts of steamy wickedness that excited poor Jasper so. Once, only once, she had caught him making eyes back across the room at a gallery launching luncheon. Promptly and prudently Erica ventured into the unknown and had a rather interesting affair with the woman herself.

Wild for a way out and someone to be wild with.

Suffocatingly bored. So when she saw Fatty she knew she looked tired and drawn in the kind of way Erica never normally allowed herself to look. The plan, tenuous and fluttery at first, had grown into something to be worked on in the few short seconds it took to recognise Fatty in the night-filled window, put the lid on the kettle and turn round.

Exhilarated, Erica realised she was actually plotting again! Plotting her way back to Farendon.

That husband of Fatty's must have been driven beyond endurance. For Fatty/Molly is the sort of person you want to be unkind to. Awful, but there are people like that. They want to be wounded. Still tempting to tease with a plump, blank face that asks to be shocked . . . given life . . . and that rather hurt, indignant expression she always wears. No, Fatty, gullible, so easily impressed, has thinned down to plumpness but other than that she hasn't changed at all.

And neither has Erica.

Three years ago Erica might have been right. But perhaps it is because of that hasty, rather sketchy summing up – and Erica was always a hasty person, they'd written on her Farendon reports, *'Must take more care'* – perhaps that's where Erica goes wrong. People may look exactly the same, but scars don't always show. And a very great deal can happen to someone during twenty-three years.

Five

Julian Tenby helps the dithering Harold from the bus while Norman Appleyard watches how his multi-coloured LSE scarf swings round Harold's face, caressingly. Norman experiences his first stab of jealousy, and winces.

Harold always gets hiccups when he is excited, hiccups that make all his body jerk and threaten to 'set him off'. It is essential that Harold should not be set off – not here, in front of the new neighbours. Norman can't see them but he knows they are watching. Norman knows those neighbours won't want hospital patients here. He quite understands that. He would prefer not to be living anywhere near Harold himself.

Julian, not knowing about Harold, isn't even trying to hurry him – far from it. He is standing back to let Harold climb down by himself, patiently, politely, and maybe that's what puts that glint of anxiety into Harold's sky-blue eyes. A fatal sign.

Nurse MacNelly would have said, 'Hey ho here we go, home sweet home at last,' but Julian kicks a tin off the path and says, 'Bloody litter louts.' And then he takes the key from between his teeth and opens the door. The letterbox snaps like a dog's mouth. Julian doesn't usher them in before him, he just lets them follow, not really knowing if they are coming or not. Not really bothered, thinks Norman, with admiration.

My hall. My door. My stairs. Norman tries saying it but it makes no sense. Walking into his new house is like walking into a coffin. If he goes this way he bangs into the wall, if he goes the other he brushes the hall table and wobbles it dangerously. And how does he know he is really there at all because he can't even hear his own feet walking on those carpets. Made dizzy and unsteady by all the walls, Norman sinks down onto the bottom stair and says, 'No, Julian, please don't close the door.'

'You wait here while I find the kitchen and go and make us

all a cup of tea.' Julian takes a milk bottle from his fascinatingly stuffed jacket pocket and passes through the hall and the door at the end, followed by Harold and Dennis. Harold, presumably to keep the ceiling off him, covers his head with both hands.

Julian looks back at Norman and decides it is probably best to leave him where he is.

The house is a square one, the sort of house children draw, with a chimney set on one side of the roof. But there should have been a cat, to balance it, on the other. Bought and furnished by the Hospital Friends, it is a house no one has ever lived in before. It smells of putty and new carpets. The weeds on the path are old weeds, ragwort and bindweed, that have withstood the slings and arrows of concrete mixers, wheelbarrows and a year's assault by the hobnailed boots of builders. And now, audaciously, they are trying to live through the autumn as well. They break through the dead space of concrete which stretches out between Norman as he sits staring out through the open door, and the road where the parked bus they came in is zebra-striped by a street light. The houses opposite loom from here like wicked castles in the fairy tales he watches on Children's Hour. A passing car catches them in headlights and, as he watches, Norman sees those houses rise from the ground to curl grotesquely across his own ceiling.

The narrow staircase ridges up behind him, hackled like the back of an angry dog before it disappears into the darkness of what Julian calls the landing.

'Norman, d'you feel like joining us in the sitting room?'

Norman doesn't, but as the other two trail up to look at him he sees Harold fumbling for his penis, finding it, and only letting go when Norman slaps him. Too late now, for Harold has been set off.

Norman sits alone on the bottom step and, finding the old bobble hat he was given by the Chaplain last Christmas – smarter than his gardening one – he takes it out of his pocket, gives it a shake and pulls it on. He does not like this pear-coloured house with its greenhousey warmth.

He wants to go home.

Julian leaves the sitting room door open and positions himself so that he can keep an eye on Norman. He knows absurdly little about him, and what he does know has been gleaned from the sporadic, rather arrogant notes in Norman's file.

When they found him he hadn't been able to speak. No reasons given . . . they hadn't bothered with those. And there's nobody there now to ask who might once have known. The five-year-old had been sent to one children's home after another and every one had found him too much to cope with so that eventually, in despair, the authorities despatched the then ten-year-old Norman Appleyard to Underwood Hospital.

No place for a child.

Treatments? Well, they came and went in phases, some, mercifully, less harmful than others. From reading through year to year it seemed to Julian as if occasionally somebody had remembered the wretched Norman and thought it was time they made an effort to try something else, because no name had been given to his condition except rather general ones like arrested development, involutional melancholia, regression and the hoary old chestnut, mentally retarded.

At times Norman had broken out, rebelled against it all with quite understandable, rather sad little acts of violence. Once he put a chair through a window and for that he was drugged to unconsciousness for a week and strapped to his bed. On another occasion he had swept all the crockery off the day-room table. One fairly serious act of arson. Only once had he gone for a nurse . . . it had been quite nasty. The nurse had left. Julian thought that was quite a commendable record, considering . . .

Early on, Julian read, Norman kept running away. On retrieval, a tall, black signature with a shadow behind it belonging to someone who called himself Mr Adam Grey, Consultant, sentenced Norman to restraint in the padded cells. On every occasion they brought Norman back and put him in those cells. And that was when he hadn't even reached his teens.

Bombarded with ECT, administered enough methadrine to turn an elephant into an addict and then a sudden withdrawal, a guinea pig for any new drug that ever came out, it was just a lucky fluke that Norman had avoided a frontal lobotomy.

But underlying everything it appeared to be the job he had been given at Farendon School that had saved him . . . if saved was a word that could be used here.

Julian watches as Norman pulls a pipe from his pocket and fills it. For a moment he thinks that Norman is going to get up and close the front door. Julian hopes he might. It would be a step in the right direction. It is very cold and Norman looks hunched and uncomfortable sitting there in the direct draught like that. Julian turns away when Norman looks furtively over. Julian hears the strike of a match. The pipe fits in the gap between Norman's two front teeth.

'Norman, your tea's getting cold. I wish you'd come and sit down with us in the warm. Harold's made himself at home already. I thought we'd stop and have a half on the way home if that's all right by everybody.'

Norman knows that Harold will be fiddling with himself underneath his trousers and that Julian won't yet have noticed. That is the only way Harold ever looks at home anywhere. Only then does he close his eyes and lie back, for all the world a happy and satisfied man.

Dennis, Norman knows, will be perched on the edge of his chair looking warily nervous so that Julian will be nice to him. Norman wants to please Julian and go in there and join them . . . but wanting to please is the start of the slippery slope. Norman hasn't wanted to please anyone for years. Not since that Nurse Mary Wellbecker . . . Norman gets his fingers out and starts counting, a sense of well-being infusing his body with the tobacco smoke. How long ago was that now? Ten, eleven years . . . He had nearly lost his job at the School over it.

If he behaves badly enough then Julian Tenby won't bother with him and the pressure will be off. So Norman sulks. And anyway, Norman knows it would be naughty to fall in love with a man. Women are the ones, and girls. Golden girls who wear tunics and cloaks with purple hoods and whose eyes are the secretive ochre of precious orchids. But there'd only ever been one girl quite like that.

He'd nearly lost his job over her as well.

Six

Erica throws a pig-skin vanity case down on Molly's spare bed. A Heidi bedroom, low beams and rugs, frill and bows. Very pretty. Very tasteful. Very Austrian cottagey.

Well, as Molly explains, Crispin and Rose have all the decent stuff at Little Court while she has been left with the holiday furniture. 'But this is a nice room with a view of the duckpond through the low window in the morning,' says Molly. 'You can lie in bed and watch them.'

How nice. Erica smiles before she remembers she mustn't. 'I'd like to have a good look round the house before we sit down,' she says, agitated and nervous once more. 'I fear they are watching my comings and goings.'

Molly is uneasy with Erica in the house. Clever, witty, humorous Erica. Erica the beautiful, the much-admired, the adored one. Nervously she glances outside but can see nothing but black. Somebody watching? Here? In Ashbury? Anyone could be lurking in the larches by the lake. Anyone could be waiting, ready to spring. The journey home had made her nervous, being next to Erica made her nervous. Their feet had crunched on horsechestnuts that littered the road. Above their heads the leaves, crimson, amber and green of traffic lights by day, were black and menacing. Erica's terror is contagious and it falls on fertile ground.

Molly is eager to get Erica sitting down with a drink in her hand . . . to hear what Erica is going to say.

They sit in corpulent chairs next to a lively fire with double scotches in their hands. Erica, comfortable at last but clearly nervous, rests her feet on a chintzy stool and wonders how far she dares go. Wonders what the point of it is. After all, they are no longer children. But can she manipulate Fatty Maguire in the way she once had done? Can she, out of nowhere, conjure up that potent mixture of sinful power that she found so elusive until Jasper came along. It seems she has been wading through her life ever since she was eighteen, trying to find something to match it. Jasper matched it. Jasper is dead.

'It started in June, three months ago, and it's only since then that I've realised that the dates are probably correct because wasn't it in June, right at the end of the summer term, that we started on Amy Macey?'

Amy . . . Amy . . . Amy . . . Amy. Molly's brain, after twenty-three years, repeats the terrible mantra. As if it's been waiting to . . .

There is no warmth coming from the fire now. You can poke it and poke it, it makes no difference. Molly's jaw goes rigid. Her regular little white teeth clink against the glass and she has to put it back on the table. She begins to feel very sick.

'I didn't get anything during the school holidays, you see.' Erica, having swigged down her drink, bangs a fist into her hand. 'If only I had an old diary. If only I knew the dates. Because then I'd know when the next one was coming – I could prepare for it. Each one, Molly, you see, is such a terrible shock.'

'What was it? What did you get?' Molly's voice is gravelly. She already knows the answer. She just hopes she might be wrong.

'It was the feather, of course . . . the black swan feather . . . and it was in the dry cleaning which was left at the bottom of the basement steps. It's always left there. They don't bother to knock. They just leave the box there. Well, it's wrapped and out of sight. When Horracks takes it upstairs he generally leaves the items out on the bed because I like to sort them out myself . . . otherwise I tend to forget what I've got!' Molly shifts in her dungarees and frilly Laura Ashley shirt that look just fine when Erica isn't sitting there. 'The black feather was in the lapel of a jacket . . . pinned to the lapel . . . just like we pinned it to Amy's blazer . . .'

As Erica speaks, as she says these dreadful things, it takes great effort of will from Molly to keep herself listening. 'And the second one?' Molly wipes her hands on her knees. On the crumpled blue and white stripes at her knees. She is no longer a two-piece person. And she has to know.

'The second one arrived a fortnight ago. It was the blood.

And it came in an eye-dropper bottle. This time I was told to collect it from the chemist . . . just the same method we used, Molly, just the same.'

Nonsense of course, but Erica warms to her subject, convincing in the telling. It requires little imagination. For this, more or less, is how they had worked on Amy Macey.

'And then yesterday. . . ?'

'Yesterday I received the bone. They told me to go to a seat in the square . . . where the tennis courts are in front of my house . . . I had to go, Molly, when this happens to you you just have to go.' Erica bites her lip and tugs at the skin with her teeth.

'But who on earth would want to harm you? Who would go to these lengths, Erica? It has to be one of us. It has to be some awful practical joke.' Even as she says it Molly knows she sounds ridiculous, knows it is much more sinister than that.

'What if it was you, Molly? What if the messages, the symbols were coming to you? What would you do?'

'Ignore them. Throw them away. Tell somebody.' But who was there who could possibly be told without confessing to . . . God! And the thought that someone out there is actually doing this. Someone out there hating you enough to do this!

And yet *they* had done it. She had done it. Erica had done it.

'There's no point in throwing them away – we both know that. Once they've arrived the damage is done. You're quite right, of course. It has to be one of us,' says Erica heavily.

Molly thinks hard with what is left of her floundering brain. 'Erica, what on earth made you trust me?'

'I didn't! I saw you in there, in the kitchen at Effie's house and I thought it was you! The shock of seeing you there like that was so awful, so overwhelming I almost fainted. But then I remembered what Effie had told me, about your divorce and your hysterical behaviour. I listened to you, watched you, and you were far too immersed in your love affair with Crispin to have room for anything else in your life! You just wouldn't have the energy, Molly, for anything else. You are consumed . . . spells . . . my God, Molly, you've been under one of your own for how long – three years? And who could I tell? I'm alone. Jasper was away when the first one came but even if he'd been there . . . even if there was someone, even if you had someone completely on your side, would you have told?'

Molly's voice is flat. 'And risk someone finding out about the most shameful, awful thing I have ever done in my life?'

'You haven't answered. For example, how would Crispin have reacted?'

Even his name, said out of the blue like that, sends a shot through Molly. She ponders. 'Told him that I caused someone else's death by whispering the name of a demon into the earth, by despatching devils under the moonlight? Well, first he wouldn't have believed me. Second, he would tell me I needed a doctor.'

'And if you'd shown him the messages and symbols you were receiving?'

'Ah, then he would have gone straight to the police. He would not have believed in it, you see. He's a barrister . . . so is Rose, very logical thinking people. Not many know the truth, they don't understand what can happen – not like we do.'

Molly and Erica go silent, both lost in thought. Erica is thinking that Crispin sounds a most interesting man. She'll have to get to meet him. She needs someone like that. Until Molly adds weakly, 'I wouldn't have been able to stop him. I know that's what he would have done.'

'I just daren't go out any more. They seem to know where I'm going. They might even be watching me now.'

Molly shifts uncomfortably, knowing that this is all part of the curse, glancing at the safely drawn curtains. 'I'm racking my brains. There's only one of us mad enough, and that was Dierdre Bott. But why would Dierdre Bott want you dead?'

'Why would anyone want me dead? Why would anyone care one way or the other?' sobs Erica, dangerously near to overdoing it.

Molly tries to cheer her up. 'There's one thing, Erica, one very important thing. One thing that's gone very wrong. You've told somebody. You've told me. Don't you see . . . the curse can't work now! It can't have the same effect on you.'

But Erica looks as if she doesn't believe her.

When the twins come home they change the subject and discuss Erica's health instead. Olly and Edward are their father's boys, they never have been Molly's. They know what they want and they 'go for it' – that terrible expression that Crispin uses – just as Crispin does. Which is why it is particularly poignant that he is talking of cutting them off in favour of Rose's baby. But the twins don't seem to mind. Crispin has spoken to them about it, has explained about some trust, and they, not sensitive as Molly is, accept it and tell her not to worry herself.

They have learnt to tread carefully round Molly when it comes to Crispin. That which had started as secret had soon come out. Everyone knows. Everyone knows about the nights Molly sat weeping in the car outside *Her* house in Godalming, glaring out from the car window with aching, bitter eyes, watched by neighbours who used to know her but didn't want to know her now. A four-hour drive was nothing to Molly then. But he, he who used to love her, had not come out. She's stopped doing that now but she does other things . . . things the twins are too embarrassed to talk about. They wish they didn't know. They think it could be to do with their mother's time of life, and they don't like to talk about that, either.

Molly can't help feeling proud when she introduces her sons to Erica. She's still amazed that she, Fatty Maguire, has managed to produce two such god-like young men. Crispin, of course. Crispin's genes overriding the fat Maguire chromosomes. Amazed, she sees the pleasing way her children kind of flirt with Erica. And Erica responds, albeit in a rather sad, muted style.

Molly is appalled to hear the number of Valium Erica gets through each day. Nor, her guest explains after the twins have gone to bed, does she sleep at night despite her reckless use of sleeping pills. Tormented by fear she forever asks the question, 'Why me, why me?'

To which Molly has to answer, 'I don't know, Erica, I just don't know.'

But it is quite apparent to Molly that Erica cannot be

allowed to go on living like this. She will have to remain in Ashbury. And it is important that Erica no longer be allowed to play the role of the passive victim. If she is going to beat this dreadful thing then she will have to fight back. The whole ghastly mess has resurfaced to haunt them. Molly can no longer bury it away, pretend it never happened.

Bereft of reason. They must have been, then, bereft of reason. For reason bars the mind from the magic world that waits. Because they had played with magic, black magic. Had struck the gavel eleven times, not seven, under the elemental flame. The witch-band met, they called their weekly esbats when the moon was waning. Scarlet, ruby, rue, the symbols of Mars. And because of them Amy Macey disappeared. Both of them know beyond doubt, no matter what games Erica might be playing, they both know that *they killed Amy Macey*. Now it has come back on them . . . as they say evil always does. Molly, for years, has been waiting for it. Now it's here. Almost a relief. And Molly, in order to rid herself forever of the haunting sight of Amy Macey's mother's face, in order to save herself now, Molly is going to have to try to neutralise this curse as quickly and efficiently as possible.

Erica's face . . . Erica's whole demeanour . . . tense, drawn. Incredibly, she is a shadow of her former self. What power there is . . . and Erica was a woman so sure, so capable, so inviolate, sophisticated . . . not given to hysterics or neurotic tendencies . . .

Just like Rose.

It is only much later, when Molly lies tossing and turning in bed, thinking, compelled to think about it because there is fascination in the horror, like gawping at an accident or reading a macabre paragraph twice, it is only then that Molly thinks of Rose again, and of how easy it would be to . . .

Rose . . . Rose . . . Rose . . .

How very easy.

But would it work on Rose – who doesn't know?

Seven

Norman eyes Harold and Dennis jealously from time to time.

The only good thing about all this as far as he can see is that for the first time in thirty-five years he will not be locked in at night. And neither will Harold or Dennis.

Patiently Julian asks them what they would like to drink.

'A chaser,' says Dennis challengingly, copying from the television. Harold plucks imaginary cotton from his trousers and says he doesn't know.

'How about you, Norman?' Julian's eyes are a twinkling brown like the crumbly earth half an inch down under the cucumber cloches. The only thing that makes Norman feel it is all right to have these thoughts, these personal thoughts, is that Julian's hair is loose-curled and long like a girl's. It hangs over his rust-coloured shirt collar and ends softly there. There are robin's feet crinkles beside his eyes and he stoops to avoid the low beams. 'I'll get you both a half of bitter,' he says as he goes away.

The feathery tickle of conversation brushes Norman's ears as he waits obediently with Harold and Dennis, their faces made sheepishly pink by the lamp-shade on the table. They sit on a settle with big coats on, the three of them perched in a hushed row like monkeys deciding how to tackle evil.

'This is the sort of thing you'll be doing all the time,' says Julian, coming back and balancing glasses between his fingers. 'This is your local. You'll come here in the evenings.'

Now Julian is back Norman feels safe to look round. He does so with his drink in his hand, which is the way he sees others doing it. All the women are covered in colours and the men use loud voices full of studied cheerfulness. Every table has its own pink lamp and a little vase of freesia, squeezed tight at the stems which is how Norman puts flowers in his jam jars in his little animal cemetery under the south-facing vegetable garden wall. Norman never lets anything die

38

without the dignity of burial, no vole, no fledgeling fallen from its nest is too small. And there'd been bigger animals, too, over the years – the fox he'd fished from the swimming pool, cats, a badger with its throat torn open on barbed wire and an old grey dog he'd retrieved from the side of the road. He trails sweet peas around the mounds when they settle, but on arrival the animals have a jam jar filled very similarly to these little table-vases.

Otherwise this room is very dark and full of trowel-shaped shadows which is just as well because Norman feels it is better if people can't see them. Because they are not right. Is it because they're not talking? He looks at Harold, whom he's never really looked at properly before – squat with a wig-like tuft of woolly hair and desperate-looking like a muppet, his herringbone coat done up childishly to his chin. And Dennis in his tartan-lined macintosh, a scarf twisted several times round his neck giving him the look of a browsing giraffe. A tired browsing giraffe who would accept any leaf, no matter how jaded, if only he could find it. Norman suddenly feels fond of them, and protective. Julian had better be careful not to hurt them because Norman would not like that. And himself? That woolly hat will be doing it. He snatches it off his head and feels the bump of his pipe in his pocket. He takes it out and fills it, feeling, with satisfaction, the astonished gaze of his companions.

Norman disagrees with Julian. He feels they probably won't come here. He thinks they will probably stay in the sitting room in the pear-house and watch television instead.

'Next week,' says Julian, 'we'll be moving into the hospital flat. But I wanted you to see the new house first so you understand what all the fuss is about. What do you think of it? Harold?'

'It's beautiful,' says Harold, with a frothy moustache on his lip.

'And you, Dennis? Are you going to like sleeping in that bedroom?'

Dennis is having trouble swallowing his chaser. But he is enjoying his crisps. So much so that he doesn't bother to answer.

Harold asks, 'Will I be able to bring friends home?'

'You'll be allowed to do what you like just so long as it's within the law,' says Julian. 'Why, do you have anyone specifically in mind, Harold?'

'Not yet. But living outside I might make friends. Look, all these people have friends.'

'Which one of these would you choose if you could? Yes, that's right, have a good look round and tell me which one.'

Harold is trying hard, eager to please. Norman prays that this won't set him off. He scratches his head and narrows his eyes to see in the dimness. The landlady's bangle attracts his eye. It burns at the bar like a darting firefly. Norman knows Harold will choose her. And he knows why, too. She looks like the piano player who comes to Underwood sometimes on Saturdays, sleazy and blue-haired with a mouth like a heart, purple eyelids when her eyes are closed. She does an hour on a Saturday night with her eyes closed, and goes. She plays old war songs mostly –'Roll out the Barrel' and 'Bye Bye Blackbird' – which ought to be sung-along-to, but no one but Harold takes any notice. Harold never moves from the piano, stands by the piano with his willy out all the while she is there. She plays on, ignoring him. Sometimes she closes her eyes just a little bit tighter.

'I'd ask that lady if she could play the piano, and if she could then I'd pick her,' says Harold.

'What about you?' Julian turns to Norman. 'Will you want friends, or are you a loner like me?' And Norman hears the bitterness although it only flavours the words very subtly, like when the kitchens use oil instead of fat. Most people can't tell, but Norman always can.

Julian is telling lies. For he is not, by choice, a loner. The agony of parting from Sylvie has turned him into one, has turned him into a four o'clock in the morning insomniac and a walker of streets at night. Eight years, after all, is a long time to be with someone, someone who can turn to you one day and say it isn't working. To see a person turn into a stranger as suddenly as that is enough to make anyone a loner – but not by nature. Not by choice.

Has he gone too far? Has he pounced too hard upon poor Norman?

'I'm like you, I'm a loner,' says Norman, copying.

'That must be hard, when you live among so many people in a hospital ward,' says Julian. 'It must be hard to find a place to be by yourself.'

'I have my job at Farendon,' Norman explains. 'I can always find somewhere to be on my own there.'

'You like going to Farendon, don't you Norman?'

It isn't smoke that crosses Norman's eyes. Norman drops them from Julian's sympathetic brown ones and whispers, too low for hearing, 'Yes, I like it, but it's not the same.' Norman is cross with Julian. For Julian is picking holes in the lined-up monkeys, testing them.

Life has never been the same at Farendon since Erica Chorley left. Norman had some sort of breakdown then, he knows he did, only nobody seemed to notice. They thought the fire was just naughtiness and punished him for it.

He remembers it all, every precious moment of it all, even Erica's first smile. How could he describe Erica to anyone, how would he describe her to Julian if he asked him? How could he do it, with the way words have of slipping from him just when he thinks he's grasped them? Well, he wouldn't join them together, that's how he'd do it. He'd just say – *leopard* – *gold* – *frosty fern* – *moon* – and hope that they knew the precise beauty of a fern gripped with hoar frost and the yearning caused by the beauty of a moonlit night behind bars. The leopard and the gold, thinks Norman, don't need joining.

River – *brown* – *minnows* – *birds* – *orchids* – *leaves*

Taller than Veronica, slenderer than Jayne, Erica's skin was as smooth as her gaze. Her hair cascaded like brown river water, full of the million lights in water, but underneath, golden brown with minnows rippling in it. She moved light-boned as a bird. Her orchid eyes shone wet with secrets and she smelled of hot leaves drying in the sun. Norman used to see her and want to run away, hide like a dog panting in the shade. But he never could run. He was drawn, as everyone was, towards Erica.

But even now, sitting sipping his half in the pub with Julian, comes the agony of the baby explosion. It always comes when

41

he thinks about Erica. That is Norman's secret name for great trauma, for what happened in the end.

For Norman believes it must be just like that when a woman has a baby. All that secret, precious joy inside, growing and pushing inside and filling up, almost right up, and then it tears away, she sees it for what it really is and she hates it . . . won't speak . . . won't look . . . won't touch . . . wants to hurt. Norman always feels very sorry for pregnant women, big, velvety ladies with secret smiles and full of love – and afterwards with their prams, thin, angry, cheated people giving sharp slaps and stinging.

Once they left the television on in the ward and Norman watched a baby being born, saw it all happen so he knows. Afterwards they found him sobbing in his chair – worse, in Arny's chair, and no one in their right mind would even approach Arny's chair. He had watched how she touched the baby clothes for the camera man in her bedroom before she left, light, deft touches like swifts' wings on water, her hands had dappled the waiting crib and the teddy bears.

Then, afterwards, the blood bang of the explosion, slack-jawed, blank-eyed. It had broken Norman's heart.

And every time he loved it happened. 'It's crappy,' he says.

'Pardon, Norman?'

'It's crappy to like anyone. It's better to be a loner.' He wishes he hasn't said it because Julian lays a hand on his arm, for the second time since he's known him he does that, and Norman feels a swell of fondness filling him up bitter as the beer, and after Julian has moved his hand Norman still feels the pressure there, the pressure of a hand speaking to him.

He sits in a chilly silence, staring hard at the picture of a hunting dog with a pheasant clamped in its teeth that hangs in the shadowy corner opposite. Shadows fascinate Norman. There aren't many shadows in Underwood, just lots of bright lights. He pities that limp-necked pheasant for he knows it is still alive. If Norman found it in his garden he would take it gently in his hands, whispering comfort while he gripped its neck and pulled. Better to be dead, far better, than to be alive and suffering.

Little fingers patting – all cake and milk.

42

Norman's back aches and he feels cramp coming to his knees. Very, very badly indeed does Norman not want to like Julian. But the enormity of the danger excites him, and it is for the excitement alone that he clenches his pipe between his teeth and deliberately lets himself slip a little further.

Norman watches, and copies Julian as he tackles a second drink and, grieving, passes the back of his hand over tired eyes.

Julian grieves most naturally. Well, he is a human being and used to being treated as one. A man of letters, he is well able to express his feelings. Julian would be the first to tell you that deep emotions, when ignored, build up inside until eventually they have to burst out. The longer they're buried away the worse it is bound to be. But there are no special wards set aside for grief in Underwood. Never have been.

Love and the loss of it. And like it or not, it forms an instinctive bond between them.

Eight

Molly is still thinking when she wakes up. When morning comes she isn't sure if she has slept or not, perhaps she has been awake all night struggling with her predicament. Her fingers fiddle with the pleats on the eiderdown. Distressed and uneasy, Molly doesn't want to get up. She doesn't want to face beautiful, suffering Erica across the breakfast table.

Rose – and what an ideal time to begin! Just as Rose is giving up work and experiencing, for the first time perhaps, those long, lone days in that monster home with nobody but the char and the radio to talk to.

Rose – she and Crispin have taken that gentle word and filled it with pain so that to Molly it sounds like 'dagger'. Rose's friends, of course, are all working. Rose, at thirty-three, is late to be a mother and her friends have all been one and gone back. Oh, no doubt she'll enjoy the life of leisure at first, and Crispin will take her coffee in bed before he leaves, kissing her a fond goodbye. Rose will be able to smell his shirt and the intriguing whiff of cologne that always comes from him after he's shaved. Rose will lie and listen and sip that coffee as Crispin's car crunches down the drive. And start thinking about herself . . .

But Rose is pregnant. To do what Molly is thinking of doing would be a monstrous thing, heinous even. If anything happened to Rose she would never forgive herself, would she? But she could start with the black feather . . . just to see . . . Lucky she hadn't dared think of it before. Lucky Erica hadn't turned up earlier because there was a time, not so long ago, when Molly wouldn't have felt any constraints at all.

Erica is right. Erica is perfectly right. Of course they have to do it.

Last night both she and Molly agreed that they would have to go back to Farendon. For once they would not refuse the

44

reunion invitation, that schooly invitation done on a faulty copier with boxes for ticks if you wanted tea on Friday, Saturday or Sunday, another box for which House you preferred to stay in, which newspaper you wanted delivered in the morning and which informal discussions you would like to attend. You could imagine these returns being marked with an acid-red pen, and finally a comment on the bottom such as *'Poor'* or *'See me'* or *'What is this meant to mean, Molly Maguire?'* Yes, all that comes back with Farendon. So real it makes you want to gasp.

That red pen, thinks Molly Tarrent, has dogged her life ever since. Striking its terrible way through all those dinner parties she was forced to put on for Crispin, slicing through her fallen summer puddings with caustic comment that showed in Crispin's eyes; deleting without mercy the floppy baked alaskas and turning the syllabubs, wiping them out forever and leaving a messy, shaming page behind it. It put hard rings round the fact that she never could properly train her cat and had to give it away. It left question marks in margins when the twins misbehaved, or failed, or came near to failing. And when Crispin left her, well then that red pen swept the page.

And what is more, as Erica suggested, they will both write to the other eleven, not saying, of course, what is happening, but to *suggest something is going on*, and the other eleven can hardly fail to attend.

To understand properly you had to have been there at Farendon, down with the maidens and mistresses in the stuffy heat among wooden desks and wide-windowed classrooms, the lush long grass of the lawns and playing fields, wet-green round the trunks of the trees.

And always, when you look back to those days, there is the heady smell of new-mown grass.

When you came downstairs you had to pass the sparse-haired matron – what she had left of it was a curiously dirty yellow – known as 'the Hydra'. Each morning she waited, resting her bolster-bosom on the bottom banister with book and pencil in her hand. She croaked, 'Tick or a cross, tick or a cross,' like some grotesquely tufted parrot.

Obsession was everywhere.

You had to run round the playing fields before a breakfast of porridge, following Miss Radley, astonishingly erect, the back of her head, shoulders, hips, shins, all an exact ninety degrees vertical to the earth, her thrusting breasts like rocks and her rugby-player legs revolving, and when she ran she rose and descended at a ninety degree angle also.

Intensity was everywhere.

Was it at Farendon that Molly learned about obsessions, learned to cope with relationships so intense it was impossible to give them up in any normal way, impossible to let go? Her love had always been flawed. To worship is not, necessarily, to love. And it's wearying to be worshipped. It was wearying for Crispin. Molly had been mad after Crispin left, hadn't she? But is she better now?

Or has Molly, clinging to the bitter residue of her love for Crispin, been trying to replace all that . . . and is that why she's persisted? Trying to simulate in some pathetic, second-class way all that consuming frenzy, the excitement, the selection of the victim, the chase, the kill? Only they hadn't meant to kill Amy Macey.

That taste of power. Power from the earth as they revelled in their femaleness and worshipped the moon . . . it was all there, from the moment of initiation, that knowledge that they had, that exultation, those ceremonies, that intimacy.

Worship was everywhere.

And how had Fatty Maguire, the fat girl, come to be included in such an exalted assembly in the first place? Surely, in the process of natural selection, *she* was a victim?

The elevation of Fatty Maguire had happened, as so many huge things in life happen, as an accident. There are always two paths to take, thinks Molly, sitting soberly up in bed now and staring blankly out of the window, but you can only see them when you look back. At the time, blinkered, you cannot see the options. Nor can you judge their worth.

The fifteen-year-old Molly had been fatly searching for a secret place to eat her cake . . . a whole cake sent from home . . . she hadn't wanted to share it, when she stumbled across the place behind the reredos. Lit by the very light of

God, a hard red glow that illuminated the northern end of the chapel, behind the altar. Down a track of beaten bluebells through the woods.

And Molly has to ask herself another question. Why, out of all of them, out of the stream of new girls that had arrived last autumn, why had they, so fatally, chosen Amy Macey? There is no answer to that one, save for the shameful thought that it might have been because she looked so like an angel that she called for desecration. A little, doll-like, Christmas tree angel with bubbly white curls. Nobody ought to look innocent like that.

There had been other victims, oh yes, there had been many, but they escaped unscathed with nothing more, presumably, than some unpleasant memories of a few short months of rather nasty persecution during their schooldays which had either fizzled out or come to nothing. Not one of them had even associated the disappearance of Amy with the witch-band. It had never got out. No one had blabbed to parents or police. But every single member, every one of those thirteen know, beyond a shadow of a doubt, that they killed Amy Macey.

There can only be two possible reasons for the curse on Erica Bryant, thinks Molly, revenge or extortion. Erica is rich, excessively rich. Already Erica would pay a tidy sum to stop the persecution, to regain her peace of mind. If extortion is the motive then presumably, before very much longer and the whole thing gets out of hand, Erica will receive some sort of demand.

If revenge is the motive it is an entirely different matter.

And there are only thirteen people, including herself and Erica, who can be doing this. All middle-aged women now, incredible, but true. For the symbols that Erica has received are the very ones they used for Amy Macey, and she is surely dead, although, of course, no body has ever been found.

These are memories that Molly has denied herself for over twenty years. Understandably. But after all that time they are still raw. They still burn. Molly eases her legs under the covers. Fat legs. Her face looks fresh and scrubbed even after sleep. Anxiety gnaws. She has remembered to leave biscuits

47

and Malvern water by Erica's bedside. She wonders whether Erica eats breakfast and thinks perhaps she would prefer coffee and a croissant . . . well . . . she has some of those in the freezer. They haven't actually bothered with breakfast since Crispin went and Molly isn't used to getting it. What time should she get up and how will Erica fit into the slow-moving pace of life in Ashbury? How long will she stay? Should Molly have invited her in the first place or will this turn out to be one of those invitations you regret the day after you issued them?

Slowly Molly realises that for the first time in three years it wasn't thoughts of Crispin that woke her, washing over her and drenching her with misery first thing in the morning. She actually feels brighter. All her thoughts, all her concerns are turned towards the curse. She is tired and confused by it all – and yet energised. That is how it works. In some way she is going to have to remain detached or be pulled into the vortex, helplessly, quite useless to poor Erica.

Molly lies in bed and thinks and listens, deciding to wait until she hears Erica up and moving about.

It doesn't take Erica all night to think and plot. She slept well, she was terribly tired, and before bed she and Molly must have put away four double scotches. She leans out of bed and raises the floral Austrian blind and yes, she can see the ducks, as promised, on the village pond.

This morning Erica's thoughts are back at Farendon, too. Back to the time they sat round listening to Dierdre Bott telling them all about being in love. That was how it started, with them all sitting round listening to Dierdre, because Dierdre was in love with the Head Girl, Alison Morgan, a colder and more unattainable creature it was impossible to imagine. As Alison Morgan was going to be a chemist this entailed long, lonely vigils outside the school labs for poor Dierdre, to be ignored or even laughed at when Alison, the adored one, finally came out.

'For the ultimate sensation,' said a suffering Dierdre, pulling up her legs and hugging them tightly, 'you have to prostrate yourself at your adored one's feet and beg to be punished.'

48

They sat round in one of the St Mary's House dormitories and listened, aghast, to the girl they called Barmy Bott. They sat on pillows on the floor. They drank Coke with aspirin in it because someone said that made it alcoholic. Pleased with the effect she was having, Dierdre carried on, 'So you have to find someone who doesn't care about you . . . someone so far, so way, way far above you that he or she would be willing to have you as slave, abjectly worshipping . . . and then you feel, then you feel this sense of giving up yourself completely to a greater being, this sense of being devoid of all lesser feelings but the complete one, the sensation of total worship . . .'

'That someone wouldn't be a very nice person, I don't think.'

Who had said that? Erica can't remember. She reaches across and takes a biscuit from Molly's tin. Bites it. Tries to think. For somebody had said that.

'Religion does that for people.' Erica thinks it must have been Jayne Cromwell who spoke then. Jayne was always fairly logical and direct in her thinking. 'Masochism. Perhaps that's how nuns get their kicks, why they go round whipping themselves and lying on the floor.'

'But you're worshipping somebody kind and gentle,' said Dierdre, thinking of cold, cold Alison. 'Jesus is no good. What you want is somebody wicked and masterful. Someone with immense power.' And Dierdre sighed and shuddered.

Silence. Awed silence. And some bewilderment. For Alison Morgan's only power was to report people, give out dinner tickets and take detention.

'Like the Devil, for instance?' It was her, Erica, who had whispered that. They all turned, chilled, to stare at her, fox-eyed in the dark.

Yes, that is how it had started. Erica realises she is not chewing her biscuit, but gripping it lightly between her teeth. What a start, what a start for something that had grown and grown into the mighty force it had eventually become. Five little girls sitting round discussing Dierdre Bott's hopeless state of love. Five little girls yearning, ripe to feel something just like it.

Hysteria was everywhere, at Farendon, that summer.

Nine

The following week Julian spends the Saturday helping his little group move into the 'flat'. It is, in fact, a three-roomed section of basement which used to house, when the Hospital was more self-sufficient, the pathology lab. Because he knows this, and only because he knows it, Julian thinks he can smell formaldehyde. But is there an atmosphere down here? Can Norman, Dennis and Harold sense it, too?

This is the first batch of men from Underwood to be eased out into the world. Julian thinks of birth. Of how babies, both animal and human, are given appeal to protect them in the most vulnerable stage of their lives. Wide eyes and snub noses. Downy skins and big, helpless wobbly heads. Well, unfortunately his little band have no such appeal. They are men. Peculiar-looking men at that. The sort of men that will attract persecution rather than what they desperately need at this stage, protection.

He even has to fight with the Almoner to get what he has been promised . . . decent warm blankets, heaters, a television that actually works, beds worthy of the name . . . not the ones stored out in the sheds which have damp, mouldy growths on the mattresses. And comfortable chairs. Proper chairs. Not waterproof chairs with wipeable seats.

'It has to be a home, God dammit,' he shouts at the jobs-worth man with the worried face. 'There's no point in the exercise, no point at all, if we're not going to do it properly. And don't talk to me about cuts . . .'

Eventually he gets his way.

Julian throws himself into his work, of course he does. He throws himself in to keep from thinking of Sylvie. There's time enough for that at night when he trails back to his flat. Empty. Silent flat. The most exciting thing in it is the leaping gas fire. It didn't look dingy like this when Sylvie lived here.

She has taken her things, and it seems that it was her things, after all, not his, that made it home.

Over-educated. Sylvie, until he got this job, called him the eternal student. She, on the other hand, worked as a speech therapist at Underwood until she left a month ago. He got a job, something she had always been on at him to do, and she promptly left him. Now she's in the private sector somewhere near York. Living in. She would rather live in than live with him! There is pain, for Julian, in that. There is pain in all of it.

Someone along the inexorable route of hospital hire and fire, somebody somewhere must have raised eyebrows at the likely practical skills of a Doctor of Philosophy. But the post of Rehabilitation Officer is poorly paid, and Julian's list of qualifications is impressive. And althought they were deluged with applications after the slim newspaper advert, there was no further interest when the job description was sent out. Underwood was too short of money to re-advertise and Julian is certainly enthusiastic. And presentable. And likeable enough. So he got the job. And no one was more surprised than he. And Sylvie, who said rather cuttingly, 'A chance to put back some of the benefits that up until now you've always been taking out of the system.'

Julian blinks her away and turns his attention to Norman Appleyard, who staggers under a bundle of bedding looking like a Portuguese donkey with hardly any part of him showing under his load. He knows it is Norman because of his ultra-clean, highly polished shoes. He feels a surprising fondness towards this handicapped man. Perhaps he sees himself there, staggering under impossible loads, an invisible hand stretched out for help. Perhaps he makes the mistake of seeing himself there. That is what comes of employing unprofessional people. They see what they want to see, not what is actually there. Yes, a trained social worker, properly paid and uninvolved, was what was needed ideally for this job.

'Dump the bedding in the lounge, Norman, and then we can take it through to where we want it bit by bit. I think it's time for coffee, don't you? Harold, would you like to make it on your first morning?'

Harold sways and pouts with his hands behind his back, his hair full of stuffing from a chair that must go back.

Julian stares hard at Harold. He's going to have to find them some different clothes. Their ill-fitting, institutionally cleaned clothes brand them for what they are, what they were, more surely than a stamp across the forehead. They look like homeless men, but they're not homeless and never will be if Julian does his job properly. And he's determined that he will. Not for them a life of seamy guest-houses, to end up in final degradation in a cardboard box with a bottle of methylated spirits in lieu of love. 'Go through to the kitchen,' says Julian gently, 'make sure the kettle is full of water and turn it on, as I showed you. Push the little red button in.'

'I'll do it,' says Dennis, striding past.

'He said I could. He said I could,' says Harold, and the two go through to the kitchen and Julian and Norman hear them arguing in there.

'Come and sit by me,' says Julian, innocently. 'Let's see how comfortable this new sofa is. At any rate it's a lot better than anything I've got at my flat.'

So far Julian has never shouted, told them off, cursed them, or insinuated in the slightest way that Norman and his companions are anything other than favourite friends of his. Well, why would he be otherwise? Far battier men than this flood academia's halls. This attitude, believe it or not, is hard for Norman to handle. Norman needs to test Julian for he feels he cannot be genuine. He has to think of something naughty to do and watch Julian's reaction carefully. He has smoked his pipe, continuously, and Julian has not even commented. He dropped a pile of plates first thing this morning, not accidentally, and Julian had merely laughed and gone off to find some more. Then Norman had hidden Julian's jacket under a pile of clothing. Julian had gone round muttering, had eventually found it, but it hadn't even crossed his mind that Norman might have deliberately hidden it. Notoriously absent-minded, which is one of the traits that drove Sylvie out, Julian is always losing his things but Norman is not to know that.

Norman pricks up his ears at mention of Julian's flat. He

goes to sit beside Julian. Julian's pale, long-fingered hand rests on the sofa arm. Norman unclenches his fist and lets his do the same on the other one. This shaggy-haired loose-limbed man in the bright red shirt, so sensual to Nurse MacNelly, this man's eyes are full of pain. Norman wants to please him, Norman wants to hurt him. Norman doesn't know what he wants to do so he sits quietly on the sofa beside him. Mimicking his exact way of sitting. Only Julian of course, being an unprofessional man, does not recognise this.

'Where do you live?' asks Norman.

'I live at number 29A bushy Grove,' says Julian, unthinkingly. 'I live in a flat, Norman, which is much smaller than yours. And I live by myself. I don't even have a dog.' Julian is pleased with Norman's evident interest.

'And how long have you lived there?'

'I have lived there for eight years. I moved into it with a friend eight years ago.'

'But the friend has gone now?' asks Norman.

'Yep, Norman. She's gone.'

'You must be lonely.'

Julian turns to look at Norman. Those guileless eyes don't fall. Julian is held to those eyes. They look empty, they could almost pull you inside them if you let them. But they're not empty . . . just veiled. Veiled by years of. . . ? Years of what? Julian thinks Norman's experiences of life must be unimaginably horrible. Just the thought of a switch, delivering two hundred milliamperes at one hundred and ten volts, all flowing through your head for half a second makes Julian pale. And three times a day for a period of five weeks! Julian, again, finds himself trying to put himself into Norman's shoes. Trying to see things Norman's way.

'I am lonely sometimes, Norman. Very lonely. But then everyone is, underneath it all, aren't they?'

'You could find someone else to share your flat with – if it's a flat for two.'

Julian sighs. 'It's not as easy as that. I wish it was. Aha, here's the coffee, and it looks great. Just what we wanted, eh, Norman?'

Dennis dithers into the room with the cups on a tray.

Harold, muttering to himself, takes them off and places them carefully on the coffee table. Julian leans forward and helps himself to two spoonfuls of sugar. Norman, who has never taken sugar in his life, does the same.

But Norman, glancing furtively towards Julian, catches the flimsy three-legged table with his sleeve (it is shaped like a piece of polished driftwood in a curious shade of woody-pink), catches and tugs so that table, coffee, sugar and teaspoons go right over and fall on the pear-coloured carpet. Flop. Splat. And the three legs point towards Norman like three stubby pig's trotters, like the underside of a handicapped pig.

Dennis leaps and Harold dances. Norman watches.

'Hell,' says Julian, balancing his own coffee which he has managed to rescue, balancing it and holding it tight to his chest. 'Hell. That'll stain. Did I order any detergent from the stores? Did I? And if I did, the big question still remains, did they bloody well bother to send it?'

So Norman tells himself it is all right.

Ten

The twins have gone. They have taken their duvets and gone.

But Molly's isn't an empty nest. There is a cuckoo in the Priest's House.

If Erica wasn't still here Molly would have the house to herself. She doesn't know if she wants that. She could have burned beef and picked off the black, crispy bits with her fingers. She could have gone barefoot and naked in her Innisfree home whenever she felt like it, able to leave the bathroom door unlocked and there must be more, much more, only Molly can't think what.

Symbols and meanings, symbols and meanings, and why would anyone be cursing Erica? They go through it and through it and through it until it makes sense no longer. Erica isn't getting any better, but so far, thank God, no worse either.

She seems cheered by thoughts of their return to Farendon.

Soon Molly is going to have to introduce Erica, properly, to her friends. To the group of village friends she has, most of them members of the writing group. Molly doesn't know how they are going to fit together, the sophisticated, worldly Erica and the Ashbury set. She wasn't friends with them either until Crispin left. She didn't have any close friends until Crispin left. And then she fell headfirst into a nest of feminists – the last outpost for dungarees, ordering bulk from *Clothkits* – who were pretty shocked at her dependency on Crispin. She doesn't talk to them about him. They won't let her. That's why she uses her writing because even they wouldn't dream of censoring that. Molly is a bit afraid of her Ashbury friends, although their brand of feminism is more to do with drinking real ale and singing bawdy songs in a corner of The Crown rather than wading through the mud at Greenham.

Last week Molly posted the feather to Rose. It wasn't a swan's feather. It came off the back of a duck but it looked just the same, small and rather bedraggled, but enough. She drove twenty miles to Exeter in order to post it. She bought special, rather strange purplish envelopes in which to put it, lined envelopes which she keeps hidden among the scarves in her wardrobe drawer. She sat for a while trying to write the word *Rose*. She couldn't do it, she just couldn't do it, so she put *Mrs Tarrent* over the familiar address and didn't look at it again.

And the reason for her shocking behaviour she lays at Erica's door, because it was after one of Erica's 'sessions' that Molly came back downstairs, slipped out of the house after dark and rooted around in the mud by the pond for the feather. The moon, she'd noticed, was waning. Until then it had only been a thought. But once that feather was in her hand, once she had taken the trouble to get it, it was too late to pull back.

Erica has made herself at home from day one. She seems enamoured of Ashbury. After breakfast on that first morning she had rung Horracks in London and dictated a list of essentials that she wanted sending on. Molly listened hard for any suggestion of a returning date but Erica didn't give one. She just told Horracks she had bumped into an old schoolfriend and that she didn't know how long she would be away.

The following day these 'essentials' arrived, piled in the back of a gold Mercedes which looked obtrusive among the Ashbury Volvos and Minis. Erica didn't care. She never had cared, that was one of the most remarkable things about her. She parked her car outside the Priest's House, having driven the agency driver to Exeter station.

All that day they talked, only leaving the fireside to pop across to The Crown for lunch. They talked at The Crown. They talked over the muffins that Molly bought at the village shop for tea. When Molly stopped to get the supper she was so immersed in Farendon she couldn't find the grater. She felt dizzy in her kitchen! Her own, familiar kitchen. As if she'd suddenly woken up and come down to make a drink, woozy with sleep. They talked through a supper of macaroni cheese. All about Farendon. Everything about Farendon.

And to Molly, talking about it at dear last was like an exorcism. The relief of it makes her light-headed. Sometimes she had begun to wonder if, after all, it hadn't all been a bad dream.

Only briefly did Erica touch on her marriage to Jasper Bryant . . . the playboy genius who built up an empire overnight, lost it and built another one. Selling designer jeans and T-shirts in every bleak town centre up and down the land alongside the Tie Rack and the Sock Shop.

Erica's marriage seems to have been a web of intrigue and deception. Molly, far from understanding, thinks Erica must be relieved to be rid of him. From what she hears, Jasper comes over as a selfish brute of a man. Erica is well out of it, Molly thinks to herself, free at last, or she would be if this awful curse wasn't hanging over her.

Molly has read that devils once disturbed never go very far away. They have always been there, in shadow, over Molly's shoulder. She always knew they would return. In some ways, in some inexplicable ways, it is a relief.

'Do you mind,' asked Erica on the second night, 'do you mind if I play some music?'

'Of course not.'

Pale, haunted Erica might find comfort in listening to music. While Molly could and did feel concerned for Erica, she did not feel sorry for her. Erica was not that sort of person. What had Molly been expecting – Mozart, Brahms?

Erica leafed through her old seventy-eights and forty-fives with a smile on her face and a gleam in her eye. 'Horracks must have been glad to see the back of these,' she said. 'He hated them. Snob.'

To start with the music was decently quiet. They sat and they sipped more scotch. Erica scorned Molly's re-corked selection of wines cluttering up the fridge behind the milk bottles. Every now and then Erica got up, moved across the low-beamed room to turn up the sound a bit. Until it was extremely loud. Louder, in fact, than Molly had ever experienced it before. Molly didn't like to comment. After all, anything that made Erica feel better must be good. In fact Molly didn't know how to do anything about it. They were the old records, the Farendon records, the ones they had danced to then. Lots of Elvis, lots of Otis Redding, lots of Little Richard. Wild music, hard and certain, more primitive than now. And some Sixties stuff. All beat. All drums.

And the next time Erica reached to turn up the volume she took off her shoes and started to dance. Without much motion. Dressed all in black, jeans, sweater and a black scarf like a band round her hair. Keeping her quick, vigorous body under tight control. Because underneath the savage frenzy was there. More of a gentle sway. And her eyes went blank. She stared at the air and she swayed, fluidly, on her own to the rhythm, as if she was dancing with a ghost. But the queer thing was that she didn't look odd dancing like that. Erica was so beautiful that she couldn't look odd doing anything. Without her make-up and with her hair so shiny and her eyes so startling in her bony face, Erica looked like a little girl, the sort of haunted, bony child you see curled up on doorsteps in charity advertisements. If anything it was the room that looked odd, the low-beamed room with its flowers, books and brasses, its rugs and Molly's precious rosewood piano. And Erica was totally insensitive to the aura of the place. On to it, on to the Priest's House she was stamping her own.

What a very good thing, Molly thought to herself, that the house is detached, and set on its own from the rest. Otherwise neighbours would certainly be banging on her Black-Death door. As it was the lights were on and it was well after midnight. It was long past her normal bedtime. There would be talk in Ashbury in the morning.

Molly watched Erica, tried to place her, to put her somewhere within her terms of reference for how, otherwise, could she cope with this? Erica, intensely vulnerable but at the same time feline and sensual. Molly was, frankly, embarrassed. There she sat, a plump woman in a plump armchair with vibrations coming up through her stockinged feet and right up to her head, to where the pale pony tail must surely be bobbing where it sprouted, feministly, from its elastic band. She felt so much older than Erica. She managed to think how shocked Crispin would be if he came in now and saw Erica dancing like that, if he heard the music loud like this. And then Molly smiled. How she wished he *would* come. How she wished he was likely to walk through that door in the stooped way he had, and be shocked. Molly had never, until lately, shocked Crispin. But if he walked in, as she dreamed he would, it would be Erica who shocked him, Erica, with her yellow eyes vacant and dilated. Not she.

So when Erica beckoned, when she inclined her head, seeming to notice Molly for the first time, Molly squeezed her inhibitions up in her fists and started to dance. Well, she could hardly make a greater fool of herself here in her own little lounge than she had done lately outside it. She'd told Erica all about that, all about her futile efforts to get Crispin back. It was funny but you could talk to Erica about things like that and know she wouldn't criticise. 'I wish I could undo them but I can't,' Molly said. 'They are things I'll never be able to laugh about. Time never erases things like that. I'll never get over the humiliation. I even . . . once . . . I even got on my knees and begged him. In the street between bollards. But there were worse things than that. Yes. Worse. I phoned the police to tell them drugs were on sale at his house. They raided it. I put an advert in *Exchange & Mart*, inviting men to ring up to listen to sexy stories. I regularly tampered with his car. He was, I suppose, when you think about it, very patient really. But humiliation like that, Erica, how do you get over it? It's pathetic, isn't it?'

And Erica hadn't contradicted her. Erica, by her silence, had agreed.

So Molly danced. And it was funny because she remembered how to do it. Twenty years on and yet she still remembered how to dance. And the same passionate feelings began to rush through her. The very same. As if she wasn't forty years old at all but fifteen still, with all the need, all the yearning, all the frenzy of the child she had been.

Discovering it still there like that was astonishing. So, all these years while she had waltzed and fox-trotted round dinner-dance floors with Crispin, feeling nothing but the constriction of her dress round her ankles, while she had sat aside smiling to watch the youngsters dance, while she had shouted up to the twins, 'Turn it down for goodness' sake, turn it down,' all those years of doing that and *this* had been churning inside her. She had denied the wildness. She had never realised.

They must have danced for two hours, those women, not speaking, not pausing, just dancing. Molly smelled her own sweat and she hadn't smelled that for years. It was nice. There was a moment when Molly cried but Erica turned her back. They didn't dance together. It was important they be apart. They were dancing for themselves . . . dancing . . . writing . . . it merged and became the same. Just a way of expressing terrible, terrible feelings, terrible memories, and achingly beautiful, secret ones as well.

Well! Debilitated, exhausted, limp, afterwards of course it was difficult to know what to say. Molly raked the fire and beat up the sofa cushions, trying to fill the room with some sound. The drums left a flaccid silence behind them. Words were impotent after the dance. So they parted under lame 'goodnights', 'sleep wells', and 'See you in the mornings'.

But Molly couldn't sleep. She didn't want to let go. She didn't know if she would ever find those feelings again. For them she was somehow dependent on Erica. Going out into the night in her dressing gown and slippers, something she wouldn't have dreamed of doing in normal circumstances suddenly seemed quite a tame proposition. Perfectly okay. Why shouldn't she do it? Dancing out her hatred had felt good. Now she only had to follow the feelings through and she would exorcise them once and for all.

Posting the letter was a different matter entirely for she was sane and sober when she did that. 'With intent', the law would call her actions. Intent to what? Molly wasn't at all sure. So she stood at the post-box and chanted under her breath the name she hadn't dared write on the envelope, *'Rose . . . Rose . . . Rose,'* until it didn't sound like a name at all, became more like a household gadget in her head like a coal-scuttle or a bag of clothes pegs. Suddenly meaning nothing. Certainly having nothing to do with the cold little false-eyed lynx who bore the name. And in that way Molly was able to put the purple envelope into the bright red letter-box, and watch it fall, hear it tickle the bottom with a feeble-sounding phutt.

'With intent'. Molly even wore gloves.

But the blame for her actions, the blame she laid squarely on Erica's shoulders. As she always had done.

Eleven

Julian Tenby is naïve in the way of people who have never quite left school, but even so he is perfectly aware of Harold's distressing little habit. Julian considers that any comfort in this cruel world must be grasped with both hands, a rather unfortunate turn of phrase in this particular context but true, nevertheless.

There is not a shade of embarrassment in Julian's bearing when he leads his little band of men into John Collier's menswear store, having obtained a chitty from the Almoner for new clothes. He is interested to see what they will choose. He has no intention of influencing them. It is something they are going to have to do, one day, on their own.

They take Harold's choice to the counter half a dozen times before he finally makes his decision. Julian raises his eyebrows not a fraction when Harold chooses a gaudy checked blazer and a pair of navy twill trousers with bright red braces. He might glow bright as an American oilman but anything is better than that conformist drabness which he was made to go about in until now. At least it looks as if he has been to a shop, a normal shop, not some nightmare warehouse where jumpers and jackets cling drably to gorilla-shaped manikins.

'What d'you think? What d'you think? Is this all right? Does it suit me?' Dennis, after an hour of browsing, picks a very smart and sensible ensemble of bottle green . . . trousers, jumper, tweed jacket. And the colour suits him. He even looks, thinks Julian summing him up, he even looks quite dignified in an abstract sort of way. Julian tells him so. If only he hadn't come out in his slippers. The slippers cast plaid aspersions over the whole effect. Dennis tells the assistant he wants to keep his new things on. The labels have to be cut off him while he bends and contorts to expose them. A customer comes in, spies the odd behaviour and walks straight out again. Eventually, straightening up, Dennis moves with considerable pride.

Norman, whom Julian imagined wouldn't be interested in clothes at all, takes the longest time to choose of all of them. Up and down the racks and rows he goes, touching and staring, pulling jackets out and holding them up in front of him, holding out his leg in a pansy, quite uncharacteristic manner and frowning to himself.

When, finally, he comes from the changing room, steps out from behind the curtain with a heavy swing, he is a mock version of Julian himself. Brown cords that will be disreputable in time, brown jacket with patches on the elbows (Julian's were sewn on by Sylvie, he didn't buy it like that) and a brown and white check Vyella shirt. In his hand he shyly holds a red cravat. Julian fingers his own, catches sight of himself in the glass doors.

He thinks he is flattered but he isn't quite sure. For the first time Julian isn't quite sure. He notices, it is blatantly apparent so that even Julian notices, that Norman has not been for his weekly haircut. It is no longer close shaved up to his ears. It is growing, slowly, but certainly it is longer than it was. Norman smiles only with his lips, and the gap between his front teeth looks very wide when he asks, 'How do I look?' There is something that is not benign about that smile. He looks like a man gripped by some intensity of feeling that I cannot place, thinks Julian, but he says, 'You look perfect.'

Julian finds he has overspent. But he is prepared for that and he is happy to pay the difference.

The first night they spent in the new 'flat' he stayed with them, slept on the sofa cuddled up and dreaming dreams he often had, in which Sylvie was back. In his dreams he sensed that Norman was staring at him, staring through the medically-suggestive glass and plywood section put up to divide the sitting room from the kitchen.

First he had taken his group to The Farmer's Arms, the soulless pub with the red patterned carpet and all the brass next to the Hospital, but he noticed uneasily that Norman matched him drink for drink and Julian felt that this was a criticism. He knows he is drinking too much lately. He doesn't need Norman to rub it in.

With great success his little band spent Monday night on their own in the spooky basement flat at Underwood Hospital. Do they feel it too? Julian asks himself. But he daren't ask them. The last thing he wants to do is to introduce anything like that. They have painted the green walls white, have moved the fluorescent lights and put ordinary hangings there, but you can lie and look up and see old screw marks in the tiled ceiling – probably asbestos – where the other lights were. If you're directly underneath, on the sofa, you have to imagine – you can't help it – you have to imagine that once there were bodies here. On a stone-cold slab.

He had left them three frozen, individual lemon mousses and a large Marks and Spencer fish pie. In the morning he noticed that the oven had not been used. They had eaten the fish pie cold, but Julian poked through the waste bin and read that it had, happily, been pre-cooked.

'It was lovely, very tasty,' said Dennis, 'with sauce on.'

Success! Julian had been worried about them. He hadn't slept properly all night. A most unprofessional man.

On a Monday and a Friday Julian lectures at the University to supplement his poor Rehabilitation Officer income. It isn't far from Bushy Grove so on a clear night he walks. Throughout that Monday evening he pondered on returning to check his men before going home. He couldn't keep his mind on his work. He gave long sighs and slow blinks, normally a signal for a change of subject and whenever he did it his students inserted long dashes and some even turned over – but that evening they had too many long dashes, wasted sheets and no changes of subject because Julian wasn't concentrating.

Back at his flat he had paused, key in hand. Should he pop back to Underwood? It wouldn't take him ten minutes. Or should he give them the benefit of the doubt and leave them to cope alone? Eventually he decided to backtrack to The Pack Horse and have a pint and a ploughman's instead. Suddenly he felt very hungry. Several times he turned round. Stopped to listen. Was there something, someone? Or was he just uneasy because of his worries? What with Sylvie leaving him and all these new pressures, Julian wasn't used to feeling responsible. He'd bought them lemon mousse and fish pie but had forgotten to get anything for his own supper. He'd never been responsible for himself before, let alone three other inadequate men. Oh yes, he identified with them. He identified most strongly.

Norman only wanted to see where Julian lived. No he didn't, he mustn't fall into the trap of telling untruths to himself, that way lies madness. He must be truthful and admit that he wanted to stay near him. That, and to see if someone would stop him, to see if he could really just 'go out' for no other reason but that he wanted to. The last time he'd been out at night, other than with an escort, was when he'd been twelve years old. He could hear himself now, his footsteps in the darkness. Then, it had been different. Then he hadn't been able to hear. And they'd thought he couldn't speak, either. Just because he didn't they thought he couldn't, although he had been able to when he first arrived. He'd asked lots of questions but no one had ever answered.

They tried to get him to speak. They sat him down.

> *There are fairies at the bottom of our garden*
> *Not so very, very far away . . .*

And Norman sat and stuck his tongue through the gap in his teeth. He could read lip-read what the therapist said but he didn't know what fairies or gardens were. He had no conception of 'far' or 'away'. As far as Norman was concerned everything that ever was or would be was here in the ward all around him. He didn't want to know. And what's more the man's hand was hurting where it squeezed his jaw trying to force the sounds out. And he saw him say, half-turned away, 'Good God give me strength!'

No one stopped him. So Norman thrust his hands deep in his pockets and enjoyed the walk. Practised walking with the long strides that Julian used. Flicked his growing hair back from his forehead in the way that Julian did. Only it wasn't quite long enough for that yet. But it was growing. He remembered, the last time, he had skipped from pool to pool of streetlight, basking in each one like a fish jumping a series of tiny falls. He couldn't do that now. It would look odd. He didn't even want to do that now, he mused with interest.

It had been easy to get out of Gladstone. You only had to force the blocks off the toilet windows with a knife you kept from supper, climb up and squeeze through. They didn't give knives in Pitt. You had to eat everything with a spoon. And you couldn't get out either because there were bars on the windows and it was three floors high.

Norman hurries and starts looking back over his shoulder. Perhaps they'll come and get him again. Big men, silent men, male nurses, mouths wide, eyes angry, arms strong picking him up and hurting him putting needles in his arms and turning his eyes into glass. Stop it, Norman! Stop it! He slows and breathes long out-breaths, letting his shoulders loosen.

He knows where Bushy Grove is. He asked the porter who came round with the laundry. Norman follows the numbers, up one side of the street, down the other, and comes to rest outside number 29. It is a tall red house with lots of storeys. Some windows have lights on and Norman can hear music and television voices. He doesn't know which window belongs to Julian but he's found the house and that's what matters.

He watches. He waits. In the fierce, guarding way he used to watch and wait for Erica. Norman hides under a mottled laurel in the bit of garden, just back from the dark bay window on the ground floor. For three hours Norman waits. The temperature falls. The autumn night starts dripping. He wishes he had his bobble hat because the top of his head feels cold. And his ears start to ache.

Finally Julian comes. Where has he been? Has he been with other people, other friends? Norman is jealous. He could have stayed with them, with Dennis and Harold and Norman. He could have stayed with them in their brand new flat, watching the new television and sharing their fish pie. They would have let him choose the programmes. They would have made him cups of coffee, as many as he wanted. But Julian had obviously decided he would rather be elsewhere, spending his time with other friends. Proper friends who talk in pubs and don't look different from everyone else.

Norman follows Julian to The Pack Horse and waits outside in the shadows. Finally, at half past eleven, he follows him home again, sees the light go on in the bottom bay window near where he has been standing. It is gone midnight before that light finally goes out and Norman Appleyard can safely return to his basement flat, only to find Dennis still up and playing Edelweiss, his favourite record, loudly, amidst the sickly-sweet, overpowering stench of formaldehyde.

Twelve

Not for the world would we want to betray poor Molly for she has enough on her plate. But it has to be said, it must be said, to keep things fair, that Rose can't be all bad for she collects Golden Retrievers – so she does have someone to talk to after all – and is a member of Animal Rights, and it is with an Animal Rights label, licked by her pretty pink tongue, that she covers the mis-directed envelope and redirects it back to the first Mrs Tarrent, the one it was obviously meant for in Ashbury. For Rose knows no one who would write to her on strange purple stationery like that. And she's not going to be accused of tampering with Molly's post and opening that whole ghastly can of worms again.

Things have gone quiet just lately. Let them stay that way.

Her mail she gives to Crispin to post in chambers. She lies in bed, Molly's bed, between Molly's sheets, safe and protected from Molly by her answerphone. She always gives him her mail. And he puts it in his pocket without bothering to look at it. He's a busy, important man. Why would he bother to check over Rose's mail? And she's not going to mention it to him either. Least said the better on the subject of Molly.

Erica has rashly immersed herself in Molly's life at Ashbury. She has forfeited the wearing of make-up in order to appear pale and wan. She insists that Molly keep both doors locked day and night. Soon she will have to manufacture another incident to keep Molly's interest alive. It will be worth it in the end. They have sent back acceptance forms to Farendon. They have written for the names and addresses of the other eleven. Erica revels in fear and apprehension . . . the antidote to boredom is already taking effect.

Erica has taken to spending the days in her dressing gown. That is more effective than anything else. On this bright winter morning she peers out of the window and screws up her eyes. Erica is a night person and Ashbury is very much a day place. How on earth, worries Erica, can Molly live like this, buried away in the backwoods, rarely venturing anywhere except to the shop and her weekly writing sessions? No wonder she went over the top living here alone but for her two aloof children. No wonder she became obsessive and ridiculous, closeted away here with those dotty women friends. The place, Molly is certain, lends itself to neuroses and madness. Erica was shocked by Molly's confessions. How can a woman think so little of herself, almost as if, without Crispin, there is nothing left of her. How could such a substantial woman get to feel that way – humble herself like that?

It isn't even as if Crispin was ever nice to her. He treated Molly as if she was a vegetable, and an off-vegetable at that. Erica tries to tell Molly that. 'He never took you anywhere. He was mean with money. He was forever eyeing other women. He was forever finding fault with your clothes, your housekeeping, your body, your lack of intellect. Molly, he was a lumbering millstone round your neck, can't you see that? Can't you see that you can lead a much more exciting life without him? Now is your opportunity!'

'But I needed him. I loved him,' whined Molly, lumbering around her kitchen in those dreadful dungarees, clumsily arranging all her little bottles and jars as if any of that was important. She even tipped her cornflakes into a plastic container. And every day, to Erica's annoyance for there is nothing worse first thing in the morning than the sound of a Hoover, she cleaned her house. You would think, the way Molly worked, she'd be thin as a rake. And she lived on her nerves, forever tugging at her lip, then biting it with those neat little teeth. 'And I thought, in spite of what he said, that he loved me. He did make me unhappy, I do admit that. In fact, quite often I prayed that he would die. But I never dreamed he'd leave me!'

Some people, thought Erica, love to play the victim.

And Molly, strangely excited, told of all those long, painful vigils outside Crispin's house. The weary drives backwards

69

and forwards. The neverending phone calls, thought Erica, could be said to be natural. After all, eighteen years is a long time to be married. But Rose had countered those with an answerphone and her own voice sweetly saying, '*Rose and Crispin are out just now but if you would like to leave your name and number one of us will catch you later.*' Ugh! Molly had dialled the number to let Erica listen to that. As Molly rightly said, it was obscene.

'All I was able to do was leave a string of recorded obscenities in return,' Molly confessed.

'But you didn't do that, Molly, tell me you didn't do that.'

'Oh, I did. And I used to get myself comfortable and read out the rude bits from Crispin's old love letters but as I was cut off after about thirty seconds it took a great deal of dialling and pausing to leave anything worth having.'

Erica cringed. If Crispin had behaved very badly, as Molly insisted he had, then so had she. The phone calls could be excused, but the box opposite theirs at Covent Garden was a different matter, so was the scene outside the Godalming newsagents, so was the business of lurking, disguised as a client, in Crispin's chambers and so were the suicide-threatening letters inserted between pages two and three of *The Times*. She shouldn't have bribed that poor little delivery boy.

'How did you possibly believe that behaving like that would get him back?' Erica asked her.

'I didn't think – I just acted. I was driven. There was a devil inside me.'

Erica hears the mail drop. She inspects the purple envelope with a speculative eye. Crispin? Would he use envelopes like that? Surely not. Molly is out, she insists on fetching her bread and vegetables daily from the village shop. 'It's important to patronise it in order to keep it open,' she says. 'I don't mind paying the higher prices. After all, at the end of the day it's Crispin who pays, isn't it?'

There are five letters, three are nasty brown buff, one gives notice of a Hoopers fashion show – hardly a suitable venue for Molly, thinks Erica unkindly – and the purple one. Erica is fascinated. She holds it to the light but it is lined so she sees nothing. Perhaps Molly is having a secret affair she has not told Erica about. There must be more to Molly's life than she's making out. It is one of those self-seal envelopes which you don't have to lick. Erica knows you can open those and seal them again very easily. She is bored. She has time on her hands. So she opens it.

And out flutters a feather. A black feather. No message. Nothing else.

My God!

Astonishment follows horror, follows disbelief. And after that, after Erica has taken the letter, and the feather – for she's thrust it back into the envelope, she doesn't want to touch it – into the warmth of the kitchen for the hall has suddenly got very cold, after that comes the worm of anxiety that seems to start in her brain and burrow its way down to her heart.

Why? Who would? Had the reunion invitation stirred something up? All the very same questions they have been asking themselves over Erica's manufactured drama, only this is real. She lifts a coffee cup and sees it tremble in her hand. The coincidence of the timing undermines her. Why should it come now, just when they are planning to return to Farendon, just after Erica's invented scenario of her own? They will both return to Farendon with a quest, Molly with a fake one, Erica with something very nastily real on her hands. Why hadn't it come eight, ten years ago? Why now? And why, of all people, had it come to the door of poor, defenceless Fatty Maguire?

Thirteen

While all this is going on all those miles away in Ashbury, Farendon, that sleepy green oasis, prepares for the return of her Old Girls. She must surely be given a gender, for she who has 'formed' so many is no less deserving than hurricanes or ships. An ancient matriarch garbed in silk, she knows that those who return are dependent on her for something, or they would not come back. In this lies her power, so she decks herself as old women do preparing for visitors, but the lipstick smears like a scar and the powder cloys deep within the broken pores and creases. She knows. She knows. Buildings always know. And her breath has the mothball smell of death. She, who sits so defensively upon the hill, employs one man in her preparations, an old retainer hunchbacked by madness, and that one man is Norman Appleyard.

He, cowering as a normal man would, works under the direction of Miss Radley, games mistress turned teacher of human biology, now in her sixtieth year but still a powerful, surprisingly upright woman. The head gardener, Hunter, left years ago, and now the estate is in the charge of Appleyard, although they never officially gave him the title of head gardener. Well, it wouldn't look very good would it, especially when you think what they pay him. Two boys come in each day to help him.

Now that indomitable woman comes out of the front door where she's been arranging pieces of abstract art, or rather censoring the stuff sent up from the art department for display in the hall for the Old Girls. You can be a little more risqué with the Old Girls than you can be with say, parents, or governors, but even so . . . Celia Pratt will have to take that one back.

'Oh, *Appleyard*!' And Miss Radley gives two short blasts on her whistle – she might be a biology teacher now but at heart she still haunts the lacrosse pitch – a signal they have agreed to use between them during this busy time.

Appleyard comes from pruning the rambler roses. He is soily from forking round the bases and filling them with slag.

Is there an insolence in the rakish angle, today, of Appleyard's bobble hat? Is there a certain jauntiness in the step of his lumbering boot? There is certainly something different about his smile, but Miss Radley – a specialist in the rooting out of insolence – can't place it. The wind chases the leaves round Miss Radley's ankles on this day so scandalously blue that it could never be honestly painted. It tugs playfully at her hair, like a naughty child determined to involve an inattentive parent. But it has picked the wrong person in Miss Radley. With her light grey tie and her Airtex shirt, her skirt is so heavy that nothing but a hurricane could lift the hem, and anyway she is safely encased in stiff, orange wool tights beneath, and her hair is so tightly pinned to her head that a silly wind like this could not raise a wisp of it.

'About the flowers, Appleyard.'

'Plenty of dahlias.'

'You know very well that I hate dahlias. And so does everybody else, everybody who has any taste at all. For what reason, for what earthly reason would anyone present anybody else with a bunch of dahlias? To say I love you? To say I miss you? To say I'm sorry? No, Norman, the only reason somebody would present anyone else with such a totally unevocative bloom, riddled with slugs and making such foul water, would be to say thank you for feeding the cat! And what we at Farendon are trying to say is welcome back. I don't know why you grow them, I really don't.'

'The Chaplain likes them,' says Norman glumly, 'for the Harvest Festival.'

'And the Harvest Festival, among the leeks and the carrots, is where they belong. At the foot of the font. They have the smell of old churches about them and I will not have them in the school.'

This annual confrontation has to be gone through before they can reach a workable relationship worthy of the name. During it Miss Radley once again asserts her authority. 'So what else is there? What else have you got growing in the garden with some colour in it? We want flowers for the bedrooms, the hall, the corridors and the dining room. What have you got in the greenhouse? I shall have to come and have a look. And the lawns need mowing again, that last burst of sunshine has brought on a flush of late grass. It looks untidy.'

Norman quickly decides that he likes the look of autumn grass when it loses that smooth, unnatural snooker-table baldness. He likes the tufts and indents in it. He decides he will like everything about autumn with its smell of decaying leaf mould, burst apples and smouldering fires. If Miss Radley dislikes these things, then he will like them. He says, 'I take my orders from Miss Blennerhassett. That's who I take them from.'

'You take them from me during the reunion. I am in charge, as always, of organising the reunion affairs. And well you know that, Appleyard. Miss Blennerhassett has enough on her plate at the moment. And Appleyard,' she adds, as Norman turns away, 'I'm not sure that I like your attitude this morning.'

Appleyard isn't worried. He has plenty of cyclamen, begonia, primula and gloxinia coming into flower in the greenhouse. Set up one end where the extra heater is, are his precious Cymbidium orchids called Erica, crossed with care until they reached the exactness of her tiger eyes – and outside in the garden a whole bed of winter-flowering pansies. In the greenhouse this morning he lifted the leaves of the dead tomatoes and thought of the sweet little ones he used to put in a brown paper bag to take home to Arny. He won't be doing that next year. He won't be seeing Arny any more. He lives in his own flat now. No, Norman isn't worried. The school will be a picture. It always is. Every year Miss Blennerhassett, whom Appleyard considers to be a real lady, not like Miss Radley, always comes up to him afterwards and says, 'Splendid, Appleyard. A really magnificent effort! First-class show.' So it isn't anything to do with Miss Radley at all. It is strictly between him and the headmistress, Miss Blennerhassett.

'I can't stop here chatting to you all day,' says Norman, raising his arm to rub the fuzz on his woolly bobble with the centre of his hand. To himself he says, 'I forgive her.' He knows that he must humour her, that she is someone who likes to believe she is in charge.

Appleyard wanders off, muttering, leaving Miss Radley to the petulant wind which knows no better.

Nothing is going to spoil this day for Appleyard. He is excited. He turns pink in patches as he heads for his shed. Because today Julian is coming to 'have a look, if you'll put up with me'. So Appleyard checks the clock, sees that lunchtime is near, and walks faster so that he can prepare the tea and condensed milk, delicious and sweet, which he will share with Julian. And he bought some special egg and cress rolls on his way to work to celebrate the occasion.

Julian hasn't arrived yet but in his head Norman can smell him – toothpaste, after-shave, linen, soap, shampoo – good smells. Norman might have got to smell like Arny but he escaped in time, didn't he. Well, last night he had forced his way into Julian's flat, easing the Yale back with his pruning knife and had gone into the bathroom where he made a careful note of the colours and shapes of the bottles in there. He had handled them with awe, all the contents of that green-glass bathroom, before putting them back exactly. And with the money they give him each week he will gradually collect them himself. One day, people will think of him and sniff and smile, as he does when he thinks of Julian.

Norman had time, before he left, to open Julian's wardrobe and touch the things in there, to ruffle them so that a sense of Julian came out into the room. To pick up his pillow and hold it. To put his foot in one of Julian's shoes. He had time to open the fridge, to take out and inspect the stone of an avocado pear and lift an asparagus spear. He had time to weigh his hairbrush in his hand, to finger the books in the shelves and to pat the papers in higgle-piggledy piles on the floor.

Julian comes. He names the plants wrongly but Norman, usually so particular on this, doesn't contradict him. He leaves the door to the orchid house ajar, letting cooler air in. Norman doesn't close it. These things aren't important.

'Ah . . . childhood,' sighs Julian, touching a leaf with a

careless finger. 'The smells of childhood. My father used to have a greenhouse like this, much smaller of course, but no matter what's growing inside them they always smell the same, don't they?'

Norman knows this is not so, but he doesn't say it.

'And then, when my father made some money, he installed an automatic sprinkler so you got drenched whenever you went inside. The whole atmosphere was suddenly changed. But Father used to sit there on a garden chair in a souwester under a golf umbrella, not caring about the sudden downpours. Revelling in them, almost. I think it was a way of keeping everyone else out of his secret place, don't you?'

Norman thinks that Julian's father must have had something wrong with his head. He loves showing people round his greenhouse. Now he gets out the egg and cress rolls, smooths the paper bag they came in and lays them proudly on it, looking at Julian for reaction.

The way that Julian makes no comment, accepts the snack as his due, pleases Norman. Julian sits on the three-legged stool with his back resting on the propagating bench, eating his rolls and looking relaxed. 'It's a big place,' he says with his mouth full. 'I've never been inside the grounds before, only seen the walls from the road outside, and the clock-tower of course, you can see that from the roundabout. How long have you been here, Norman? It must be quite hard work, keeping all this up.'

'Mr Hunter took me on when I was fifteen,' says Norman, pouring the tea into two enamel mugs, one red, one blue. Which one should he give to Julian? Which one would Julian prefer? 'Mrs Hunter was a cleaner at Underwood. She was a nice woman and I liked her. One day she asked her husband if I could come and help him sometimes.'

Good God. So, in the end, it had been left to the cleaner. 'So they took you to see him?' Julian sips his tea and winces. He takes sugar in coffee, not in tea, and this is sweet, sweet as syrup. He takes another bite of egg and cress.

'He didn't want me,' says Norman. 'I could tell. He stood just here, just where we are now, talking to the nurse, Carnaby, it was, male nurse Carnaby. He left a long time ago.

I couldn't hear what they were saying because I was deaf then. I left them talking and I walked through there, into Hunter's orchid house. Hunter was an expert with orchids.'

Norman blinks and Julian thinks he's stopped. Norman tends to stop in the middle of conversations like that, almost as if he feels he's suddenly gone too far and is angry with you for asking in the first place. So Julian studies his roll and, forgetting, takes a second sip of tea. He doesn't want to push Norman. He doesn't want to take him back to days that Julian considers are probably best forgotten. It is enough that Norman has allowed him to come here today, allowed him to enter what Julian considers is a very private, special domain.

Norman pushes aside a packet of slug pellets and sits on an enormous upturned flower-pot. With hard eyes, in the solid way Norman always turns them to look towards the past, he starts to say in a rush, as if, if he doesn't say it now it will never come, 'Mr Hunter suddenly realised where I was. He pushed past Carnaby and flung open the orchid house door. Probably afraid I was doing something to the orchids . . . killing them maybe or pulling the petals off. He must have been shouting very loudly but of course I couldn't hear. I could see that Carnaby was laughing, he was standing outside, having a cigarette and laughing. I was afraid of Mr Hunter. He was big and brown like a bear, he walked like a bear as if he found it difficult to balance on two legs like everyone else, and he crossed his arms over his chest a lot, just like bears do. But even when I saw him coming in, filling the door with his hairiness, I couldn't stop from staring at the orchids.'

Norman brings his eyes right round the greenhouse and then rests them on Julian steadily. 'I turned my back to him. I didn't want to see him. And Mr Hunter came in, came up to me and looked right down at me and then he moved an arm and I thought he was going to hit me. I spoke then. I spoke and I said fuck off bastard, fuck off. That pulled him up. He stopped in his tracks. But his finger on my cheek was gentle, and he brought it up from the side of my mouth where the tears were and back to my eyes as if he wanted to put them back.' Norman follows the same route on his face, wonderingly, with a grubby, soil-encrusted finger. 'Then he looked very angry and rushed back out again. But he closed the door, very carefully and quietly, behind him. And that was that. He let me come. Because his orchids made me cry and I told him to fuck off he let me come. There! So that's how I started coming every day. And since then I've been very happy. Very happy indeed. And I'm very happy now, too!' People like to know that Norman feels happy. Happy is good. Sad is bad. But Julian is allowed to be sad. Julian looks sad now.

Julian, unprofessional so hardly able to endure Norman's reminiscences, says softly, 'I didn't close the door, did I?'

'They won't hurt,' says Norman, nodding at the orchids. 'They're tougher than they look.'

But there is something . . . Julian regards Norman's smooth, unlined face, his cherubic face, he studies it carefully. This is a face uniquely designed for keeping secrets. A face you'd think had never been lived in. It must have been a shock for Mr Hunter to hear such obscenities coming out of that inscrutable face. But Julian has noticed something so delicately flawed in the tale, or in the telling of it, that it is almost indetectable. It is, incredibly, almost as if Norman has deliberately recounted it and coloured it in such a way as to pre-empt Julian's reaction, as if he understands full well the tragic poignancy behind it and is using it to manipulate.

But why shouldn't Norman manipulate Julian? It isn't the prerogative of the experts. Norman is practised at it, has had to be in order to get where he is today. So why shouldn't he put a little gentle pressure on the areas where he thinks Julian might care? It's called smiling for the doctor, smile nicely and the doctor might not hurt you.

But Julian doesn't think of it quite that way. In some instances, manipulation is acceptable, in others it certainly is not. Not when it is so subtly used by a defective man.

So, surely not, surely not, thinks Julian. Surely Norman Appleyard doesn't possess the cunning. He looks and moves and behaves like a totally innocent man. Julian wants Norman to be an innocent man. But just then he didn't talk like one. There is something unsavoury about this, like finding a bug on a lettuce, although, if the lettuce is fresh, you ought to expect the bug to be there. It begins to look as if *Norman is able to choose how to behave* . . . shit!

And before Julian can stop him Norman is pouring more tea and spooning in the condensed milk with a dessert spoon.

Fourteen

Molly sends the blood to Rose. It is pig's blood, sticky and black, and she drains it from one of the Tupperware containers in her fridge. Ugh!

She finds a useful glass tube with a cork stopper in Edward's old chemistry set while she's clearing out junk from the attic. A sad business, clearing the attic, clearing out the children. She fills it with blood and wraps the whole thing in a strip of corrugated cardboard before popping it in a purple envelope. Then she drives to Exeter and posts it.

She feels less guilty about the blood than she did about the feather. In fact she feels quite light-hearted. The blood is merely a consequence of the feather, while the feather was a consequence of her own hatred.

Within a week it is back on her mat. She might have picked it up herself had she not so carefully developed the habit of missing the post and going to the shop the moment she sees the post van stopped on the corner. She'd taken to doing that last year when she realised how dependent she was becoming on the post, how eagerly she waited for THE LETTER. The letter, of course, from Crispin; the letter full of remorse, that tells her what a fool he's been, what a blind, unhappy fool; the begging letter asking her if she might, in time, feel able to forgive him and take him back.

Would she though, would she?

'*I now see Rose for what she really is,*' this mythical letter goes, '*I see her for what she is, a scheming, despicable, evil-minded bitch!*'

So it is Erica, once again, dressing-gowned, who collects the post. Who opens the purple envelope and finds the blood, somewhat congealed, but otherwise none the worse for its journey.

Damn! Blast! This is going too far.

*

80

'That woman is having the most extraordinary effect on poor Molly.'

'She had an effect on all of us, Jessie. The atmosphere tonight was not the same.'

'What is it about her? What is it?'

'She doesn't care if she's liked or not. That's what it is. She doesn't even try.'

The writing group has finished early. There didn't seem, after Erica's contribution, much point in going on. If someone's ignorant enough to refuse to take anything seriously, then of course there's no point. So they are congregated, the women who are left, in their own special corner at The Crown.

A fuming Effie Tate asks the question of all of them, 'How long is she intending to stay in Ashbury with Molly?' They cannot answer. They are silent. They fiddle with their real ale. Effie's got a gin. Now that the holiday season is over The Crown has been reclaimed by its locals again. They have removed the à la carte menu and reverted to the blackboard which advertises home-made soup and prawns in garlic, fisherman's pie and vegetable stew. With side salads. The microwave hums in the kitchen.

The corner where the writers sit is dark and by the fire. They miss Molly who usually sits at the end of the oblong table. Jessica, in this leaderless group, is in fact the leader. Now she says, running an anxious hand through bright red curls, 'I've never heard Molly write like that before. She seems, well, almost happy! There's none of the old blackness there. Is she writing like this for Erica? Afraid, perhaps, to let those deep feelings out? Or is she really feeling light-hearted and happy?'

'Whatever it is,' says Effie darkly, 'it is her influence that's causing it.'

The subject tonight was 'Magic', set naughtily by Linda French because she had already written a piece on it which she considered was rather good. They had started by reading their pieces, all very nice, except that Fleur always tended to get overinvolved and had clearly delved a little too deeply into *The Golden Bough* – because it wasn't really *facts* they were

81

after, as Jessica considerately told her. Although of course the facts are terribly interesting.

Erica, being a visitor, hadn't been required to bring any writing. But Molly, who would normally have made a meal of the subject, Molly's effort was empty. 'She never touched the subject, not really,' says Fleur, now, 'Going on like that about that ghastly little conjuror on TV . . . who calls that sort of thing magic? What a waste of a subject!'

Afterwards it had been even worse, when they passed two lines of a 'magic' poem round like consequences, folded over, to be followed by another two lines and then passed on. Everyone else's two lines were serious, but when the poem got to Erica or to Molly they inserted such ludicrous nonsense that all the poems, when read whole at the end, made no sense. No sense at all.

'We should have said something. We should not have accepted it.'

'But it's difficult – with Erica being Molly's friend. Under all that aloof sophistication she does look drawn and ill. And she might be nervous, of course, being among people she doesn't know. People react in different ways. She, obviously, becomes cynical and derisive. She's desperately upset, of course, by the death of her husband. He left her an absolute fortune, by the way. And whatever's going on, it has to be said, Molly looks so much happier.'

'She's changed,' says Effie, wonderingly. 'I've never seen anyone change so fast. It felt as if they were both laughing at us!'

'You didn't know her, did you Fleur, when they first came to Ashbury, Molly and Crispin?' Effie shakes her head, remembering. 'Well, she was very different then, or that's what we gathered from what we saw of her, which wasn't much, admittedly. Crispin didn't approve of us. He made that quite clear. Oh, he was a most objectionable man. But he was a powerful man, mentally powerful I mean – beside him she was a sorry creature, yes Crispin, no Crispin, and she held all his views, I mean she wasn't her own person. She belonged to that terrible man . . . body and soul. Molly seems to be a kind of chameleon, able to change according to circumstances, almost as if she's made of water, almost as if she wants to get out of her own shape and become somebody else! You know . . .'

'Well, I'm sorry,' says Jessica firmly, 'but I think I preferred the old Molly. Miserable, yes, positively morbid at times, but at least you knew where you were.'

'Now I've upset them!'

Molly sighs as she opens the door.

'Why worry. What do you want with people like that anyway?'

'They are my friends.' There is accusation in Molly's tone. 'We've had some good times together, good laughs. Good cries. You should have been kinder, Erica. I don't like the way you walk all over people. There's too much pain in the world already without going round creating it. You'll be gone one day. I'll be here on my own and I'll want them back.'

But Erica kicks off her shoes and laughs. Hah! If Jasper's looking down, if there's an after-life and Jasper's watching her now he would be furious! Sod you Jasper, I don't need you to get my kicks! Erica sits in the tall chair, Molly's chair that used to be Crispin's chair. Molly takes the other one after automatically fetching the scotch from the cupboard. They don't bother with water any more.

What will they do this evening? Will they pore over the old album again, the old Farendon album that Molly found along with the chemistry set in the attic? It is up to Erica. Please, Erica, please suggest the album! Or will Erica, in that evocative way she has, take Molly back to Farendon with memories that she pretends to have forgotten?

Or will they dance? Draw the curtains, turn off the lights, light the candles and dance?

What they do is up to Erica.

The feather, the blood and the bone. They had trodden on the cross and repeated the oath. '*I will abjure the Faith, forsake the Holy Religion and the worship of the Anomalous Woman. I will never venerate the Sacraments and I swear to keep that covenant.*' Now they both wait for the stone, and after that, no more. Even Erica will not send to herself the Crow Biddy, the little doll just two fingers high made by simply winding straw round your fingers and binding the ends for hands, legs and head. One eye, no nose, no mouth. They only used the Crow Biddy once, when they sent it to Amy Macey. The faceless doll could be anyone, but the person who gets it knows who it is, knows why the pin is clipped to the heart. And once the Crow Biddy has been sent the spell cannot be revoked.

They found out about the Crow Biddy in the city museum. She sat with her one eye staring out angrily above a plaque which read in old English *A wicket dol of evill purpose maad with wex or strawe.* Over the ages the straw had faded from gold to grey. Round its waist – for decency? – was a rag like a dirty old handkerchief, and you knew what it smelled like without being able to hold it. Its hands and feet were roughly cut and its eye was a dull black bead which drooped across the flat face and lay off-centre. And you had to wonder, when you stared, if anything lived in it, if mites had got in it and, eating away inside, had moved the eye to that more sinister position. But you wouldn't have wanted to poke it and see. There it was, displayed under glass and with it the story told by the chronicler of St Jude's Abbey in a yellowed leather book opened at the page. Bridget Alnwick, spinster, being accused of witchcraft and taken to the place of reckoning, had cut off one of her own hands – a dramatic gesture which seemed pretty pointless, because the action only confirmed her guilt. The wound did not bleed, so they burnt her. They probably would have burnt her anyway. But ever after, said the spidery writing, she ill-wished the people of the town and wicked people used effigies of her to bring down their enemies. Her familiar, according to the chronicler, was a crow.

No, Erica will not send herself the Crow Biddy. But by the time she sends herself the stone Molly will be totally convinced – if she isn't already. She will be in exactly the right frame of mind to return to Farendon.

As for the purple envelopes well, Erica is saying nothing about those. Erica is fascinated, excited and eager to discover who is doing it and why. Is there really someone else as wicked as she? Will it, perhaps, be possible to start something off again at Farendon? She will find out when she gets there. She watches Molly carefully for signs of distress. The curse will be working shortly – but how long will it take without the victim knowing? It makes for interesting speculation. It is something worth finding out. If the books are right it doesn't matter who collects the mail. The name on the envelope is enough.

Certainly, Erica calculates correctly, if Molly knew she would by now be destroyed.

Instead, and Erica glances across at Molly sitting there plumply and expectantly in the lesser chair, she looks better than she has ever been. She is almost radiant!

Fifteen

'Norman has changed. He is not the person he was.'

Dennis has been thinking a long time before he manages to put those thoughts that have been nagging him for weeks into words. And now he hears them he doesn't like them. They frighten him. It is almost as if, by saying it, he has made it irrefutably so.

Of course he is talking to himself so no one else has heard him. But even so . . . even so . . .

Dennis puts his record on again and opens the doors so the smooth strains of 'Edelweiss' echo beautifully in the deserted parts of the old pathology wing. He tries to think. He can just remember another time when Norman took on like this and started behaving strangely. And that was, oh years ago, when he was only a lad and Dennis, ten years older, sometimes tried to look after him. And that business had certainly ended in tears if he remembers rightly.

Dennis thinks, rolling his uneasy mind around as a mongoose tackles an egg. What happened then? It's no good. He can't remember.

The more urgent thought that springs easily to mind is that it isn't Dennis's turn to do the tea. It is Norman's. But Norman will be late and so Dennis has volunteered to take his place.

Dennis has baked a cake. He is exhausted. This afternoon he made a cake after watching a cake-baking demonstration on the television. He was alerted to the programme by the woman's tone of voice. Normally Dennis just has it on and lets it go by. But the woman with the apron and the basin had glared at him and talked to him just in the way he was used to being glared at and talked at . . . had even told him off for his likely clumsiness before he started. And so Dennis had paid attention and not dared ignore the instructions after the woman had gone off the screen. Something in her bearing told him she might, at any moment, pop back. And how affronted she would be to discover she'd been turned off. No, there was nothing else for it but to do what she told him. The cake turned out trumps. He has hidden it under his bed because he knows that if he leaves it out then someone will eat it. Well look! He buys real coffee and they drink it, he cleans the toilets and they crap in them, he makes the beds and they mess them all up again.

Something else has tired Dennis. He has taken the opportunity, while everyone is out, of having a good old poke round the flat. He crept, listening, afraid of being discovered, into Harold's room. He picked up and inspected the ornaments on Harold's chest of drawers, the shepherdess and the Scottie dogs, the wedding photographs – old sepia photographs of men with swords outside a church door. He often asks Harold about them but Harold says he can't remember who the people are, he keeps them because he likes them.

Then Dennis wandered off down the corridor of frosted glass into Norman's room. He tutted when he saw that Norman hadn't made his bed – again. No nice rug in here by the bed like there is in Harold's room. Harold made it himself and said he would teach Dennis how to do it so he could make one too. Ticking in here, loud ticking from a Mickey Mouse clock. Dennis opened Norman's drawers and rifled through, felt in pockets. Then he put his hand under Norman's pillow and brought out the raffia doll. He'd known it would be here. Norman calls it his Jennie doll and won't let anyone touch it. Dennis brings it up to have a good look. He can't think why Norman keeps it, ugly, tatty thing with its one eye and its bound limbs. But Norman has had the doll for oh, years and years and years.

Dennis goes back to his own room. Dennis listens to 'Edelweiss', sits on his bed and brings his head between his knees in order to view his wondrous cake one more time. Vaguely he wonders whether he ought to have a word with Julian about Norman.

They will both be late for tea tonight because Harold is

sweeping leaves in the Hospital grounds for five pence a bag and Norman is cutting dahlias to take to the chapel for the Farendon Chaplain.

He wheels them in a barrow through the track in the woods, two buckets of water swinging on the handles. The chapel door is never locked and when you go in you walk into silence. The organ pipes gleam and play the thumping chord of silence. Norman goes in and shuts the door behind him; stone is all around him, his eyes are wide and his face is a question. He listens. He listens carefully. For the slightest movement, in here, can be heard.

Nothing.

If *she* was here you would hear her laugh. Just a little giggle, like water running, icy water in the coldness of the place.

It was here he used to come before he left, every evening, bringing red wine, toads and lizards, an occasional grass snake, even bags of dried blood fertiliser, for Erica. To be 'blessed' she said. He obeyed happily, like a man in a dream, hoping she'd be here to receive them, to thank him with a kiss and a hug, her eyes bright and her hair smelling so sweet . . .

He loved to be able to do things for her.

'You see that red light burning there,' she told him, pointing to it, her other hand round his shoulders so that he was very close to her. 'Well that,' she told him, 'is the eye of God. Watching you, Norman. See how it never blinks, but just watches, watches. And even when you go away He can see you. Now you try this, when you get home tonight. You lie in bed and rub your eyes hard, then lie back on your bed, or cot, or whatever they give you where you live, and you'll be able to see God's eye, red lights, still watching you.'

She used to face him to talk, bringing her face very close so he could read her lips. She mouthed her words out carefully so that to Norman they were very clear. They even rang. He couldn't hear but they rang. And he went home that night and he did try it out, and she was right, God's eye was there, watching him.

The others used to watch and smile, nudging each other. Giggling. But Erica was never like that to him. If he caught sight of her on the games fields, on the tennis courts, going backwards and forwards between the school Houses, her cloak swinging behind her, if he raised his arm, then Erica always waved back. And smiled at him.

Oh yes, he learned what a garden was when he came to Farendon and soon after that he learned about the fairies. But they weren't at the bottom of the garden, they were in the woods, in the old bricked-up copse behind the chapel. You had to crawl through a drainage tunnel to get in. Hunter had told him what it was. Hunter had told him not to go near it, for once it had been an ancient burial ground, a place where, years ago, felons and suicides were put, far enough away from the church so as not to offend the righteous sleeping there. And for decency's sake, when the Founder bought the land, before Farendon was built, she had to promise to cordon it off from general use.

Norman, intrigued by the place, had ignored Hunter and gone there, just once, to see. It was like walking on the foundations of an old country cottage, and about the same size. But the stones that tried to trip you were not tumbled-down walls, but markers, hardly gravestones – more like Arny's teeth – markers to the wretches who had been put here. Brambles, leathery-leaved and angry, wrestled with the ivy that clawed the broken walls, dripping dew loudly, green tears from leaf to leaf which finally went dry on the dank and mouldy floor. The old stones, crumbly and worn, rucked the earth as if they stirred with life still, like bulbs, and were trying to push their old grey heads up once more to the sky. If you wet your finger and rubbed them, you could see old letters there.

Well it was here, Norman knew, that the fairies came – Erica and her friends. They had cleared the ground of undergrowth so that you could see the briar roses on the walls. He watched them from a high hump of stones left from the ruined abbey. He knelt between clumps of ragwort and cow parsley and they couldn't see him. Fairies, naked, dancing. In the early morning and, he was sure, at night in moonlight, only he wasn't ever allowed out at night.

Erica became, to Norman, his life. If he saw her and she smiled then the sun shone and he was warm and cheerful all day. If she frowned or ignored him then winter came to Norman Appleyard and his heart dripped sadness like an icicle into his bones.

He tried to emulate her breezy way of being; he moved fast, thought fast, held his body higher. He took more interest in the garden things she wanted, filling his bag with spiders and moles as he went about his work, certain that Erica would never hurt them. Once he found a baby robin, fed it with a dropper, kept it warm in his shed and picked choice worms and grubs for it while he dug. It grew tame and strong, it came when he called it. 'Tick, tick, tick,' he called, and it came to him, perched on his fist. Its tiny feet tickled him as it walked up his arm. When it was grown strong enough, he put it in a box and took it, as an offering, to Erica.

She smiled at it and kissed him, in here, behind the reredos. Norman is about to tiptoe through to get nearer to his memories, when the chapel door opens and the whispering sound of the woods comes in. 'Ah, Appleyard, good man!'

Norman shakes himself and prepares, like a pine tree lowering its branches, to take the pain. If he thinks of Erica then he must afterwards expect the baby explosion, and here it comes. He shivers.

Little fingers patting, all cake and milk, and that thin, sharp scream must be his . . .

'Are you well?' asks the Chaplain, concerned. There's work to be done yet and he doesn't want Norman ill in bed.

'I've brought them,' says Appleyard, pointing to the buckets. 'Six bucketfuls like you asked me.'

'Very fine specimens, very fine indeed. You have green fingers, Norman,' says the Chaplain, thinking to himself how marvellous is the way God compensates. 'I've decided that this year it might be nice to deck the chapel with a display of autumn branches, browns and bronzes, golds and silvers. Think how beautifully they would go with the colours you've chosen. Have you any ideas, Appleyard? Any thoughts on that?'

Appleyard wants to get away. Julian is coming to tea at the flat and he doesn't want to be late. He wants to prevent Dennis from cooking something revolting. If Julian doesn't enjoy it then he won't come so often.

'I'll talk to you about it tomorrow. I have to get home early tonight.'

'Ah! I have heard about that,' says the Chaplain. 'Got your own place now, Appleyard, I believe. And how are you coping with that?'

'We are enjoying it very much indeed, sir.' Norman pushes his tongue through the gap in his teeth.

'And then, I understand, having proved yourselves, you will be moving into town!'

'Yes, sir, I understand that we will.' Norman stamps his soily boots on the clean chapel floor.

'But we mustn't neglect our work here in all the excitement, Appleyard, must we? The ladies have been good to us at Farendon, haven't they?'

'I'll collect the wood tomorrow, first thing tomorrow, after I've taken Miss Radley's plants inside. I'll get Peter and Joe to go round the grounds with a saw.' And Norman removes his hat, scratches his head and stares at something under his nail. Then he puts his finger in his mouth and chews.

'Right then, Appleyard.' The Chaplain closes his eyes. 'I mustn't detain you any longer. I can see you're in a hurry. Good night to you and God bless.'

'God bless you too, sir,' says Appleyard as he backs away.

The Chaplain, who is a good man and always feels inadequate when faced with Appleyard, turns towards the cross. He crosses himself, genuflects and quotes out loud three lines of a poem that once moved him profoundly.

> *'Oh Lord, tell me what is said*
> *By these men in a turnip field*
> *And their unleavened bread.'*

Sixteen

Poor little rich girl – ah! Was she born bad? Very probably.

The hot smell of Weatherstone exterior gloss – aaah! Fornicating, at twelve, with a painter named Ginge.

Poor little Erica.

It went, her childhood, like this but not as quickly . . .

'Erica is here, Mr Chorley.'

'Well, let her wait another few minutes, Angela. Another few minutes won't hurt her.'

Miss Phillips came back from the company director's office and gave a strict yet sympathetic smile. Erica didn't smile back. She pulled a rude face. Miss Phillips, dear Angela, the *pp* on Daddy's letters, the birthday card and present sender. Miss Phillips smelled of lily of the valley. Miss Phillips licked her lily of the valley handkerchief and wiped Erica's eyes when Mummy went through the purple curtain.

Little Erica, suspended from Farendon, snapped the elastic on her hat, twisted it tight under her chin till it hurt her and then she lifted each leg, slowly, so that it ripped off the leather on the waiting room chair. She stared at the space in front of her, taking no notice when people walked through and, to be polite, tried to say something. She knew Miss Phillips was watching her through the glass. Miss Phillips, who called Daddy 'poor thing' in front of her.

Erica heard the buzz, she saw dear Angela's head go down. She felt her eyes on her. Erica was up before Miss Phillips came in. She was up and knocking at the door. Later in life, when people talked of gentlemen's clubs, she always thought of Daddy's office.

His face was all that she hoped for and yet not at all. The room was full of under-lit pictures of ships, sailing ships with full rigging and one two-funnelled liner, the water always a sinister yellow, a blazing sun going down. The strong, stale smell of cigar smoke filled the air.

They said, everyone said she was like him. Daddy was wearing blue socks. Nobody had bothered to tell him about *that*. She could have done . . . if anyone wanted her to . . .

'Now then, Erica.' Daddy looked cross. He picked up a letter and held it in front of his face. 'What's this I'm being told now? This . . . this . . . this,' and he can't give it a word, 'This has got to stop!'

'It's only for a week, that's all. I've been banned for a week.'

'And is that, Erica, going to be your attitude – insolence? Is that what it's going to be?'

'I didn't do anything. It wasn't my fault,' said Erica, with a shudder in her chest she made sure she didn't show.

Years ago, when she was tiny and Mummy was alive, Mummy used to bring her here and leave her crayoning on the floor in front of the fire while she went shopping in Liverpool. She always asked, when she came to collect her, 'Well, was she good?' and Daddy always said, 'Perfect. My perfect, my pretty princess.' Sometimes he'd put her on his shoulders and carry her round the offices, showing her to people. She hadn't been made to wait in the waiting room then.

Mr Chorley sighed, smacked the letter down on the desk between them and sat back. He stared at his daughter and drew his lips together tightly. 'I have telephoned Miss Potts at Farendon. I have just this minute come off the telephone from Miss Potts. You can't go home. I won't be there, I have to be in Capetown tomorrow. And the Browns aren't keen to look after you on their own. D'you hear that, Erica . . . the Browns, after last time, aren't keen to manage you alone. You're eleven years old, Erica, eleven! You've been away at school since you were seven, the best education money can buy, hell, you ought to have learnt the rules by now.'

'What did she say?'

'Who?'

'Miss Potts. What did she say?'

'Roberts is going to take you back there this afternoon, but Miss Potts expects an apology and that's why you're going to sit in that chair now and write one so that I can see it and sign it!'

Mr Adrian Chorley pressed a button with his finger and said, 'Angela, one minute . . .' Then he stood up, stiffly heavy in his three-piece suit, and paced his office high up in the Liver building and stared out disconsolately at the slow-flowing Mersey. He turned his back on his daughter. From where she looked it seemed as if he didn't have a head, just a back and long, dark legs, and hands that wrestled with each other at the base of his jacket.

Not until the door opened did he turn round. His black hair tickled the bright, white collar. He was brown from being in Africa. 'Angela, some suitable sort of paper to write to a headmistress on, and some suitable remarks to make.' Miss Phillips sat down.

'This is the letter of apology, is it?' she said, looking closely at Erica.

'This is,' Daddy said, sitting down again. Raising his eyelids slowly as if the weight of the world was caught on the ends of them.

'Well, I think it ought to come from Erica, not you or I,' she said.

'Well – we're waiting. What do you think you ought to say? And a thank you at the end, to Miss Potts I think, for being so amenable. This time at any rate,' and Daddy rolled his eyes and sat back again, rocking.

Miss Phillips set the paper down in front of Erica and tapped it with a pen which she then put, lid off, pointing towards the child.

'Dear Miss Potts dear Miss Potts dear Miss Potts, come on, surely even that must be obvious to you!' said Daddy, driven by impatience. 'The start of a letter, Erica! The normal start to a letter!'

'*Dear Miss Potts,*' wrote Erica, biting the end of the pen. Indifferent clouds floated by in the high sky outside the window.

'Now then,' said Daddy.

'I am writing to apologise . . .' prompted Miss Phillips.

'*I am writing to apologise,*' wrote Erica.

'For cutting up Sheila Brand's dress with scissors . . .'

'Wait a minute, Angela,' said Daddy. 'Wait a minute. Hell, I am writing to apologise for my bad behaviour would surely sound better. We don't want to get into that . . .'

'*For my bad behaviour*,' wrote Erica . . .

'On September the sixteenth last . . .'

'No,' interrupted Miss Phillips. 'Scribble that out, Erica. You can't write it like that.'

Erica scribbled it out.

'. . . for my bad behaviour, which I understand is inexcusable. I have spoken with my father and he agrees with me that the money for the damaged article will be compensated out of my own pocket money over the weeks left this term. I am most grateful for the second chance you have given me and I promise to be on my best behaviour from now on.'

'Got that?' asked Daddy.

'No, you went too fast,' said Erica.

'She can come and do it in my office,' said Miss Phillips in a weak, troubled voice. 'Don't forget Brian and Andrew are waiting downstairs.'

So Erica, swinging her hat, went first, pushing Miss Phillips's hands off her shoulders. She didn't have to marshall her out like that! She was going . . . she was going . . . she was going . . . She didn't like Miss Phillips's room. It smelled of brown windsor soup and Erica knew it was because Miss Phillips was always drinking Bovril.

'Erica is outside, Mr Chorley.'

'Help her to get rid of it, do whatever you have to, Angela.'

'Erica is outside, Mr Chorley.'

'God help us not that jobbing gardener again? Or was it the painter this time?'

'Erica is outside, Mr Chorley.'

'Get hold of Miss Potts for me, will you.'

'Erica is outside, Mr Chorley.'

'How much is it going to cost me this time?'

So naturally Daddy was thrilled when Erica married Jasper, 'the elegant bastard', he called him behind his back. They had so much in common. And it put an end to the trouble he was sick of paying for – someone else could take her over, get her out of it. They had managed to keep her at school – just – with the odd hefty contribution towards a science lab here and a restocked library there.

After that came Europe. Adrian Chorley had, for months at a time, lost track of his daughter. And how many marriages had there been, five? Five in ten years, God dammit. He doesn't even remember half the blighters' names. But Jasper was different, no playboy he, or if he was he behaved himself about it. Didn't bob up in every tabloid you happened to pick up at the airport.

A romantic meeting, some said . . . those who didn't know Erica. She'd been miles from land, still swimming, swimming off Skiros, her strength nearly gone when he'd picked her up. Taken her on board, lock, stock and barrel. Plied her with brandy. Saved her life in every sense.

Yes, Adrian Chorley approved of Jasper Bryant. Incredibly, astonishingly, the man seemed to love Erica. So he felt he could, at last, wash his hands of his recalcitrant child.

There is no more Daddy, no more Jasper, but there are still letters.

Every letter was a little different – Erica wrote in green ink, Molly in blue. Molly didn't want to go down as Fatty Maguire but Erica said, 'That's how they know you, that's how you must sign.' And to be honest, Molly was feeling like Fatty Maguire again. To sign Molly. Tarrent would have been cheating. So this is the gist of the letters that Molly and Erica sent from the Priest's House, Ashbury.

'*Dear Jayne (or Wendy or Charlotte . . .)*' There were eleven in all, but four were living abroad. They didn't bother to write to the ones living abroad. '*No doubt by now you will have received your Farendon reunion invitation. No doubt, like us, you have never been back. But this time we are writing, with good reasons, to ask if you would, this once. Something has happened that makes it imperative we meet. It isn't possible to write more in a letter, suffice it to say it is urgent or we wouldn't have dreamed of contacting you.*

'Please reply and give us some idea of your decision.

'We thought we should meet at The Royal Clarence first, twelve-thirty on Thursday.

'All good wishes from . . . Horse Chorley and Fatty Maguire.'

And the gist of the letters they received back was this, *'Dear Horse and Fatty, Surprise! You're telling me something must have happened. I never thought I'd hear from either of you two again.*

'Naturally I am reluctant to return but I am far too fascinated to refuse. I don't know what other reactions you'll get, after all this time. I can't say I'm looking forward to it so I'll just say until the thirty-first . . .'

Jayne Cromwell, Dierdre Bott, Harriet Tyeson, Moaning Little . . . Nine replied, two were dead, four couldn't or didn't want to come, so that left five who were willing, five and the two of them, to meet at The Royal Clarence Hotel for lunch on Thursday next.

Molly's friends go by, but they see the gold Mercedes and they don't knock any more. Molly doesn't care. She can't bear to go back to being herself again. She is happy to be dazzled by, to be possessed by Erica.

Seventeen

Julian glances into other people's faces. Is there anyone else on this road tonight as disappointed, wistful or solitary as he?

A wintry haze obscures the Hospital trees, horse chestnuts and sycamores coming up through asphalt, rendering them other-worldly and missing something, like the men with missing teeth and missing stares, the few bent men who walk round them as Julian makes his way to the basement flat where he's promised to spend this evening. No word at all, then, from Sylvie. He'd been thinking of Sylvie on his way here, thinking so hard he had bumped into scurrying pedestrians, he'd even been hooted at by a nervous van driver as he tried to step into the road. Every morning he half-expects something – a postcard – just something to ask how he is, how he's coping without her. But nothing. Hell.

The grass is cordoned off like park grass by fluted railings shin high – the sort of railings you don't know whether to cross or not. He follows the road up where it winds steeply and turns into a kind of curved ramp, round the main Hospital block sprinkled with signposts that originate from a more mentally-propitious age. Now they are tatty and wind-stripped, pointing to departments and strangely-named annexes which no longer exist. Through ground-floor windows of this red-bricked temple to insanity he can see trolleys, stacked, rubber-wheeled trolleys, waiting for people who, thank God perhaps, will never come. The windows glint back at him brazenly, for they have seen grief and misfortune brought past by ambulance in such a steady flow they must long ago have become immune. Unlike Julian, who shivers.

'Julian, I was wondering,' starts Norman, pink-cheeked and embarrassed. He has obviously only just arrived home himself, for his coat is still on and his bobble hat sits at a happy angle. He has been waiting behind the door, Julian realises, ready to open it. Something is burning in the kitchen. Dennis must be cooking again. Julian edges his way into the flat and makes for a chair. Norman follows Julian, hanging about above the chair, crossing his legs. 'I was wondering if you would like to come with me to the first night dinner at Farendon.' And he thrusts the invitation at Julian, lets it drop in his lap and immediately leaves the room, unable to bear to wait for Julian's reply.

Julian picks it up and looks at it. He hasn't got his coat off yet. He hates social occasions – of any sort. His unrelenting unsociability was another of the reasons why Sylvie left him. Oh, he doesn't mind being with friends, or colleagues, people he knows. But not dinner with a table-full of strangers. And this sounds worse than the general run of ghastliness. An Old Girl reunion . . . God . . . a dinner. The thought of the speeches makes him wince, all referring to old times, good times, times he, Julian, would know nothing at all about. He is surprised that Norman has been invited. Do they always ask the gardener? How about the cooks and the cleaners? Do they get to go, too?

Julian cannot refuse. Not without hurting Norman. And that's the last thing he wants to do with everything going so well. Too well? No, Julian mustn't be pessimistic. He sighs, rises stiffly from his chair, and goes to find Norman who is sulking in his bedroom, expecting a refusal.

'Of course I'd love to come,' lies Julian, sitting himself down on the edge of Norman's bed. 'I can't say I promise to enjoy myself, though. These things aren't exactly my cup of tea.'

Norman pretends not to be pleased. Pictures obscure almost every inch of Norman's walls, pictures he has purloined from the stores department, pictures that used to hang, for relief, on doctors' walls, in waiting rooms and treatment rooms. Hospital pictures, for you never see those lazy fisherfolk anywhere else, or those terrible bridges – where are they, Rome? Venice? Where in the world are there places as starkly forbidding as these?

'What's it like? What was it like last year? Do you always go, Norman?'

'First time I've been asked,' says Norman, plaiting his sheet diffidently. 'Miss Blennerhassett called me in yesterday. She told me it was a way of saying thank you for all my hard work over the years. Miss Radley would never have asked me, not if it had been left up to her.'

Did she now? Julian thinks that a more realistic pay cheque would be a better expression of gratitude but of course he doesn't say so. He has never seen Norman proud before. Now he gets a full smile so the gap in the teeth seems wider.

'I expect you'll know most of the people there.'

'By name, by sight, but not to talk to,' says Norman. 'I haven't spoken to all of them.'

'Well, you'll have a chance to rectify that on Thursday night, won't you?' says Julian.

'And you'll be there to help me,' Norman replies. 'For a start you can tell me what to wear.'

'You're going to need a suit,' says Julian dolefully. 'And I haven't got one to fit you.'

'They've got one in the ward, in Pitt – they keep one there in case it's ever needed.'

'What? One suit for everyone?'

'They take it up and let it out, depending. But I've only known one person wear it and that's when they let Clem Weiner out for his wife's funeral.'

'It sounds to me as if this suit might well be out of fashion.'

'We could look at it,' says Norman hopefully.

'Well yes, yes we could.'

Harold has overheard. He has been standing outside Norman's room, listening. Now he comes in and hovers by the door. 'Are you going back, then?'

'Back?'

'Are you going back to the Hospital to get it?'

'Yes, to have a look at a suit for Norman.'

'Can I come?'

'Do you want to go back then, Harold?'

Harold rubs his hands hard together. 'Yes, for a visit. Yes, I want to go back.'

'You could go back any time for a visit you know, Harold. It's only two minutes across the road. It isn't exactly forbidden.'

100

'You have to get permission,' says Harold, 'to go onto that ward. You have to ring up first. And Dennis will want to come.'

'No problem,' says Julian, mystified.

'No problem,' says Norman under his breath.

Julian hasn't seen Harold this excited before. He's like a child being offered a treat. Julian can't understand it. 'Fine, then! Dennis can come. You can come. Norman can come. We'll all go back. Perhaps they'll give us tea!'

And Norman laughs. He is excited, too.

Later that evening, after a meal of burnt beefburgers and beans, Julian leads his little troop into the Hospital reception where he telephones Pitt ward to try to talk about a suit for Norman's dinner.

Nurse MacNelly, that brassy blonde, seems to be in charge and quite willing, she says, to receive them, only she can't imagine where the suit is. 'Are you sure?' she asks on the end of the phone. 'Are you sure we keep a suit for general use? I've certainly never heard of it.'

'Well, they all agree that there is one somewhere,' says Julian. 'And if you don't mind we'd like to come up and look for it.'

'Someone probably died in it,' quips Nurse MacNelly, 'because I can't imagine anyone buying a suit specially. Not for the wearing it would get. Hardly worth it, I wouldn't have thought.'

They start the long walk. Julian realises that for the first time since he's known them, he's not leading. He trails along behind, willing to follow them through the devious system of passages, up steps that smell of Dettol, along more corridors, up more steps. Everything about them echoes, their voices, their footsteps, even their breathing. Julian is reminded of school, of his first day at school, of the sinking realisation that no matter how long he stayed there he would never get to know his way round. And they remind him of schoolboys – eager, clattering, no longer wary. No longer, it would seem, dependent on him!

He tries to imagine – he has time to imagine – what it must

be like to be brought here as a patient. What it must be like to be engulfed in this great place so full of pipes, inside and out. Pipes that rumble and steam, letting off waste that seems to come from nowhere, lagged pipes, rusty pipes, pipes that click grotesquely like an old man cracking fingerbones, that hang wherever you look like Sylvie's dripping stockings on the bathroom rack. They follow the pipes, which are in the ceilings and in the walls. There is no escape for the pipes, they turn and turn back, daunted by the gracelessness of this terrible place.

His men break into a run when they reach the outer limits of Pitt ward. They stoop to peer through the gingham-curtained door windows. Norman taps, turns to beckon Julian, and taps again. Dennis bobs up and down in excitement and Harold childishly picks at his lip, very much in danger of being set off.

Always warm, pale nights. Never different in here, the seasons pass unnoticed save for the changing colours on the tops of the trees and the force of the rain beating on the windows. But Norman doesn't seem to mind. The keys turn and the men go in, acting like visitors all of a sudden, now that they're here. Strangely shy.

'Well, well, well,' says Nurse MacNelly. 'Look who it is!'

And Norman, Julian's Norman, looks bashful! Julian smiles and shakes his head. I need them, he thinks to himself as he sees them suddenly independent. *I need them*.

But although she speaks to the men, the nurse's eyes are fixed upon Julian. So much so that he has to frown. She's a little over the top. He's always known he is attractive to women. Men do, if they are. It's no good pretending otherwise. Thirty-five yet he could be any age, child-like in one way, wise in another. All right, Sylvie's departure deflated him a little, but even that can't take away the fact. He sees it in his mirror every morning even if there's nobody there to tell him.

'Come into the office,' she says to Julian. 'I've got the kettle on.'

'What about. . . ?'

'Oh, they'll be all right,' says Nurse MacNelly, bending to

102

re-lock the door. She rises, her head tilts, her little teeth bite the edge of her lip. 'They can look for the suit while you come and tell me how they're all getting on.'

And Julian, following as her crêpe soles squish across the floor, feels strangely trapped.

Dennis and Harold don't move. They stand there, so keen to come, now they wait to go.

Norman walks through the ward, nods to Arny who is screwed in his chair, and makes for his bed. 'How you doing, Arny?' It is still there just as he left it. He climbs up onto it and lies down, hands behind his head, staring at the ceiling. Same ceiling. Same pattern you can make pictures with.

After the fire he kept waking up. But just as he formed a world again they came with needles and sent it away once more. He clenches his fists behind his head. Once he sat up, the little boy he was sat up, and was sick, hot, sweet sick, sticky on his hands and heavy in his lap like bath water in a flannel, slopping. They came and put him to sleep again before he could clean himself up.

He lit the fire because they put him in the padded cells – they never thought to check him for matches. They put him in the padded cells because he tried to run away – after Erica. They found him on the station and they brought him back and put him in the padded cells.

He'd sat on the floor and struck match after match, not thinking, then, of setting the cell alight. But when the thought came to him it made him excited. So, kneeling, he carefully held the match to the thick, mattress material. It went out. So he poked a hole in it first and thrust the match inside. It took. Black smoke came out of the hole, wisped out of the hole and filled the tiny room. Norman had to lie on the floor in order to see. After that the flames came. Just little white flames that tickled the walls first before turning into red ones. He watched them. Then, when he couldn't breathe, he went to bang on the door but nobody came. He banged again. And again. And then he went and lay down in a corner.

They came and they dragged him out. They dragged him up to Pitt and they stripped him. They searched him for matches then, when it was too late. They jabbed him with a needle and sent him to sleep. He woke up and they came again. And again. And again. It must have been a week. And when he went back to work Erica was gone. Everyone was gone. And no one had asked him anything.

Here, on this bed, that had happened to him.

They hadn't asked him anything because how could Norman, poor deaf mute, know anything? But he wasn't deaf, was he? They had come to syringe his ears just a couple of days before. That's when he heard what Erica was really telling him, underneath the smiles, when her head was turned away.

She would kiss him first, mouth her pleasantries, and then, thinking him deaf, she would say to her friends, 'That's it you stupid, retarded cretin. You just do what you're told and beat it! You disgusting, smelly spastic with your imbecilic smile. Get back to your ward where you belong!'

That's what Erica had been saying – what she must have been saying about him all the time. She hadn't really liked him after all.

And no wonder. No wonder.

Now if he had been like Julian – Norman clings to his bed, his knuckles white against the black iron. Dressed in Julian's clothes, smelling of Julian, yet not Julian, he clings to the memories that obsess him. There is pleasure in pain, for Norman. Pleasure in fear, for Norman. For when they came to cause him pain they were nice to him, said, 'It's going to be all right, Norman,' when they took him down for treatment. Smiled at him and hugged him sometimes when they took him down, when they frightened him.

On those days Norman used to feel special.

But now he knows they were saying Erica things behind their smiles.

Norman tries to switch off his head as he sits up on the bed, breathing the place again. He used to be frightened, just as the outside world frightens him now. Pitt, Gladstone, they used to frighten him. Not now. Now he is terrified of being outside, of the flat that smells of formaldehyde, of the new, pear-coloured house that is waiting. But above all, above all of these things, he is afraid of his feelings for Julian. What can he do with these feelings? Where should he put them? How is he to know that love can stay as a state of yearning if it has to – that love can be anything – but never to be ashamed of.

If he was a child he might have clung on and refused to leave. He might have stamped at them and shouted, backing up against the wall, 'Fuck you bastard, fuck you!' and caused the reaction he wanted. He can't shout at Julian like that. Julian, Norman is sure, wouldn't know how to respond. Julian wouldn't hit him and lock him up, which is what Norman needs to have done to him now. Julian would probably look sad and be hurt. Would shy away from Norman, thinking him disgusting. Norman doesn't want Julian to think that.

Here, in Pitt, he feels safe. They all feel safe here, him and Harold and Dennis. No wonder they were eager to come back. There are monsters outside these red brick walls.

Things aren't as simple as they used to be.

Eighteen

Who do you think you are, Molly Maguire, going on a diet and wearing those clothes again? Go back to your smocks for goodness' sake and take those jeans off. The people of Ashbury will call you mutton dressed as lamb. It's no good you trying to be like Erica. You are a world away from Erica. As far away from Erica as Norman is from Julian.

Fat is beautiful, Molly. You should be remembering that. But how can you, when Rose has taken your husband away?

Molly sends Rose the bone, and when she finds it, when she picks the little grey stalky thing from the compost heap between finger and thumb in order to bring it in and dry it out, she thinks of the Crow Biddy. How can she help it? Can she honestly bring herself to send such a thing to Rose, who is pregnant? Does she really hate her that much?

Yes. Yes, she does.

There are only a few occasions when Molly has met Rose. The first was during a brave attempt of Crispin's to 'do this properly'. Over lunch. In a dark little basement restaurant in Beauchamp Place. Molly grew so huge on her way down the steps she felt she wouldn't be able to squeeze through the door. Up until that day she had never seen Rose before. Then she appeared through candle smoke, as wispy and intangible as the smoke itself, and Molly wanted to put out a hand and snuff her out.

She tried to behave herself, of course she did, because she was still intent on getting Crispin back. Rose was the sort of person who couldn't be bothered to fill silences. Shy, people called it, but Molly knew better. So, through that terrible lunch, through the Petites Pâtés à la Provençale, the Brandade de Saumon and (she was the only one who had pudding) through her Timbale de Fruits à la Parisienne, Molly heard herself speak like the Holy Ghost, in many, very foolish tongues, desperately talking to cover the silence, for Crispin's sake. And all the while Rose sat back behind the candle smoke and appraised her.

Cow.

She very nearly delved in with her hands that day, delved into the food without knife or fork, because she was the pig at the table, the rough-necked, fat-faced pig with trotters for hands . . . snort snort grunt grunt . . . Rose put her, by her attitude, firmly in the trough.

They called a taxi for her afterwards. They saw her on her way. She looked back through the taxi window and saw them smiling, holding hands on the pavement.

The next time they met was when Molly called at Little Court. Drove up the drive, parked, noting that Rose's neat little red Lancia was under the trees in the Volvo's place, and, using her key, walked right in through the front door, knowing, of course, that Crispin was out.

'Well, this is unexpected.'

Deliberately, Molly forced herself to say nothing, to let Rose speak first, and 'This is unexpected' is what she'd said. Rose had friends round. They were sitting in the conservatory drinking Dubonnet with ice. They all looked round when Molly walked in. Rose stood up.

'You should have told me you were coming,' said Rose, in that little girl voice of hers. She was wearing something vast and African and her head looked very little coming up out of it. 'Join us. Have a drink. By the way,' and Rose turned to her friends, 'let me introduce you. I don't believe you know . . .'

'Mrs Tarrent,' said Molly, her fog-horn voice contrasting horribly with Rose's tuneful one. She saw a plate of figs on the rush-glass table and stifled a frantic urge to stoop, right here in front of everyone, and gobble them all up. Fat swung on her every time she moved her face, so much so that her eyes were nearly put out and she could hardly see.

And then Rose changed. Her face hardened, her eyes narrowed, her voice became terribly controlled. 'Do you want to talk to me, Molly? Shall we go into the drawing room?'

And by now Molly, who was Fatty Maguire again, couldn't

remember what she'd come to say and so she shouted, 'Bitch! Cow!'

'This is Crispin's wife,' said Rose, calmly, to her friends. 'She sits outside on the road for hours at night. Just sits outside, waiting.'

'Rose, I think we ought to . . .' said one of them.

'No. Don't go. She'll be gone in a minute.'

'Oh . . . I'll be gone, will I? I'll be gone, will I?' What were all those clever things she'd worked out to say on her journey up here? Where were they now? Molly saw the terrible picture of herself on her sad journey back, knowing she would hear her own pathetic words, her inadequate words ring in her head as she hurtled past the services, past the eighty miles to Exeter signs, eighty, sixty, forty, while the words grew louder and louder. 'I'll be gone, will I?' Surely, surely she could do better than that! In front of these people! Surely those weren't the words that would rock her, ring in her ears?

'Look, Molly, I'm quite prepared to talk sensibly with you if you are willing to do the same. We can't go on like this . . .'

'Oh we can't, can't we?'

Oh Molly oh Molly! Come on! You are not Fatty Maguire!

'We are both sensible, intelligent women . . .' said Rose.

'Oh, is that what we are?'

'Yes, we are.'

'The only difference between us is that you have Crispin and I don't.'

'You make it sound as if he had no choice in it. As if he's a parcel to be handed out . . .'

'Sod off you thin, mean, stick of a woman. Sod off!'

Oh Molly! No! *'See me, Molly Maguire.' 'Poor effort – where is your imagination?'* And on that note, on that really shameful note, not clever, not witty, not saying what she wanted to say in any way at all, on that note she flounced from the house, backed the Volvo treacherously so that it tore into the Lancia's bumper and dented it, then drove off into that lonely four-hour journey, absorbed in her humiliation. Loathing herself.

The house had let her down. She had hoped that Little Court would remind her of who she was, but it hadn't. Instead it had conspired with Rose and her friends against her.

And I'm afraid that there were other incidents, too dreadful to repeat.

Oh yes, Molly will send the Crow Biddy to Rose. No doubt about it. She is strong now. She is strong and powerful, inspired and bewitched by Erica.

Nineteen

It would seem that there never was a suit. Or if there was then it couldn't be found. Perhaps it was a figment of Norman's imagination.

So the next day Julian tries the Oxfam shop. Takes Norman along to root through all the cardboard boxes. By now he regards him as his little lap dog, always there, always staring at him adoringly out of those wide brown eyes, copying everything he says or does, ready to obey his every command. Flattering? Well, yes, in a way it is. Disconcerting, too, of course. Hard, sometimes, to know quite how to handle it.

Sometimes Norman gets on Julian's nerves, but on those occasions he seems to sense it and obligingly slips away. Julian has dealt with this sort of thing before, many times, except that female students make up his previous experience, never handicapped men. The main thing, Julian tells himself unworriedly, is to retain, at all times, his sense of humour.

However it is quite clear that Dennis does not approve. Is it jealousy, Julian wonders, or is there another reason? Either way Dennis, when he can, comes between him and Norman – sits between them at The Hand, interrupts conversations in a barely civil manner and demands Julian's instant attention whenever he starts concentrating on Norman. In some ways Dennis's attitude, furious though it makes Norman – he's getting very sulky lately – is a relief and a help.

But now, on the day before the reunion dinner, Julian and Norman walk back from the Oxfam shop together, Norman holding a remarkably distinguished suit in a carrier bag, far more distinguished than Julian's, but very similar. And a perfect fit, too. Norman is happy, happy and whistling to himself as he goes, busily absorbing all he can of Julian to fill the empty space inside him. Quite naturally, for he is the missing opposite, the dimwitted man living totally inside his body as Julian lives inside his intellectual head. Norman doesn't know about these things. All he has on his mind this evening is that he's got tomorrow night to look forward to, a whole glorious evening with Julian being next to him and talking to him without that interfering Dennis forever thrusting his oar in.

Julian looks down at his smaller friend stepping out briskly to keep pace beside him. Norman is so easy to please. He is thrilled and excited about his suit as a child might be with his presents on Christmas morning. So Julian decides to invite him back to his flat for a nightcap, as he would invite any other friend on a chill October evening.

It is a spacious flat, basically of two large rooms divided by an arch, and off the bedroom is the bathroom and off the sitting room is the kitchen. It is comfortably furnished with large, shabby sofas and chairs, rugs that fall on top of one another and book-shelves from floor to ceiling along one wall. Lamps, not ceiling lights, give it a cosy warmth and keep the grimness at bay, but it is a man's flat. The things women put about are strikingly not in it. And even Norman knows that the little red fleur-de-lys on the wallpaper in here must have been Sylvie's choice.

Julian is unnerved to find that Norman, who has never been here before, seems to know his way round. Yes, he puts down his carrier bag and goes to the bathroom uncannily as if he knows exactly where it is.

Julian goes to the fridge and pulls the tags off a couple of cans of lager.

When he returns with crisps and glasses Norman is going round the room fingering his things. Julian has noticed before how all three men tend to do that, as if they need to get to know a place, as a blind man might, with the tips of their fingers instead of their eyes. But Norman has paused before a photograph. He picks it up and studies it hard. It is a picture of Julian at the seaside, sitting there with his brother and two sisters, staring cheekily at the camera with a bucket on his head. Handsome even then, he looked at the camera as a child in the way that now he looks at women. A confident, well-proportioned child, at ease within his body.

111

'This is you,' says Norman awkwardly, as Julian sets the drinks down.

'That's me, when I was about ten, on holiday in Brittany.'

'And these other people. Who are they?'

Julian goes over and stands beside Norman. 'Well, that's my brother Michael, he lives in Canada now, and those are my two sisters Tess and Josie. Both are younger than me, both married and with children of their own about that age.'

Norman says nothing. Just stares.

Talk to him, Julian, go on, ask him! But I don't want to upset him. If I ask that question, he might not even know the answer!

'Are you an only child, Norman?' Julian tries to make his voice casual. Goes to the table and pretends to take an interest in something else. Pours the drinks. Wanders across the room, shaking his pockets for matches to light the gas fire.

It doesn't cross Julian's mind, when he makes his innocent, well-intentioned enquiry, that he might not want to know the answer. But it crosses Norman's.

Little fingers patting, all cake and milk, and that thin, sharp scream must be his as he slips like ice into uniformed hands and his five-year-old heart burns like a wound . . .

He used to ask, 'Is my mother coming today?' And then, in later years, when there was no one left to ask he used to ask himself, 'Is Erica coming back?' He'd soon stopped.

Stuttering shyly Norman replies, 'I think I had a sister, called Jennie.'

There is nothing in his file about a sister. Nothing about Norman's family at all. Julian's voice is gentle. 'Do you know where she is now, Norman?'

'Yes,' says Norman unexpectedly. 'Yes, I know where she is.' And he smiles as if he hides a mischievous secret.

Enough, Julian! Enough! And so he says, 'Come and have a drink and some nuts, and do you like olives?'

Norman's eyes light up. 'With red bits inside?'

Julian nods. 'Yes, if you like.'

'I've only had them once.'

Norman is so pathetically easy to please! 'Well, have some again. Hang on while I fetch them from the kitchen.' Back

112

and relaxed and sitting down, and Norman tucking into the olives, 'Norman, how did you know where my bathroom was? It's as if you've been here before but I can't remember . . .'

'I have.'

'What?'

'I have been here before. Several times. I came here when you were out.' Norman's smile, now, is not so child-like.

'You can't have been here. I keep my door locked.' But even while he is denying it, Julian's mind automatically takes him back to the times he has come home and felt someone here. Stood outside with his key in the lock and felt another presence near by.

'Huh. That sort of lock is no use. That sort of lock is easy to force.'

'You're telling me you came here when I was out and forced my lock?' Julian turns to face him, pushing tiredly at his hair. 'Is this some sort of joke?'

'No. Not a joke.' And Norman takes another olive. He must have five in his mouth already. The jar is nearly empty.

For Christ's sake! 'How many times have you been here, Norman?'

'I dunno how many times it was,' says Norman, casually. 'Two, maybe three, I didn't count. Are you mad?'

Julian controls a laugh because he is tempted to take the question literally. And if he did, he reasons to himself, he wouldn't be able honestly to answer it. Julian is probably mad, but he is also very surprised. But why is Julian so surprised? He had spent last night telling his students, a little group of students here in his flat, that the biggest mistake human beings make is to have expectations of each other. Life, he hears himself saying, is shit, people are shit, and the second big mistake we make is to assume we deserve to be happy. Why should we be happy? And why should we utilise so much energy in the pursuit of such a doubtful benefit?

So why is Julian surprised that Norman has been coming into his flat at night and rooting around, no doubt taking his things out of his drawers, having a good look at everything? Why, in fact, should he have expected him not to? What were his expectations of Norman? That he should behave in the way of a 'normal' human being? If so, why is he doing this job in the first place? How little talk and reasoned argument matter in real life.

Julian looks hard at Norman. Takes in the innocent eyes and the gentle, guileless expression, an expression quite embarrassingly full of open admiration. Is Norman playing games with him? Norman doesn't seem to know he has done anything wrong. 'If you'd asked me, Norman, if you'd told me you wanted to come here, then I would have given you a key.'

Norman knows perfectly well he has done wrong. This is Norman's last test. And Julian passes it, unaware, with flying colours. Norman sticks his tongue in his gap when Julian smiles ruefully and says, 'Well, I'd much prefer it if you didn't do it again. If you tell me you're coming I'll leave the key under the mat.'

Norman tries his suit on again and poses proudly in front of the mirror in Julian's bedroom, asking over and over if he looks all right, if he'll do.

'You look just fine, Norman. Just fine.'

They settle down to their second beer, and during their third Julian begins to tell Norman about Sylvie. He talks about pain and grief as if it is the sort of thing people talk about all the time – like the weather. He talks as if Norman is his equal, as if Norman knows all about these sorts of feelings. As if Norman might even have an opinion. Norman listens, spellbound.

'Eight years, Norman,' Julian repeats himself. 'She calls it an estrangement you know, a queer word to use. Eight good years, and now my life is just a series of small, false hopes, while over my head looms this awful, vast certainty that I'll never see her again. The flat still breathes her, can you smell it?'

'She'll come back – one day,' says Norman quickly, hoping she won't.

'But I'm boring you, Norman, aren't I? I've run out of olives and I'm boring you. Not a very good host tonight, I'm afraid. And talking of people disappearing, talking about estrangements, you must have been working at Farendon when that young girl went missing. I was in The Hand the other day and overheard somebody telling what happened . . .'

'I was ill. I was in bed. Asleep for a week. I heard stories, too, when they let me go back to work. Of course Erica had left by then . . . never got to say goodbye.'

'Erica?'

'Just someone who used to be there who I liked. We,' says Norman seriously, 'we became estranged.'

'Oh? So Erica was somebody special?'

'She didn't like me. I thought she did but she didn't. She said terrible things about me when she thought I couldn't hear.'

'Snap, Norman,' says Julian. 'Let's drink to it then, and after this you must get home.'

So they clink their glasses to Julian's meaning of the word 'estrangement'.

Twenty

Fate sent Erica to Molly, but would anyone have done? Erica sits waiting for Molly to come back, her soul craving that enthralling mixture of wickedness and danger that a return to Farendon is going to give her. And is Molly her missing opposite? – somewhere inside all that cool confidence does she need that insecure fat child, for balance?

Well, need her or not she's got her.

Erica sits by the fire and contemplates the stone. The stone she's just gone outside to pick up. The stone that comes before the Crow Biddy.

They are close now, she and Molly, close as they were at school, and intense like they were. Molly does not want to go back to Farendon. Molly is always looking for an excuse to chicken out. 'I don't know quite what we think we are going to achieve,' she moans. 'And there's still time. We could always call everyone up and cancel.'

And then Erica sighs and says, 'It has to be one of them. Look at me, Molly, look at me! How long do you think I can go on like this?'

'You don't eat enough,' says Molly, looking worried. 'You don't eat enough to keep a bird alive.'

'I don't want to go back either, Molly. I have the same abhorrence as you do, but I don't see any other way. I have to find out what's going on and stop it before it's too late.'

Molly is terrified, limp with fear when she thinks about the menace. She tries so hard to forget what's happening to Erica that sometimes she manages. She has another reason, one of her own, for going back to Farendon, but she doesn't like it, she doesn't like herself for having it. Because there, in the home town of the witch Bridget Alnwick, Molly is going to make and send her Crow Biddy, to be sure it has all the power it needs to strike effectively home. But now she goes back to saying, 'Who could it be, and why are they doing this to you?

And how do we know that the person who's doing it is going to be there?'

Erica thanks God Molly knows nothing of the purple envelopes dropping through her door. She'd never cope with that.

Erica hears the key in the lock. She pinches her cheeks and opens her eyes startlingly wide. She clenches her fists, gripping the arms of her chair. When Molly comes in she frees one hand and points to the thing on the floor.

Molly drops her basket. Oranges roll all over the rug. 'What is it?' she hisses. 'What's happened?'

'There,' shouts Erica, pointing. 'There! Look!'

Never has Molly seen anything so simple appear so sinister. It is small and round and black and seems to have two grooved eyes that stare, like an uncurled spider, about to unwind and scuttle, not away, but towards them. Molly turns white. Her freckles act as a dark shadow through which startled eyes peer out.

'How did it get here?' she asks in a whisper, as if the stone might hear and jump. 'And how . . . how do they know you're not in London?'

'Because of the letters we sent.'

Molly bites her lip, her little teeth fierce on the skin. 'Of course.'

'I went to pick up the post,' says Erica, 'like I always do, and it was there, on the mat. Someone had obviously put it through the letter box. As simple as that.' She starts to shake. She makes her teeth chatter.

'So whoever it was has been here – this morning – here in Ashbury!'

'Did you see anyone, Molly – on your way to the shop and back? Anyone different from normal?'

Molly sinks to her chair, keeping her eyes fixed on the stone. She runs distracted fingers through her hair, tearing at it, tearing off the rubber band from the end of her pony tail and pulling the elastic between nervous fingers, stretching it to snapping point like her own nerves. 'I don't know,' she moans. 'I can't remember anything. I can't even remember what I bought, why I went. This is terrible!'

'I picked it up. I took it with me to the bathroom. I was sick . . . so sick . . . I couldn't stop retching. And when I came in here it seemed to burn my hand so I threw it down and I haven't been able to bring myself to touch it since. Molly, I daren't even move out of this chair.' And Erica tucks her legs tightly under her and breaks into heartrending sobs.

'No wonder! No wonder! I shouldn't have left you. We knew this would happen. We knew that one day this was going to come.'

'I'm really frightened now, Molly. You think! You just think about it for a moment. You know what's coming next, don't you?'

Molly shakes her head. It feels big and dream-like on her shoulders. 'They can't. Nobody would do that . . . nobody would. Not after Amy.'

'If someone can be heartless enough to do this, they can do anything.'

'But why? Why?' Molly is nearly crying. Anger, fear and frustration meet in a knot to twist her face.

'Get it out of here, Molly, please get it out.'

Molly clenches her teeth. She reaches carefully round the stone for the fire-tongs as if its very aura is dangerous. With her shoulders hunched and her arm outstretched, her face a study in absolute horror, she touches the foul, offensive thing. It rolls. She jumps and seems to steel herself. Comes back for another go. Gets it. And holding it out at arm's length she hurries through to the kitchen, opens the back door, runs to the end of the garden and throws it over the hedge into the field.

Just as if she was dealing with a wormy cat turd, thinks Erica, trying to mask the grin on her face and bring on some tears before Molly gets back. She's never seen anything quite so funny. It would have made a hilarious video.

That, thinks Erica calmly to herself when she hears the water running in the kitchen and Molly washing her hands, that should stop any talk of not returning to Farendon, of cancelling the next day's trip.

Thank God it is tomorrow, because she couldn't stand one more day in Ashbury. The two weeks she's been here have been bad enough. Going round without make-up, feeling ugly, catching alarming glances of her own haunted face in the mirror. Eating nothing but drinking far too much. But it's all been necessary, she tells herself now – yes, very necessary.

Erica knows it can't be like it was before. For a start, only half the witch-band will be there. But even so, even so . . . she wonders how much they all will have changed. Twenty-three years is a very long time. Will she still have that power over them, will she still be able to manipulate and compel? Why not? It worked very easily with Molly, although, admittedly, Molly was down when she found her, down and with all her old props, husband, children, missing. Molly was easy. Molly was always easy.

They heard her coming, creeping down the aisle in the Chapel. They heard the door squeak first, the iron ring turning, then they heard the footsteps.

It was right at the beginning, when they were first starting. They were twelve, an eager, committed twelve, and they needed a thirteenth. But no one would have dreamed of choosing Fatty Maguire.

'Get her out of here,' mouthed Dierdre Bott, peering round the edge of the reredos, her tumble of red hair clashing shockingly with the scarlet altar cloth.

'Who is it?'

'That fat Maguire girl.'

'No, wait . . . wait a minute,' said Erica.

And while they hesitated Fatty steamed on, intent upon a safe place for her and her madeira cake, knowing about the circular place behind the altar, knowing, through her fear, all the hiding places in the school.

Fatty was in the middle of feeling warm and content. When Erica moved out Fatty jumped, guilt and fear turning her into jelly as she tried to back away, shaking her head. She wasn't quite Bunterish enough to hide the cake behind her back, but she almost did – almost.

119

'I didn't know anyone was in here,' she said. 'If I had known I wouldn't have come . . . honestly.'

'You were wrong,' Erica told her. 'There's quite a few of us in here.'

Fatty's eyes widened as they all came out, sly looks on their faces. Immediately she wondered what was going on. What could this particular group of girls possibly be doing here in the Chapel? Normally she kept her distance from them. They could be unkind. They were the school bullies, every one of them a terror to somebody else, every one of them capable and clever at something – work, or games – drama, or music – or merely good at being nasty. Not like herself – bad at everything, fat and stupid, hadn't even learnt to swim until last year, too embarrassed to be seen in the pool. All Molly wanted to do was get out of the Chapel and go to find somewhere else before the break-bell went.

She hated school. Every letter she sent home begged for her to be taken away, but they took no notice. It was good for her . . . how she hated anything that was supposed to be good for her. Now the warning bells clanged in her brain for she had stumbled upon something she should not have stumbled upon, something that was very definitely not going to be good for her at all.

But Erica, in the few seconds it took to decide, thought that Fatty could be useful. It was always good to have someone not of the same mould, someone who could be used and dropped, used and picked up, someone who was afraid. In any venture there is always the boring, repetitious side of things, stuff at which the other eleven would balk. Fatty would make a very firm base in any established pecking order. She, Erica, at the top of course, Fatty at the bottom.

At that time, right at the beginning, none of them had expected the thing to last. It was just a craze, this Devil-worshipping, a craze like yo-yos, that would pass. It didn't turn out that way. The witch-band lasted for three years, until they left, until Amy Macey disappeared.

But then they didn't know any of these things. So she told Fatty to wait. 'Sit in the front pew and eat your cake if you have to. No one here wants to touch it, don't worry. We have to talk.'

Fatty continued to shake her head. 'I won't say anything, Erica, honestly. Heck – you know I won't say anything.'

'Shut up and sit down. Eat and wait.'

And all twelve of them retired behind the reredos again and discussed the pros and cons of allowing Fatty Maguire to join this most exclusive circle.

'Someone to do the donkey work?' said the sharp, no-nonsense Jayne Cromwell. 'Is that it? And is that a good enough reason?'

'I think it is,' said Erica.

'Actually, she's okay when you get to know her,' said Marian Blake. 'She's quite nice really. She can't help being fat.'

'She probably wouldn't want to join. She'd be scared. She probably says her prayers every night, kneels by her bed, you know, and says her prayers. And then there's always the danger she might go and tell somebody. She's a bit of an unknown quantity.'

'She's not like that,' said Marian, defending Fatty again. 'She's not at all like that. You want to talk to her before you say things like that. I think she would like to join.'

'Even knowing what we plan to do?' asked Erica, narrow-eyed.

'Yep, even knowing that. I think she'd want to.'

'Bring her round then,' said Erica, smiling a deep, warm smile. 'Tell her to come round. But make her leave that disgusting cake behind, for God's sake.'

Yes, having Fatty join the gang had proved, again and again, a most useful move. Because from that moment on, Fatty worshipped Erica. Worshipped and feared her with that peculiar, submissive sort of love reserved for the frightened, but none the weaker for that. Quite glorious, in its way.

Oh yes, some people want to be wounded. They wander vacantly into chapels and they hover outside other women's houses, in cars.

At risk. Like Molly is.

Twenty-One

The scandal, the whole ghastly business of the disappearance of Amy Macey, knocked Farendon back. Parents didn't like it. Well, naturally they didn't like it. Where was she? People don't just disappear. Parents sent their daughters here to be cared for and turned into young ladies. If they wanted a vanishing act then they might as well save their money, bring them up at home and take their chances.

The school tried to hush it up but Mr Macey wasn't having it. He made his wife appeal on the wireless news. Yes, it was that big a scandal. With Mrs Macey saying, tearfully, 'No, Amy was not the sort of child to run off without telling anyone.' And, 'Why should she go without taking any of her things? Why would a girl run away and leave her night-clothes behind?' And in those days, girls like Amy wouldn't have.

It was unfortunate for Farendon that Amy looked like a Margaret Tarrant Christmas fairy. And worse, she was a quiet, obedient child, small for her age, appealing and sweet. She had no close friends. She was quiet and shy. To be truthful she had never settled well and the school realised, too late of course, that they should have done something about it.

They discovered her missing at supper-time. But she'd missed classes all day and nobody had done anything about it. They all just assumed she must have had a good reason – been ill, gone to the dentist, or her parents must have arrived from Uganda and taken her out to tea. They weren't suspicious like they would have been if Erica, or Dierdre, or Jayne – any of the well-known skivers – was missing. They would have sent out messages, scoured the school for them.

Extraordinary, but no one had seen her. Her photograph was up all over the town; HAVE YOU SEEN THIS GIRL? The police didn't even have to deal with mistakes. Amy was so striking she couldn't be mistaken for anyone else. Only one girl at a time could possibly look like she did.

Of course they searched. They searched every inch of the place . . . nearly every inch. They brought dogs. They sniffed about for disaster. Mr Macey was a powerful man in the Foreign Office. Mrs Macey couldn't bear to believe that her child had run away. 'Something has happened to her,' she used to say, making the then-Headmistress, the portly Miss Potts, wince every time. 'She wouldn't go off on her own, she wasn't that sort of child.'

'But what can have happened?' Miss Potts asked back, beside herself with worry. She drooped, she drooped most terribly, eyes, mouth, neck, arms, stomach, and under her desk, her legs, they drooped unseen.

'She's been abducted.' Mrs Macey sat up straight, her eyes grief-stricken. 'Taken off. By some man.'

Miss Potts wrung her hands. 'But Mrs Macey, someone would have seen! There are always people about! There were no strange cars . . . no strange man was seen about the place . . .'

'Well, you tell us, Miss Potts. You tell us,' said Mr Macey, unhelpfully.

Yes, Amy seemed to have disappeared, not even in a puff of smoke, but into thin air. They were forced into holding meetings, parents' meetings, unheard-of then, at Farendon. And of course it was in the school's interest to lean towards the theory that Amy had, quite out of character, quite out of the blue, run away.

'What about bullying in the school?' One shrill woman put her hand up, forgetting she was a parent now and didn't need to do that. 'What about bullying? Could the poor child have been bullied by other girls and could nobody have known?'

Miss Potts on the podium, looked out over thick, blue-tinted spectacles, down her line of mistresses for an answer. 'Bullying, anybody?' she enquired. 'Have there been any reports of bullying lately?'

Down the line came an identical shaking of heads. Miss Potts shook hers. She gazed at the questioner sorrowfully. She had fortified herself with two sizeable gins before she arrived. 'It is something that we at Farendon have always been very sensitive to,' she told the hall, fugged with cigar smoke and perfume. 'And we have always prided ourselves on the very lack of such behaviour here. We don't tolerate bullies at Farendon, Mrs Braithwaite.'

'But would you know?' Mrs Braithwaite had the floor and wasn't about to give it up. She was a most stubborn woman, and she wore a stubborn hat.

'Of course we would know,' said Miss Potts abrasively. 'There is nothing that goes on here that does not get reported back to me.'

'What about employees, gardeners, cleaners, workmen and such-like?' Dr Murray's voice was quiet and authoritative. The hall was hushed. Silenced by his sinister little smile.

'The police, naturally, have questioned all our employees, from myself down. And I think it can be said that aspersions such as that cannot be cast on any member of my staff.'

'But the fact of the matter is, Miss Potts, that you cannot give us any sort of assurance that such a terrible thing might not happen again.' Bunny Armitage's father, sitting at the front, spoke but dared not look Miss Potts in the eye.

'Nor can I assure you, Mr Armitage, that your Armstrong Sapphire will not go off the road on your journey home from here, and that you and your family will not be instantly wiped off the face of the earth.'

'Point taken, point taken,' said Mr Armitage, wishing he hadn't spoken. He'd only done it, really, to impress his new young wife.

Finally Miss Potts summed up. 'All I can say is how much we all abhor this tragic event which has cast such a cloud over our school. All that could be done has been done. The police, the girls, and you yourselves have been wonderfully supportive through this whole ghastly nightmare. We can only offer our prayers for Mr and Mrs Macey, and for Amy, wherever, poor child, she might be, and try to get on with our lives as best we can, hoping for news, always hoping for positive news.

'I also regret that we have been subjected to such disruption during the last few days of the summer term. For some of our girls in the upper-sixth forms these have been their last days with us, and I would have hoped that term could have ended on a happier note. Let us hope that the strong sense of moral and Christian duty which has been imbued in them during their years here with us will provide a steady foundation, the fountain-head from which they will drink in years to come, unsoured by recent happenings.

'And we would be most grateful if you would all refrain from talking to the press who, I have just been informed, are encamped at the bottom of the drive.'

So spoke Miss Potts. Managing not to add, with great strength of will, 'Don't push.'

The numbers teetered, but did not fall. Hilary Park's father, from the north, told Miss Potts she'd done 'a grand job'.

Some of the same staff are still there now, preparing for the reunion. Miss Potts, of course, has gone – well, she was ancient when Molly and Erica were there. Miss Blennerhassett was her replacement. But Miss Butler – English – and still slashing away with the red pen, Mrs Delaney – History – and of course Miss Radley – Biology – they are there and can remember that time.

They are stitting in the staffroom which is full of Norman's flowers, making out a seating plan for the Thursday night dinner. Mrs Delaney stands at the window and considers the faded hydrangeas, wonders if her apples will still be all right for apple sauce tonight, and if she can put off her husband's attentions until the weekend, when she will be stronger to withstand them.

'Have you seen who's coming back this year?'

'Who?'

'Look.' Miss Butler, long, black hair rolled into a bun, pen between her teeth, leans back and points the names out to Miss Radley.

'My God! Not that lot. Lord behold us and Lord protect us.' Miss Radley's eyes are not what they were. She holds the paper away from her, stands squarely as she always does, and reads from the list, 'Erica Chorley, Molly Maguire, Dierdre Bott, Jayne Cromwell, Harriet Tyeson, Minnie Little and Marian Blake. How extraordinary! I wonder what's got into them. Not the sort, I wouldn't have thought.'

125

Mrs Delaney, moving from the window, frowns. Remembers Amy Macey. 'Perhaps, finally, the urge for reminiscence has overcome them. It happens to us all, in time.'

'Not this lot,' says Miss Radley flatly.

'They weren't that bad.'

'Think about it,' says Miss Radley.

And Miss Butler taps her teeth with her pen, looking for something to strike. But Miss Butler doesn't strike, not this time. Instead she gets up and takes Mrs Delaney's place at the window. Thinking, again, about that girl Molly Maguire's last essay.

She'd been in a hurry because of the end of term party. They were having one even though Amy Macey was gone – it was only fair, they told themselves, for the sake of the leavers. She was sitting at her desk with a pile of papers to mark and Molly Maguire's came to the top. Ten pages from Molly Maguire – wow – the lumpy, unimaginative fat child, in that stubby, blotchy writing so messy and bold. What was the point? She'd let her eyes rest on page one, picked out a few misspelt words, thought to herself how typical, just the sort of girl to succumb to this type of morbid hysteria at a time like this. Miss Butler hadn't had the heart to mark it. She'd screwed it up and thrown it away.

Well, what was the point?

Molly came stuttering up to her later that evening stuffed into her party dress, saying, 'Did you . . . did you have time to read. . . ?'

'No, Molly, I'm afraid I didn't. I just couldn't face it,' she'd told her.

And Molly had nodded, understanding. And left.

Twenty-Two

Norman Appleyard's thoughts are on love as he walks home from Julian's flat. Love, and the different kinds there are, and what it has done to him – to Julian, even.

'Skip to my lou my golden one – skip to my lou my golden one – skip to my lou my golden one – skip to my lou, my darling.' He kicks a stone along the pavement and pulls faces into the dressing-table mirrors in the furniture shop.

'Flies in the sugar bowl . . .'

Norman loves Julian. How much? Well, let's see. Norman plays games. It is easier, sometimes, to think this way.

Would he, Norman, for instance, give Julian his new suit if he wanted it?

Yes.

Right then. Would he, Norman, not watch television any more if Julian asked him not to?

Yes.

His orchids then. Would Norman throw them all out of the greenhouse and dump them on the rubbish tip, *jump up and down on them even*, if Julian asked him to?

Yes. Yes, he would. He might not like doing that but he would.

What about Dennis and Harold? Would Norman do something, leave them alone, abandon them, knowing how upset they'd be, *in the middle of the town centre, for instance*, if Julian said so?

Yes.

Would Norman be able to give up thinking of Erica?

Another question . . . another one . . . that one's not fair.

Right then. Would he be prepared to have his leg cut off in order to save him?

Yes.

Last one. A real tester. *Would Norman be prepared to kill someone, someone he doesn't know, if Julian asked him to?*

127

Yes.

Really?

This is a silly game, but it gets him home without letting in the darker thoughts that always lurk at night-time.

So. He loves Julian just as much as he loved Erica. Which was much, much more than he'd loved Mary Wellbecker. In fact, he probably didn't really love Nurse Wellbecker at all. He was probably going through a bad patch, just bored, yearning for that moonlight to mean something again.

Norman makes a detour. Instead of going straight up the drive and round the ramp to the flat, he steps over the railings and onto the grass. He takes twenty steps forward, and twenty-five to the side, stands with his back to the main Hospital building with his head down, like someone in prayer. Suddenly he turns round. Jerks his head up. And there they are, light-dimmed, the night windows of Pitt. Norman brings his head down to his shoes, sees them dewy with grass. Looks up again. Down. Looks up to find the moon. There it is. And here he is, standing in moonlight. Free as a moonbeam. Hands, look, his hands are blue with moonlight. He is bathing in it. He lifts his head for a last time, letting himself go dizzy with the stars. He thinks he sees a shooting star, screws his eyes up tight to make a wish, looks again but it is an aeroplane. Doesn't matter. He holds his arms out and swirls round, once, twice, three times. Then he walks away.

Dennis is still up. How annoying it is to get home and find him up every time, almost as if he's been waiting. All fussy. Dennis is not a moon person. Dennis has possibly never noticed the moon.

'I'll put the kettle on,' says Dennis. 'I want to talk to you.'

Norman sighs as he hangs up his coat, 'I'm very tired, Dennis, and I want to go to bed.'

Dennis comes up and sniffs him. 'You've been drinking,' he says disapprovingly.

'What is this? What are you? My wife or something? I'm allowed to drink if I like. I'm allowed to smoke, to drink, to go out at night, to buy new suits . . .'

'What new suit?'

'Here.' And Norman opens his carrier bag just a little so Dennis can peep. 'Shall I put it on?'

'How much did that cost you?'

'It cost me three pounds ninety-nine pence. From the Oxfam shop.'

'It looks new,' says Dennis, suspiciously.

'I think you're right. I think it is new. Wait here. I'll go and put it on.'

'I'll make some coffee,' says Dennis, who is now an expert at it.

They sit in the kitchen because Dennis says he's given the sitting room a clean and he doesn't want anyone going in there. Norman wears his new suit. Dennis is in his pyjamas.

'I am worried about you,' says Dennis, not prepared to beat about the bush, for he has been worrying all day.

'Well, that's silly, for you to be worrying about me. That's just silly.'

'I don't think it is.' Dennis isn't going to be silenced on this. He's worked out exactly what he's got to say and he's going to say it. 'You have been,' he says, slowly and clearly, 'in Julian's flat.'

Norman nods.

'With Julian.'

Norman nods again.

'You're getting very fond of Julian.'

'Don't you like him, Dennis? He's been very good to us, to all of us.'

Dennis screws up his face. He won't be diverted. Or confused. There is one way he has to go and he doesn't want obstacles to contend with.

'It isn't that,' Dennis manages to ad lib. 'It's got nothing to do with liking.'

'What has it got to do with then, Dennis?'

'It's got to do with you being silly again.' There! It's out! Dennis has said it. He gets up and wanders round the room, all nervy, banging his fist into his hand. He carefully avoids looking at Norman. There is something more he might add, if he dare. He is heady with success so he adds it. 'And I think I ought to say something to Mr Robbie.'

129

Norman sighs so heavily it looks as if his sigh will slip off his feet and slide all over the floor. Dennis is his friend. A very old friend. When Norman was in Gladstone Dennis was there. He used to come and sit by his bed and talk to him. When they moved him, they moved Dennis, too, and when he came out of the cells for running away it was always Dennis who came and told him, 'Behave yourself boy. Do as they say and nothing will happen to you. When will you learn that? When? When?'

'Is my mother coming today?' Dennis was the one who put his finger over Norman's mouth and hushed him.

Nobody wanted him to be in Underwood for the rest of his life so they had to try. They gave Norman the intensive ECT treatment when he was twelve, and although they never let Dennis go down with him, he was always there, waiting, when they helped him back. And holding his hand when he knew it was time for them to come and get him again . . . three times a day . . . breakfast, dinner, teatime. Dennis must have missed his meals to be with him. Sometimes he only sat there, holding his hand and looking down into his eyes. Never had to speak, really. Just Dennis being there with his familiar face was a kind of comfort.

Later, after the fire and all that business with Erica, Dennis had come to stand with him. Not say anything, just stand with him, for hours, sometimes, looking out of the window, warming his hands on the radiator. Norman will never forget all that friendly standing that Dennis did.

Same with Nurse Wellbecker. He had flown at her in the end, wanted to destroy the part of her that made him behave so badly. Dennis again. Dennis had been there when they came with their needles. Not stopping them – no one could do that. But just, you know, just there.

Norman knew nothing at all about Dennis. It seemed that he had always looked the same, tall and vaguely bewildered all the time, looking out over the top of everything. Never totally involved. A good way to be, thought Norman, many times. Because he couldn't be like that.

So he can't just shout at Dennis, tell him to turn it off, like he does with his 'Edelweiss'. It's not quite as easy as that. He has

130

to try and explain something, something he doesn't even understand himself. And Dennis, let's face it, Dennis isn't all that bright.

So Norman has to look at Dennis, with his mournful, rubbery face and his bewildered hair. 'I wouldn't leave you, ever, in the town centre, alone,' he tells him. 'Not for anyone. I just wouldn't do that.'

'I don't know anything about the town centre, Norman,' says Dennis. 'But I am worried that you are going to get yourself into big trouble again. You know what this sort of thing leads to.'

'Dennis, it isn't anything like that. I wouldn't care if I never saw Julian Tenby again. I need him, that's all. We all need him, for a little while. Until we get used to coping on our own. Perhaps I need him more than you and Harold do. And anyway, how could it be like you're saying it is? I am a man. Julian Tenby is a man. How could it be like you're trying to say it is?'

'I am worried about you,' says Dennis, mournfully, not skilled enough to argue.

'Well, don't be. There's no need to be. And there's certainly no need to say anything to Robbie. Look, if you start talking to him we'll be back in there before you can say Jack Robinson. That's what'll happen if you say anything to him.'

Dennis doesn't look too upset by the prospect. And nor would Norman have been if it wasn't for Julian.

Harold's snores are loud through the wall. The partition boards they have used are not thick. His snores and his breathing sound like waves rattling onto a shingly beach. 'He's not worried,' says Norman. He raises his eyebrows and smiles at Dennis. Dennis smiles back. At the same time, together they put out their hands and ruffle each other's hair – a gesture of love learnt by children, from passing nurses.

Twenty-Three

The Royal Clarence, stuffed with glass-eyed pike and foxes padding nowhere.

Molly and Erica drive through an archway into a courtyard. Molly opens her door on arrival, leans out and is instantly sick. Her beads and her earrings, her perfume and her 'Erica clothes' have combined to make her feel wretched. Those, and the hundred and twenty miles an hour Erica insisted on doing on the M5.

The legs she puts out onto the cobbles don't feel or look like her legs. To start with they are jammed into high-heeled shoes, and high-heels have always made her feel dizzy.

Erica looks at her crossly.

A boy dressed as Buttons comes to take their bags.

'We're not staying, we're only here for lunch,' Erica tells him.

'Then by rights you shouldn't be parking here,' says the boy, eyeing the brand new car with reverence.

'I will park where I like,' says Erica briskly. Molly groans.

'Is your . . . companion . . . is she all right?' asks the boy.

'She's fine, just car sick. She'll be better when she gets some air.'

Molly sits with both legs out of the car, breathing deeply. What is she doing here? What is she doing here, dressed like this, and with Erica? Suddenly she craves the Priest's House and Ashbury and her friends in the corner of The Crown. Suddenly she knows what she would do in a house all to herself. She would sleep, she would sleep and sleep and never get up. She starts to cry.

'Oh Molly, come on, this has to be done.'

'I know, I know, I know. It's not that. I just can't bear these shoes. Pass me the flat ones, Erica, please. I put a pair in the back, with the cases.'

So Erica rummages through the boot and Molly's untidily

packed things. She brings forward a pair of nondescript flat ones. The bell-boy goes off and sends Molly a look that tells her he thinks her insane. 'And I really think I am,' she says to herself as she wearily changes her shoes. 'Something seems to have snapped.' But she sniffs and wipes her eyes, for Erica. And the thought of the Crow Biddy and Rose seems to give her the courage she needs to carry on.

They are the first to arrive because Erica wanted to make sure her instructions have been carried out. She has booked a side-room for the meal, she has ordered the food and the wine and it is only eleven o'clock. An hour and a half to go before anyone else arrives. Erica wants to wait in the bar but Molly has other plans.

'I need to get some fresh air,' she tells her. 'I need to walk around a bit. Get my bearings. Coming back to this place has unnerved me. I have to get out and look at it, not through a hotel window.'

'Shall I come with you?'

'I'd rather be by myself.'

Erica watches as Molly walks away. She narrows her eyes and watches. Really, she looks better in her country clothes. She shouldn't have tried to smarten herself up like this. They had gone to the fashion show at Hoopers, Molly had insisted, saying, 'You'll enjoy it, Erica, it'll take you out of yourself.' There was a dress, a black, strapless dress that swathed down to the hips and then cascaded out into a shower of sequinned net. Molly saw it and gasped, a melon ball in each cheek. 'Wow! Look at that! Do you like it?' she asked.

'Yes, I do, I like it very much.'

'What do you think it would look like on me?'

Erica had to think quickly. It was the sort of thing she would wear, but she couldn't imagine it on Molly. It wasn't Molly's style at all. 'Go and try it on,' she said. 'Then you'll be able to see what it looks like.'

And Molly had done, afterwards. Breathing in hard to get the zip up. Black and purple, flouncy and sparkling.

'Well?' Pleading.

'You'd have to have your hair different . . .'

'Yes? And if I did?' Shiny-faced. Eager.

'Well then I think it would look very effective.'

Molly had taken one look at the tag, gasped, and bought it. 'One less for Rose,' she said with aplomb. And that was the first time she'd mentioned Rose for days.

She's going to wear it at the reunion dinner tonight. She's off to have her hair done this afternoon.

But now – the arrival – the tears. Could the curse be having its effect? Erica had begun to think it wasn't working, for Molly has been cheerful, almost chirpy, lately. She'd stopped her woeful tales about Crispin, stopped castigating Rose every time she poked the fire or gutted a chicken. Her face had taken on an almost peaceful look. And now, they arrive, and she starts to cry. Erica is going to have to watch her carefully. Erica is going to have to find out who is doing this, and stop them.

The Royal Clarence is up a side street in the old town. The sign outside swings, nearly meeting the one from the Dickensian bookshop over the road, or alley. This is the street of the delicatessen, the posh jumper shop, *Naome's Crafts* and the dark, mean-looking bistro that is hardly ever open. Molly passes them by without a glance. They have made the centre into a traffic-free arcade but she isn't confused by that. She has a good sense of direction. She knows where she's going.

At the museum she stops. Pauses. Looks about her. Thank God it's open. She walks straight in and pays her money at the door. She passes the shiny literature and cardboard cut-out houses – it looks as though a National Trust shop has taken over the ground floor, it smells of herbs. Up the wooden stairs she goes, leaving the herb smell behind, and the shiny things. She goes into a matt place, danker, darker. They haven't changed the uneven wooden floor, probably haven't the money. It is long like a warehouse up here, with brickwork arches every now and then. The museum spreads itself like a shadow over the fiercely-lit shops beneath it.

They haven't changed the Crow Biddy. She was afraid they might have done, afraid that in this day and age, maybe, it might have lost its appeal to children brought up on materialistic things. When they were younger and brought

134

here on school outings the Crow Biddy was the first and almost the only thing they bothered with. There was always a crowd of wide-eyed children around it, gaping, attracted by horror, scorning the bones and ancient tools, ignoring the battered coins and bent-up bangles which meant nothing to them. She was afraid that some good-thinking churchman might have insisted they move it, maintaining that its influence was bad, that ouija boards and effigies and stories of Devil worship would corrupt the young and vacant-minded. Not knowing, or being too old to remember, the substance of childhood dreams. She was afraid they might have replaced it with a piece of moon rock, or even a sample of bakelite or a silicon chip – that's the sort of odd thing people tend to do.

But it's there. The same one. And the book open at the same page. Molly is aware that she is trembling. She is the only one up here. She grips the edge of the display case while she makes herself read the words, forcing herself to go over and over them until she's sure she's taken it all in.

1610. And eighteen deaths were ascribed to Bridget Alnwick and her malicious powers, as well as the bewitching of cattle and other kinds of property.

The woman established a reign of terror over the region before she was arrested and taken to the Assizes. She broke down and confessed under examination. Denied it in the dock where she took to 'frenzied ravings and cursings'. And it was in the dock, in front of everyone, that she cut off her hand. But many people testified against her. She had been seen feeding her crow on beer and reciting the Lord's Prayer backwards while kneeling in front of a stone.

Molly stares at the doll. Its one eye looks wary. It follows you round like the eyes in a photograph. The silence in here! Where is the traffic's hum, the click of footsteps on the pavement? The silence in here sounds like a hiss.

Suddenly making up her mind Molly lets go of the case – her fingers are stuck to it, they leave wet marks behind them – and makes her way down the stairs again. The man behind the counter is overlooked by a calendar of owls. 'Excuse me,' she says, 'but I am interested in an item you have upstairs.'

'Nothing for sale upstairs, I'm afraid.'

'I know that. It's something that interested me years ago, when I was very young. And I wondered if it might be possible . . .'

'You'll have to see Chris,' the young man says. 'I can't leave the till.'

'Shall I wait?' asks Molly, never one to push herself forward, always aware that, to others with more important things to do, she is nothing but a nuisance. But this time she is not going to back down. If it means waiting all day, if it means missing the lunch, the whole reunion for that matter, she will wait here for Chris.

Her determination must have communicated itself to the young man in the guernsey because he says, 'Put your head through that door and shout.'

She hasn't even seen the door. You wouldn't, for it is behind a display of natural soaps. Now she eases herself behind them, which is difficult for she is a large person and not in her usual casual clothes, knocks, opens the door and calls down into some sort of basement area, 'Excuse me . . .'

'Yes?'

Molly blushes. 'I was wondering if I could have a word . . .'

'Hang on, I'll come up.'

Together they go up the stairs, Molly working out in her mind what she is going to say. This young man looks like a student – perhaps he is doing a thesis on the local museum or perhaps he is on a YTS, it's impossible to tell. He is tremendously tall, wears a dirty overall, and has to duck at the low-beamed turn of the stair.

Molly leads the way feeling uncomfortable, like a voyeur. Knowing that he will think her morbid, she leads the way to the display case. 'This,' she says pointing. 'I wondered if it might be possible to get the case unlocked so that I could read the next page.'

He looks at her oddly as she knew he would. She needs to give an explanation. Mere interest is not going to be enough. 'I am trying to find out more about the old Abbey,' she says, 'and about John Luciens, the chronicler.'

'This book?' he asks her. 'It's this book you're interested in?'

'Well yes, really, that book.'

The young man wipes his hands on a rag he has brought from his pocket. She can smell linseed oil. 'We're not allowed to open the cases,' he says, staring now at the Crow Biddy as if he's seen her for the first time. Molly feels the strength drain out of her. 'But you can buy it downstairs,' he says. 'There's a copy, in the shop downstairs. It's got photographs of that thing in it, too.'

Molly wants to kneel down and kiss his feet. 'I'm so sorry,' she flusters, 'I didn't see it. I didn't stop to look at the books.'

'Well, it's down there,' says the young man, leading the way down again. 'It's quite expensive but then these old things are quite hard to reproduce.'

The young man disappears into his basement once more. She wouldn't have noticed the book, of course, because she's never seen the front cover. Now she rubs wet hands on her coat before she fingers the smart covers laid out before her. John Luciens. John Luciens. The picture on the front is of a medieval window – the sort of ghastly thing she would never normally look twice at. It is heavy. She takes it to the counter and smiles apologetically.

'Thirty-five pounds ninety-five.'

'Do you do Access?'

'But of course.'

Hah! Crispin pays her Access bills. And Molly hurries away to the tea house that is still on the corner, the tea house which served toasted tea cakes in her childhood, and picks a booth at the back in order to turn the page over.

And there it is, clearly decipherable. Something she's always known and yet never known.

They scraped up the ashes of Bridget Alnwick and took them to be put with the felons and tykes in unhallowed ground behind the Abbey wall up at the Farendon Cross.' There is even a nasty picture, one of those sharp little etchings, of them taking her, carried aloft in what must be a seventeenth-century version of a bit-bin. But the man in front carries the hand, prances ahead like a jester, with the hand that was not burnt.

'Can I help you, Madam?'

'Oh, just a pot of tea, please.'

'This area of the room is reserved for diners at lunch-time, I'm afraid.'

'Oh, I'm sorry. So sorry. I'll move.'

All those times. All those wild, wonderful times. The moon that gazed so unblinkingly down had been tarnished. They had danced on the Crow Biddy's grave.

Twenty-Four

Norman goes to check the field he has delegated for a car park. It is raining, just breezy rain borne on the air but enough to make the grass greasy. They are rolling in now, the Old Girls; a few have escorts, but they are reluctant escorts for it is not really a suitable event for men.

'Be around, be visible, help them with their bags,' Miss Radley had told him. 'Make yourself useful.'

But Norman knows Miss Blennerhassett would not expect him to do that. That's not his job. So he skulks and he lurks, head down, answering with a few polite pokes at his bobble hat the many exclamations, 'Oh, hello Appleyard! How are you? Still here then! Still keeping the old place shipshape.'

They fall into each other's arms when they see one another, with screams and tears of laughter. As if the outside world is some terrible ordeal they must get through in order to return, once more, here to be themselves again. Known once more by familiar nicknames like Barmy or Chubb or Mottles, instead of Harriet's mother or Charles's wife or the woman who runs the play-group.

Happy days!

Days when Tescos, hoovers, Benylin, Gumption, and diaphragms were just words used by people they wouldn't have given the time of day to. Boring people. People in ruts. People they were never going to grow up to be. For who was going to tell them, who was going to betray the secret – that one uninterrupted *Woman's Hour* would turn out to be the highlight of the week, that they would make gravy every Sunday, while from their various drawing rooms would come the roar and rev of racing cars, meeting the gravy fragrance in the hall around about *Songs of Praise* time? Farendon girls are good at singing along to *Songs of Praise*. They know all the words.

No one was going to tell them that. No one would be so uncircumspect.

139

Here at Farendon was where they had left their hopes behind. All those mountains they had been exhorted to climb. All those oceans to conquer.

> *Hark to the sound of voices!*
> *Hark to the tramp of feet!*
> *Is it a mighty army*
> *Treading the busy street?*

No. It is I. Stirring the gravy.

To be fair, some of the younger ones have made it. And you can tell who they are by their bearing. Their forms are at the top of Miss Blennerhassett's pile. Some of them have been picked out to talk to the others about the interesting work they do. After all, it's never too late! Universities are keen on mature students these days. Those who retain still a smattering of education . . . the date of the spinning jenny, a few fuzzy facts about the Jacobite rebellion, the complete role of Bottom the weaver from *A Midsummer Night's Dream*.

But what have they to be bitter about? Norman never learnt to read. He can't escape that way.

They wander in in groups of two or three, laughing, talking, their arms round each other. They come to attention when they meet Miss Radley, standing there at the door with her hand stretched out to shake. Coming out of the abstract art, the wired arms and the snake-bowls and the tube of crimson daffodils. She wouldn't dream of asking them now if they have any good reason not to go swimming. Or would she? They are grown up people, adults, to be respected, aren't they? They remind themselves that they are by giggling and nudging each other when they get past her.

She offers them nuts and a glass of sherry. Norman wanders in. He is not the Norman he was and he won't be treated like that. He is Norman the householder, friend and confidant of Julian Tenby, visitor to his flat and his companion at dinner tonight. His hair is growing long and he rests his brown corduroy jacket casually over his shoulders. His red cravat is neat round his very short neck and he holds his pipe in his hand.

'Ah, Appleyard,' blinks Miss Radley, taken aback.

Norman smiles and nods. Then ignores her. He walks across to the table and picks up a glass of sherry. Pops a nut in his mouth. The biology mistress looks at his shoes, fearful that he will be trailing in soil. They are clean, very clean: suede, they match his trousers. In fact Appleyard looks quite decent, a little peculiar perhaps but certainly acceptable. He leans his head on one side while listening to Trisha Thomas who has wandered over to speak to him. He strokes his chin with his hand, thoughtfully. Not Appleyard's gestures at all.

The fact that he shouldn't be here, that he hasn't been asked, is beside the point. He is here and he looks determined to stay. Miss Radley can hardly ask him to leave. Not in front of everyone. And there is quite a crowd around him. Everyone knows Appleyard. He is part of every childhood.

Twenty-Five

What is it they want – these women who come scurrying back, puffing back through the russet roundabout doors of The Royal Clarence Hotel, anxiety and wonder on their faces?

After years of shame, years of guilt, what could possibly bring them back to face each other again? It only took a letter from Erica.

And no wonder. To taste, again, however shameful, something of that time. To receive a call from that age of clarity, intensity, that time when their whole lives lay ahead of them and they knew all the secrets. What, oh what has happened to them? Look! Oh, look at them! What has happened? They were fearless and reckless then, full of power and hope. Daughters of the moon, the world was before them. They had the power to conquer it. With Erica.

Dierdre Bott. Harriet Tyeson. Moaning Little. Marian Blake. Jayne Cromwell. In quiet conversation, grouped in a ring. They knock back pre-luncheon drinks as if there is no tomorrow, while Erica watches them. She started this, now, has somebody else taken it over?

They are there, gathered, when Molly walks in. Their eyes, when they greet her, are shaded and cautious. Only Erica looks triumphant. Already she knows she has them.

Erica buys them drinks. They accept with nervous smiles on their faces. It is a small moment of sacrifice.

Rubrum a iugulo. Ut tibi supplex donem honorem.

They turn when Molly enters the room, expressions of interest put on their faces. Molly has never been important. Molly has always been just there. Often late. Often dishevelled.

Molly confides. 'Have you told them yet?'

'No, not yet. Do you feel better now after your outburst? You've bought a book. Let's see.'

142

'You wouldn't be interested, Erica. It's just a history book, a present for Edward.'

Molly won't join the ring. Molly goes to sit down, at the far end of the room. Nearest the curtain.

'Hello, Molly. How are you?' Dierdre Bott comes to sit beside her. Dierdre Bott looks like a huntsman in hunter's green that feels like felt, long brown boots and a hat with a bronze feather in it. A pair of brown gloves rest neatly on her handbag. Dierdre, who started it all with her love for the star chemistry pupil, who told them of love dressed in fluffy pyjamas with kittens on and elasticated sleeves. But it is Molly who spent her life on her knees, Molly who carried it through to serve a master. Who did Dierdre love in the end? Has she changed her mind about adulation?

Dierdre slides a manicured hand in a leather purse and brings out a picture. 'Not Bott now, of course,' she says with measured relief. 'But Barrington-Jones. This is Alistair.' Molly looks. The frazzled little man stands beside Dierdre in the picture, on a moor with a gun over his shoulder, wearing plus-fours. He has a goatee beard with a red tip. No, Dierdre has not spent her time in worship.

No wonder Dierdre has come back.

Jayne Cromwell is grey-haired and comes to sit beside them. How has she fared? She, who came top whether she worked or not. She, who took all the glittering prizes. Many was the time that Jayne was singled out as someone they might all like to emulate.

Intelligent and wise, she has lived in her face and it shows. She wears culottes and thick black tights and a very sophisticated jerkin. Tall and slim. 'I never thought I'd ever come here again.' The hand with which she smoothes her hair is shaking. There is no vodka in her tomato juice. Never one for pretence she says, 'I'm on the wagon. Got to be. Can't take the stuff.' She turns to Molly and her smile is weak as she says, 'You look just the same! Of all of us you look just the same.'

'And Erica,' says Molly.

'Oh yes, of course, and Erica.'

'I've lost weight. I'm not as fat as I was.'

Jayne smiles again. 'Erica was telling us about that husband of yours. Said to keep off the subject. You were upset. Bad luck, old bean. It happened to me. Took me years to recover.'

'But what about work?' Molly asks her, determined to know what the scholarships led to. 'What did you do . . . before you were married?'

'I worked as a singer on a liner.' Jayne stubs out her cigarette. The tip is ringed with red lipstick. 'I married a steward. Lived in America for five years, came home, had kids, got drunk, lost them.'

'Oh. I expected . . .'

'Didn't we all.'

'Shall we go through?' Erica interrupts. 'I thought we'd be better in a room on our own. A little, confidential chat, you know, before we get down to it. Preparation for the old alma mater.'

They follow her. As they have always followed her.

In Dei santo nomine. Gratias ago sine fraue. Umbris omnibus tenibus. Et lucem claram ferentibus. Hoc templo vos dimitto. Abite nunce opere facto.

The Royal Clarence is an old hotel with beams painted black. They look like gibbets where they meet the ceiling and hold it. The ceilings are limed. They will have to put paper up if they ever want to paint it, for paint won't stick to lime. The passages are narrow and thickly carpeted. The floor creaks as they go, in line over the patterns, to the private dining room with the oval table, the pristine white cloths and the sparkling glasses. It smells, as these hotels do, of tweed and sprouts.

They sit at low-level and through mullioned windows watch legs and shopping baskets go by. They watch dogs on leads and tartan trolleys, newspapers tapping against pin-striped trousers and a blind man with a white stick. Everything ordinary. So very ordinary.

They pour red wine and raise their glasses.

They hang their bags on their chairs. They fiddle with spilt salt. They look at each other and they remember.

They used to climb out of St Mary's House and St Claire's House windows – the houses opposite the School at the far side of the quad – the houses that backed onto the woods. Naked, wrapped in rugs, to be caught would mean suspension, maybe even expulsion. Just being out at night would be reason enough for that. Let alone the trauma of having to face the wrath of women like Potts, Radley and Butler and others of that ilk.

So it was no mean thing that they did. Before they began their throats were dry, their hearts were beating and their hands were wet.

FEAR

They made their own candles with moulds and wax and a slimy black dye. They went to the Cathedral shop, or sent Appleyard, to buy their incense and the crucifixes. The wine Erica used to bring from home, and the purple hearts came free from Moaning Little's brother. The vestments and the sacramental items were already in the Chapel, in a cupboard in the tiny vestry.

The Chapel, at night, was a chilling place. They moved by candlelight and the red eye over the altar. The effects these gave to the silent, vaulted stone was menacing and unreal. So were the sounds their feet made, bare, on the floor, feet on stone, living on dead, a whispering, sheeted sound.

APPREHENSION

They made a salt circle where Erica stood to light the candles and evoke the forces. Later, they would join her, and close the gap. Safe, they thought, in this other underworld. Half out of their minds already they swayed and chanted, hands clasped tightly in a ring, holding tightly, hanging on. Needing each other.

EXPECTANCY

First she followed the books . . . most freely available from secondhand shops in the old part of the city, some from a mail order magazine which also sold whips and shackles. She learnt what she wanted off by heart and mixed the mass for best effect. It was boring if followed to the letter. Erica should have been an actress – that might have filled the need and it might have been less dangerous. She loosened her hair so it flowed down her back, and in her eyes the scar down the centre was a black seam in pools of speckled gold. She moved

145

like a serpent before the inverted Cross – animal, not human, and quite without reserve.

MAGIC

When they levitated Wendy Cross, when they lifted her without using their fingers but just by directing the cone of force underneath her, it was nothing . . . it was normal. When they moved the chalice across the floor no one raised an eyebrow. They played games with it – games of catch – games guessing who could bang it hardest on the floor – dent it perhaps. It was funny! When the voice came out of the earth they didn't run away; it came where the breeze came from, and the breeze had never been frightening. Not at all. They used to call it up and stand by it, letting their hair flow in it, cooling their faces by it. When the voice came, no, they didn't run away, but several put hands over faces, not from fear, but because of the smell. It was an old woman's voice, softly savage, quietly contained. It told them to do things. Things that even then were shameful, that it wouldn't do now to think about. Things to each other. Things to themselves.

EVIL

Oh no, there was no pretence about it.

They played games until they grew bored with them, the girls from St Claire's and St Mary's. Erica. Molly. Dierdre. Jayne. Minnie. Charlotte. Harriet. Wendy. Kate. Marian. Sophie. Hilary. Caroline. They moved to the copse and they danced in the moonlight until they fell, until their feet bled and their long hair stuck to their backs and their faces. Erica mixed dry blood fertiliser with water and they slipped and covered themselves in it. It mixed with the rain over the seasons and left a hard, crusty surface on the rough grass and stones. Erica killed things. They watched. They gritted their teeth and they watched, and afterwards they felt great, secret, shameful love for each other.

And it was eighteen months before they turned their attentions to anybody else.

'There is a reason why we asked you here.'

Yes, there is a reason. Erica wants it back. She wants her power back. She wants to feel it again . . . something of it. She had to invent an excuse, or thought she did. They would have come without reason, they would have come at her bidding . . . they all want it back. She is interested to know which one is cursing Molly Maguire, but only interested. She doesn't care for Molly. If Molly knew about the purple envelopes then Molly wouldn't have come.

'Someone has evoked the curse again. The Crow Biddy curse. And we know it.'

Molly blinks. Molly has drunk far too much wine. She has talked too much and drunk too much and there is too much going on inside her head.

'I'm not saying who is the victim, the one who is doing it knows that. I'm not playing games with you. I want to know the answer and I want to know the reason for it.'

She sits in the chair at the end of the table and looks at every single one. Each in their turn, looks down. Looks at the remains of the meal, the knives and the forks and the messy cloth, and thinks how incredible, how incredible that they should be eating and smoking and drinking like this as if twenty years has not gone by. Twenty quite irrelevant years. Whatever has happened means nothing. Not now. Nothing. They are back to the start again, back where it can all begin.

'We need to meet.' As she says this Erica looks tired, looks as if she doesn't want to, hasn't the strength or the inclination to fire them all again. They sit forward, eager and alert, willing her on, giving her their own strength, if necessary, to say what she's got to say. What they've come back to hear her say.

She lifts her eyes slowly and sighs. 'So what I propose we do is this. We call a meeting for tomorrow night, Friday, same place, same time, and there we will see if we can't find out who is evoking the force, and even,' and here she smiles, a soft, kindly smile, 'and even see if we can't, perhaps, lift it. There's life in us yet. Let's prove it.'

After the lunch is a little like stopping the dance. Not quite knowing what to say or even what was said in that little private room down from the hall. They are making their own ways to Farendon. They will sleep in the Houses they slept in then.

The present boarders are moving out, putting up camp beds to accommodate them. It is the same every year. This is the way it is always done, only the Royal Clarence party doesn't know that. None of them has ever been back.

'I'd like to walk,' Molly tells Erica. 'I have to get my hair done so I might as well walk. I can easily walk from the town up the drive and be there in time for supper.'

'You never walk anywhere. Why do you want to walk?'

Molly smiles. 'I have drunk too much. I have smoked too much. And after all that I need some fresh air.'

Erica relaxes. Ah! Fresh-faced, country-loving Molly. She worries about what they might do to her hair. Fancy booking up with a hairdresser who doesn't know you. Erica would never do that. Molly would. Molly has.

'If you're sure.'

'I'm sure.'

'Let me take the book. Let me put it in the back of the car. You can't possibly lug that round with you.'

'I want it with me.' Molly has spoken too tersely. She softens. 'I want to have a look at it in the hairdresser's,' she says.

'It doesn't look quite the sort of book . . .'

'I know it doesn't but I'm taking it with me.'

Erica sniffs. 'Fine. Well, far be it from me. I'll see you later, then. Telephone if you change your mind – I can always come and pick you up from the hairdresser's.'

'I might,' says Molly obediently, knowing full well she won't. There is something else she needs to do while she's still her own person. Something for herself. Being with Erica tends to divert her from her own purposes. This, she thinks, if they are going to be busy all weekend, is her last opportunity.

The bell-boy helps her through the roundabout door. 'Better now, madam?' he asks her cockily.

'There was never anything wrong with me,' says Molly, in Erica's voice. 'That was me you saw being sick, being who I normally am.'

And he nods his head as he watches the fat woman with the book passing down the road out of sight.

Twenty-Six

'Promise me this,' says Norman, in a tizzy, adjusting his tie for the umpteenth time. 'Promise me you won't let Harold out of your sight tonight. He keeps asking me where I'm going and the thought of him trailing his way over to Farendon, getting himself into the dining room and being set off by all the excitement is enough to put me off going.'

'Calm down,' says Dennis, brushing the back of Norman's brown jacket with a shoe-blacking brush. 'Harold knows he's upsetting you. That's why he's saying it. He never goes out at night. He daren't. He's terrified of the dark.'

'Well, just as long as you keep an eye on him, that's all.'

'What time is Julian coming?'

'Half past seven. He's coming at half past seven. And I have to be ready because if we don't leave then we'll be late.'

'You won't be late. He'll be on time. He always is.'

'How do I look?'

This is the tenth time Dennis has had to answer this question tonight. Once again he gives Norman the once over. 'Very good,' he says, meaning it, 'Very good indeed. But different.'

'How? Different?'

Dennis shakes his head worriedly. 'I dunno. Just different. Not like you any more.'

This is what Norman has been waiting to hear. He has peered at himself in the mirror for hours on end, the long mirror in his bedroom, practising Julian's posture and gestures, practising his mannerisms, the way he moves his mouth, shifts his shoulders, stands with his ankles crossed. Norman has it all off by heart. Not only that, but slimmed down as he is he looks taller, and he has been able to comb back the hair that at last flops over his eyes, and over to one side like Julian does. His suit looks good. His collar is white and his hair touches it. His tie is straight. Norman Appleyard is ready for his first big event.

Julian arrives feeling uncomfortable and they walk the route that Norman has taken for the last twenty-five years, down the road and over the bridge and up the Farendon drive. It is nice walking like this with somebody next to you, specially with Julian. They talk as they walk – just as Norman's seen other people doing – about all sorts of things, things that wouldn't be interesting to anyone else, but are interesting to Julian and Norman.

The rain of the morning has cleared away leaving the night crisp and dry. Every leaf, every twig they step on, crackles. The moon is nearly full. It will be full tomorrow night. They can see their breaths as they go, and Norman tries to breathe in rhythm with Julian. Step in time to Julian. Move his arms like Julian.

'I'm not looking forward to this, Norman,' says Julian as they get nearer, as the Farendon windows get bigger and the Farendon lights burn brighter. 'I have to be truthful, I'm not looking forward to it at all.'

'You'll be all right,' Norman replies. 'You're with me.'

And Julian smiles to himself in the dark. Missing Sylvie like an ache that walking quickly seems to help. This experience, he knows full well, is going to be absolutely ghastly. He's wished, many times, he could ring up Sylvie and tell her. She would have loved it. And afterwards she would have wanted to know all about it. He could have borne it knowing that every little event could be turned and told in his dry, cynical way, told when he got home, sitting by the gas fire with a brandy in his hand, and Sylvie. In that way he could make himself a member of the audience. Uninvolved. Watching. Now, without his audience, he can't. He is really here. In it.

They are at the door. There is no turning back.

'Come on,' says Norman. Proud to be here. 'I want to show you to Miss Blennerhassett.'

'Ah, Appleyard,' says Miss Radley, easily recognisable in spite of her glitzy bronze boiler suit.

'Excuse me,' says Norman, 'but Miss Blennerhassett is calling me over there.'

And it is left to Julian to give the embarrassed shrug. It pleases Miss Radley very much.

*

The Farendon hall. Bedecked with flowers. They hang from the rafters and trail down the walls. The top table stands at the far end of the room and three long tables come off it, tables with names propped on plates. They are Old Girls now but they still cannot choose where they sit.

By a corner table with drinks on it stands Miss Blennerhassett, resplendent in grey lace, Flapper-style, with sleeves like wide-open lilies and little thin arms that come out of the ends like stamens. Naturally she is worried about Norman. She wonders if she hasn't been a little foolish to invite him, a little patronising, perhaps. Will he be able to cope? Only after she'd issued the double invitation did the terrible thought strike her that he might decide to bring one of his friends to accompany him tonight. Now Miss Blennerhassett knows Norman, but she does not know his friends. She does not even know the sort of people Norman's friends might be. So when she sees him she naturally signals, the stamen in her sleeve twisting like a periscope, which is her way of saying, 'Hello there, come over.' And she stares hard at Julian as she thinks to herself, 'Thank the Lord for that.'

Norman strolls up to her, not the normal, stumbling Norman, breathless and eager and little boyish, no, a Norman who strolls with his arms behind his back. A Norman who nods to her nicely, says, 'Good evening, let me introduce you to my friend, Julian Tenby.'

Miss Blennerhassett frowns. She is not to know this has been rehearsed for hours in front of Norman's mirror, between pictures of bridges in the most Godforsaken cities in the world. She smiles quickly. 'Well Norman, how nice,' she says. 'Pleased to meet you, good evening Mr Tenby.' She wants to ask how on earth Norman has found such a friend but of course she doesn't. She can't, now, can she?

Julian, adept in such situations, uses polite conversation as a cover to allow his eyes to wander over the assembly. They are nearly all women; the odd man stands out darkly and rigidly, laughing sillily here and there for there is little that can be sensibly said, man to man. Or man to woman. Not here.

151

And then Norman sees Erica.

River – brown – minnows – birds – orchids – leaves

Not the Erica of his dreams. Not the girl, but the woman. Wearing green. Green silk flows down her back and across her chest. Her hair is piled up high on her head and trembles of it tumble round her face in coils.

He moves to take Julian's hand, touches it and starts away. He can't do that. This isn't Dennis or Harold standing here beside him, either of whom would submit to having their hands held, at a push.

'Here, Norman, here, have a drink. It looks a bit pissy but it's better than nothing. I don't think they've got any beer. Norman! Norman! What's the matter?'

Norman is standing with his mouth wide open, drooping, head down, shoulders hunched, fists clenched.

'Hey, Norman, wake up. What is it?'

'It's her. She there. That one. It's Erica.'

A wrinkle of amusement moves across Julian's brows. 'Oh, *that* Erica! Well! What a surprise! And how convenient. All on her own and the prettiest lady in the room. Now then, Norman. Now's your chance to renew old acquaintance. Now's your chance to go over and speak to her again. How long is it since you've seen her?'

'I can't. I can't possibly go over. You don't know the things she said about me. You don't know how much she hates me.'

Julian catches hold of Norman's arm and pulls him to the side of the hall. He looks down upon his friend with stern disapproval. 'This isn't the Norman that I have come to know,' he says, humour flickering the edges of his mouth. 'I can't believe that you, of all people, could suddenly turn into a wimp! Wait till I get back to that flat and tell Harold and Dennis about your reaction! Pull yourself together, man! You're not going to let a woman defeat you like that, are you? She's forgotten what she said, women do. She probably never meant it anyway. She's probably spent the last twenty years of her life regretting having said it. Be fair to her, Norman. Give her a chance to make amends. Come on! We're going over and we're going to introduce ourselves. Right now!'

152

Norman cringes. He tries to smile at Julian but Julian doesn't smile back. How can he tell him that it just isn't possible for him to go over there and face Erica? Julian doesn't seem to understand, doesn't seem to see the significance of this at all. Julian thinks him feeble. Julian thinks him feeble and timid. Afraid. Back as he was, a patient from Pitt. To be pitied and scorned. No! No! Norman can't bear that. Can't bear to see that look in Julian's eyes.

Norman downs his wine in one and reaches for another. He gulps that and snatches a third, to the horror of Miss Blennerhassett, before he precedes Julian across the room towards Erica. She stands there like a queen, regal, beautiful. Her cold eyes slither in the light. My God, Julian thinks to himself . . . poor old Norman. What a one to pick! Of all the women in the world, what a one to pick!

They approach together. Erica frowns. Well, well, well, if it isn't little Norman Appleyard. Still free then. They haven't locked him up for good, shut the door of the padded cell and thrown away the key! What fun! And who on earth is that Adonis walking with him? What a stunner for Farendon! What on earth is he doing here? Somebody's husband? Doubt it. He doesn't look like a husband. The way he's eyeing her up doesn't put him as somebody's husband.

Norman stands before her, before the great love of his life, trembling, Julian by his side. He can, he knows he can be Julian if he tries. Now is the time to try, Norman. Now!

Norman is Julian. He smiles like Julian, holds out his hand like Julian, wrinkles his eyes up like Julian, straightens his mouth like Julian, rocks back a little on his heels like Julian, and Norman flows towards Erica like Julian, says, 'Hello Erica.'

And she lifts her eyebrows and brings her mouth together into a sort of kiss before she says, 'Hello, Norman! What a surprise. I never expected to see you here. How nice. How very nice.'

'Let me fetch you a drink,' says Norman. 'Oh, but first of all, let me introduce you to a friend of mine, this is Julian . . .'

But Julian has gone. Julian has left Norman to it. Julian is over there, talking to someone else. Confident that Norman can handle it, Julian has left him like a real friend would and is *talking to someone else*.

'I can handle it,' says Norman to himself, seeing the sweetness in Erica's eyes. Yes, yes, he rejoices, this is how it was. Really how it was. This is how I remember it. And this is how, now I am different, I can make it always be.

Absurd? No, not absurd. Just Norman trying very hard, standing as tall as he possibly can.

Julian turns from his conversation, raises his glass, and winks at Erica.

And Erica, over the top of Norman's head, sends a deadly wink back.

Twenty-Seven

And now here comes Molly to the ball.

Molly is late arriving. Molly has been busy. Molly has been very busy all afternoon.

First she went to the hairdresser's. 'Cut it off,' she told them determinedly, pointing at a magazine, 'and restyle it. I want it cut to look like that.' I want it cut like Erica's.

'It might not quite look like that, madam. Your face hasn't really got the shape for it. And your hair isn't straight enough.'

'Well, do your best,' said Molly, settling herself in the chair. Opening her new book in the chair so that it stretched arm to arm and caught pieces of hair as the stylist did his best behind her. 'I want it coming straight down the sides, kind of in like that,' she said.

She came out disappointed. But it was better than it was before. It was nothing before, Ashbury nothing, frizzy and nothing.

As an early dusk fell she made her way up the Farendon drive, splashed her way up between puddles that never dried, standing back and trying not to look when cars inched by. She didn't want, at this stage, to see anyone she knew.

She was carrying a Union Jack carrier bag, a huge one that she'd bought. In it was the John Luciens book and the bits and pieces she had bought from the craft shop. Before she reached the entrance, the wide space of garden and the Founder, she took a route across the grass, behind the trees between the rhododendrons. Memories. With every step across that grass they flooded back. Even the grass did that. It wasn't like ordinary grass, it was Farendon grass, and these dark bushes, their shadows and their shiverings, they were Farendon bushes. There was nothing like this in Godalming. Nothing like this in Ashbury either.

She was panting and puffing by the time she reached the greenhouses, the potting shed, the vegetable garden which she circumnavigated, her bag feeling painfully heavy. Molly was fat. Molly was unfit, unused to exercise of any sort except for the bit of dancing she had done of late. She came to the track of the Chapel, walked down it, telling herself, 'It's all right, Molly, it's all right. Nothing, now, is going to hurt you.' She followed the track to the Chapel door, left it and went round the side, and on. Down into the woods where the darkness was sudden and only broken by gaps in the treetops through which glowered a dirty sky.

The walled-up copse was in a sorry state. One wall in particular was nearly down. It fell to a messy V of rocks in the middle, over which it was easy to step. In she went, glad she did not have to squeeze through the brick drainage tunnel. She could have made it . . . it was a very wide tunnel, but it wouldn't have done much for her dress, for her tights, for her new hair-style.

Dank and mouldy smelling, just as Molly remembered. A faint pit-pat of water dripping somewhere, old water. A worn-out place with snails on the walls and patches of mildew, bulbous growths of sickly yellow on the stones. Over the Crow Biddy's grave she made her doll, sitting on a piece of broken drainpipe, the carrier bag at her feet. She wound the raffia round her hand, tied it, she'd even remembered scissors and a needle. She sewed the one eye in place, simple, only a blob of felt. Her fingers moved deftly, she could be making a toy, a golliwog for the village fête, except that she didn't cut the hair to make it frizzy. She left it smooth. She stuck a pin in the finished article and clipped it together neatly. She thought of Rose. She sat and she thought about Rose, and whether or not she ought to say a few words. She hung her head, not because she was ashamed, this middle-aged woman, to be sitting here and thinking wicked thoughts – no, not because of that. She hung her head because she couldn't remember what she should say.

After that she put the thing in a purple envelope and addressed it, writing, as she always did, *Mrs Tarrent*, on the front. She would post it in the box on the Farendon front wall, surely it was still there. Nothing else seemed to have changed here.

Then she felt exhausted. She had been driven . . . driven to do this . . . almost at a trot. Once the idea had found its way into her head she became obsessed with it, afraid, even, that she might die before she carried it out. It was suddenly the most important thing to do in the world. And when it was done she felt there was nothing left inside her.

Until she got up to go. It didn't feel that way when she got up to go. Instead she was flushed with a powerful lifting of spirit, a lightness that made her want to cry it was so beautiful to feel inside. She breathed out as if she'd suddenly been struck by a magnificent view. It was a little like that, but stronger. Much. Much.

She breathed out again, looked round the place before she left it, and smiled. Wonderful! Freedom! Escape from the hatred. Light she was, not heavy. Where had the fat, wounded woman gone? Gone? Had she gone?

Molly dressed carefully for the dinner. Erica was out when she reached the bedroom so she could relax and have a bath and not have her new feelings interrupted. She scented herself. She touched her hair, pushed it until it was right. Not bad – they hadn't done a bad job at all, considering. She made up her face with care. She even put lines under her eyes and she hadn't done that since Crispin . . .

Molly stepped into her dress and looked at herself in the mirror. The look she gave her reflection was full of love. Big-eyed and swollen, a look of total love. She had power. She had magic at the ends of her fingers.

Down into the hall. Years since she'd been here. Years and years. Not since the end of term leaving party when she'd gone up to Miss Butler and asked if she'd read her essay, breathing relief when she said she had not. It was better, much better that nobody knew.

She should have been shy. She was not. She should have felt ugly and fat. She didn't. She should have gone straight over to Erica who was talking to that funny little gardener, Norman Appleyard. God, she was a user. She'd used him . . . she'd used everyone to achieve her own ends. Molly didn't go over to Erica. She spotted an extraordinarily good-looking

157

young man searching in a box for beer. Molly walked across the room and immediately joined him.

'Well,' said Julian as he rose from the box, successful, with a can of lager in his hand. 'Well, I bend down and close my eyes and what happens? A gorgeous woman flies in from nowhere, looking like a breath of air in this cloistered, stuffy place.'

He stared at Molly as he stared at all women. His dark eyes were suggestive, full of promises he didn't mean. He didn't know they were there. His lips, too, broke into a straight, open smile. Beneath them his teeth were sharp, a triangle of tongue parted them. Suggestive? No, not suggestive at all. That was because he was concentrating very hard on pulling the tag off the lid of his beer. Nothing to do with Molly.

But Molly didn't think so. Molly knew that from now on, for her, things were going to be very different. She could bewitch and ensnare at will, she had power – her sexuality, at last, was something she could take and use fearlessly. And look! Look at the result when she did it.

Molly is a beautiful woman.

Julian came closer. He touched her. He is a toucher, that's all, an intruder into private spaces. He doesn't know he does it. He just does it. 'Let's go and see if we can find something to nibble,' he said. 'I don't know that I can wait for the main bash. I haven't touched anything all day.'

Things had changed simply because Molly wanted them to. They had changed because she willed it, and she willed it because she had the power. The secrets were hers.

Molly cast speculative glances at Erica. She smiled to herself. Molly didn't need Erica any more. She could get Crispin back without her.

Twenty-Eight

The speeches are long and boring but Norman doesn't mind. Norman is in his element. Norman is delighted. He swathes himself in smiles.

He is sitting next to Erica. And she is talking to him, just as she talks to Julian who is on her other side. So Norman doesn't have to worry about Julian, either, because with Erica on one side, Molly on the other, he has two nice people to talk to.

All around them are the girls he remembers from Erica's day. The fairies. On their table they talk and laugh louder than anyone else. It is the best table to be on. Norman feels sorry for everyone else, sitting there dully on the others. His people are alight tonight, radiant with their conversation and their sparkling eyes. And so is Norman. He is one of them. Included. Every now and then he sends a look of concern across the front of Erica to Julian, who is his responsibility, and Julian smiles back at him happily.

By sliding his eyes along and copying Julian Norman has managed to sip his soup properly, find his fish knife and fork, and the special small one for his bread roll. He breaks this into little pieces as he goes as he sees Julian do. It's easy. Nor has he knocked anything over yet. Every now and then he brings up his napkin to pat at his mouth. It's easy when you have the confidence that Norman has.

'So Julian tells me you're moving out, Norman, out of the Hospital and into a nice little house of your own?' Erica talks like the silk of her dress. She smiles like the silk and she smells smoothly of it.

Norman blushes. 'It's quite a small house,' he says, 'and I will be sharing it.'

'You will be free,' says Erica, glancing at him from the sides of her eyes, smiling and resting her long, graceful arm along the white cloth as she toys with the stem of her wine glass.

159

The silk sleeve stains the white cloth with a green shadow. 'You will be free to live as you like for the very first time.'

'I am used to it already,' says Norman. 'We're practising at the moment, you see.'

'I shall have to come and visit you one day Norman, won't I?' says Erica, joking, quite well aware of the effect she is having on the poor little man beside her. She has to flirt with someone to egg Julian on, and there's nobody else, so it might as well be Norman, who's almost a man.

Norman, his napkin on his knee, realises he has screwed it up so hard it resembles a knotted old ivy root, a snowy ivy root climbing up the wall of his thumping chest.

'Don't do that,' says Erica. 'Here, let me help you tuck it in.' And she tries to stick it in his collar like a bib which is what they do in Pitt, so Norman says, scrabbling to pull it down, 'I don't want it like that, I don't want it like that,' and Erica answers, 'Well, you don't want to spill all over that smart suit now do you?'

It is all right during the food, but Norman finds the speeches difficult. Julian passes him a pen and he scribbles on his menu. If he wasn't sitting next to Erica he doesn't know if he could have coped with the speeches. After all that food he needed to get up and walk around. But you can't. You're not allowed to. Once he pushed his chair right back and tried to ease his shoes off but Julian frowned at him behind Erica's back so he pulled back to the table and sat still. On his right-hand side is a dusty Old Girl who he knows is called Veronica Engles, but he ignores her completely. And anyway, she is deep in conversation with her other neighbour.

'Chockies, yummy,' says Erica when little silver bowls of mints come wrapped in green. 'Here, Norman, open your mouth, let me pop one in.'

'I don't want one,' he tells her, leaning forward and taking a handful to put in his pocket. Shoving them deep in his pocket. 'I want to save them and take them back to the flat for Dennis and Harold.'

Erica sits high and queenly in her chair. 'Norman!' she exclaims. 'What are you doing? What about me? Don't you think I might want a chocolate? Aren't I as important as

Dennis and Harold?' Her ochre eyes flash and cut themselves in half as she brings her gaze down on him.

Norman struggles with his shame. 'Oh, yes, yes.' He stands up and tries to tip himself up to empty his pocket more quickly. 'Oh, yes, yes, I just thought there were more up your end.'

'Well, there aren't,' says Erica, smiling her wide cat smile again. So Norman counts them out and puts them into her open handbag.

Norman listens to Miss Blennerhassett. Not to the words, for they are too difficult, but to the tone and the way she has of swinging her body this way and that as she talks. Through the holes in her dress you can just about see the pink petticoat underneath. Or is it her body? Out of the corner of his eye he can see that, without either of them knowing it, Erica's hand and Julian's hand are playing little games with each other on the cloth. Erica lays hers out, and Julian's comes near it. Erica's moves to her glass and Julian's follows. Erica splays her fingers, and Julian's hand catches the tip of a sharp finger-end before it moves off again, seeming to roam the cloth. Funny, thinks Norman to himself, how people's hands behave.

Does she remember, he wonders to himself, daring a glance at her face, the things he used to bring her? Does she remember those days, and how grateful she used to be when he found something special, like the robin? That's probably why she's so glad to see him again, why she's being so nice. Because she remembers and is grateful for what he did. But what about the things she said, so suddenly, when he could hear? 'You stupid, retarded cretin. You disgusting, smelly spastic with your imbecilic smile.' And that was after he had done the big thing for her, made sure she was safe and would not be taken away like his mother was.

She'd gone, later on, when he went back to Farendon to find her. Unable to bear the pain, wanting to hear something else from her lips before she left, having to hear something else or he felt that his mind would break open. He had tried to follow her. Gone to the station. Tried to buy a ticket, tried to

161

get on any train. Any train that might take him to Erica. They had come onto the platform, reminding him of how it was when he was smaller and huddled there in the station master's office beside the fire, or curled up on the big wire parcel trolley.

Padded people. You could never hear them coming; they wore soft ward shoes, and they held out their hands first, to approach him, as he'd seen them doing on television when they came near to stray dogs. If Norman finds a stray dog, if Norman finds any wounded animal he doesn't do it that way. He walks right up to it, cheerfully, talking all the time, and when he gets there he strokes it and soothes it, loving the fear away. If he can. When he'd been little he'd backed away and done his shouting, 'Fuck you bastard fuck you,' biting and snarling, flailing his fists, knowing that he would be taken back to the cells, bundled in there and left, sometimes without his clothes on, to cuddle into the mattress room and try and bury himself, to find some comfort within the mattress walls.

Metal people. Once a train had come in at the same time as he saw the white uniforms marching down the station steps towards him. Norman had stepped toward the platform edge, had felt the rumble of the monster beneath his feet as it hurtled towards him, its snub nose under the spindly bridge in the distance, trailing behind it all those tons of sparking metal, roaring and glaring with its headlights. Moving the air. Moving the hairs on Norman's head, moving his heart to his throat. They had blown a whistle then and started running. He'd been what – eleven, twelve? Still in his pyjamas. And he'd felt very little, very little and puny compared with all that train, all that noise coming towards him.

Crushing. He'd stood on the edge of the platform and held out his arms, wanting someone to pick him up. And then he'd known they were the same – the train and Underwood. Under either he would be crushed, dragged, bundled, scorched, under either the light would go out behind his eyes for a while or for ever. It didn't matter if he threw himself down on the track or down on the platform in front of the nurses. It was all the same.

Fire. Erica. And now she is here. Back again. Nothing

162

matters. Norman is glad that the little boy he was had stepped back from the train. Trembling, stepped back from the train.

On and on and on go the speeches. After the speeches, Norman might just ask Erica, if he can pluck up the courage, if she wants to come back to the flat – for a drink, for a cup of cocoa. Dennis would make it for her, he would be glad to make it. And Norman would love to show Erica to Dennis.

He has got to pop back quickly to the flat when the speeches have finished, anyway. It won't take him long – ten minutes at the most. Norman has something of Erica's that he has been keeping for her, keeping safe for her all these years, in the safest place he can think of – under his pillow.

At times it wasn't easy. Many times they tried to take it from him, but he never let them. He had the doll with him when he'd gone to the station to find her. Kept it by his side in the fire, and afterwards, when they drugged him. Now is the time to return it. How pleased she will be with him. He knows how fond girls are of their dolls. Jennie had a doll like that but Jennie's was made of blue wool and it had two eyes. He used to make it dance for Jennie then.

Little fingers patting, all cake and milk, and that thin, sharp scream must be his as he slips like ice into uniformed hands and his five-year-old heart burns like a wound. Two big tears roll from his eyes as he cries . . .

Yes, he's going to go and fetch the doll straight after the speeches. He's going to give it to her and ask her if she wants to come and have a mug of cocoa. Julian will come, too. They will have visitors at the flat. Their first proper visitors. Dennis can play his 'Edelweiss', but very softly. Dennis is bound to have some tasty snack hidden under his bed, he usually does. He's taken to watching some cooking programme on TV in the afternoons. Dennis is probably going to be very happy when they reach the pear house. Pottering, cleaning, cooking and playing his music.

Yes, cocoa at the flat with Julian and Erica. Erica might not like the smell, though.

Twenty-Nine

'One of your sons is on the telephone, Mrs Tarrent.'

'What?' Molly has always wanted to be the sort of person called out of dinners, but why oh why did it have to be this one, and now, at such an exciting time? She is sitting next to Julian. Erica is on the other side, but it is Molly at whom Julian glances so intimately from time to time; he smiles with her, knowingly with her, as he passes the salt or pours more wine in her glass.

'Oliver Tarrent. He says it's urgent.'

And Julian has just asked if she would like a liqueur. 'Oh yes, please,' she manages to say as she gets up in a flurry. 'Yes, please, I'd love a crême de cacao. With cream on top. If you can.'

Molly, quite frankly, is drunk. And not just with drink, oh no.

She is led to the telephone by a tall, blonde girl who is in the sixth form and will be leaving next year. She is taking her A-levels next summer. Molly can't concentrate on this, she can hardly answer politely. She has never met a man as attractive as Julian Tenby. She feels passionate about him and they've only just met. And why would anyone be phoning her here? She told the twins she was coming in her last postcard but she never expected . . .

'Oliver? What's the matter?' The phone is in the staff-room. The curtains have not been drawn and outside it is very black. You can just see the outline of the Founder standing out there in the cold, pointing down, eternally reading her book, lit by the front porch-lights. Molly props herself on the arm of a chair, leaning forward with her elbows on the table to handle the phone.

'I thought I ought to phone you. I knew that nobody else would.'

'I'm in the middle of a dinner.' Molly picks at a sequin. Delves deep into purple net and picks at a sequin.

'Well, I didn't know. You should have said you'd call me back.'

'I can never reach you. You know that. You have to phone me.'

'Mum, Rose is very ill.' Her sons never sound like her sons on the phone. They sound like people she's never met. Do they love her, her children, and if so, how – in what way do they love her?

Rose is very ill. The message takes time to get through. Molly reels. Molly is drunk. Worse than that, Molly is intoxicated by Châteauneuf du Pape and Julian Tenby. But the smile on her face is not a drunken smile, it is the smile of the vanquisher, the exultant smile of one who knows many things and holds the secrets of the earth in the palm of her hand. 'So!' She smiles into the darkened window with bared teeth, twists her fingers viciously and the tortured sequin comes off the dress. She presses it carefully down on the table. It sticks to her fingers. She presses it off.

'What?' she asks. She must have this news repeated so she uses a little, light-weight 'What?' with a giggle on the end of it.

'I've just rung Dad and he's in a terrible state. They've taken Rose to hospital. She's been ill for some time but now she's haemorrhaging, badly. They are frightened about the baby. And they are fighting to save Rose's life.'

How really awful, says Molly to herself, chuckling. How really, absolutely terrible. Poor Rose. Hah! But she must conceal her feelings, especially to her sons. Responses come slowly. The first one is, 'Why, Oliver, have you fetched me out of a dinner to tell me this?'

Oliver's silence conveys shock. He starts to stutter, a childhood weakness they paid a lot of money to get corrected. He stops and starts again. 'I thought you might want to get in touch with Dad. He's upset. In need, I would have thought, of a little comfort. I would go home for a while, but I can't.'

'Me – get in touch with Crispin?'

'Well, in the circumstances, yes. And I thought you would want to know. I thought you might be able, by now, to feel sorry. To help in some way, perhaps.'

165

Oliver always was a fool. How he got himself into university Molly can't think. But it's often the way that people with no commonsense have the most intelligence. Perhaps the two don't gel.

'How are you, Oliver?' Molly's words are slurred.

'I'm all right. Are you?'

'Perfectly all right, thank you very much. In fact I am better than I have been in years and years.'

'Perhaps I shouldn't have rung. I think it might have been better if I'd just left it.'

'Why do you say that?' Now her tone, to her son, is sharp.

'Because you don't seem to have taken it in. You don't seem to mind. I rang, Mum, because I thought you would want to contact him, at least to write him a note. Let him know you're thinking of him. He's pretty desperate.' Oliver is hurt. Oliver is confused.

'Is he really?' Molly stifles a hiccup. Presses the hiccup into her hand.

'Well yes, he is. Naturally he is.'

Molly puts down the phone, doesn't even say goodbye. Something is pressing on her chest, grief or joy, it could be either. She runs her eyes over magazines, staff magazines, about children, teaching, education in general. Fuck. She laughs. She laughs. Fat, she wobbles when she laughs. There are flowers arranged in a vase on the table. Someone has tried to make it nice in here, nice and homely and cosy. Fuck. Carefully she puts the phone back on the table and goes to stand at the window. She wobbles to the window on high heels, her shoulders shaking with laughter.

So – success! Rose is ill and in hospital. Does Molly care? Is Molly interested in Crispin any more – was she ever? Wasn't it only revenge she was after?

She wriggles her shoulders, straightens her dress and gazes out into the darkness. Julian Tenby does not have a home. He rents a flat in the city. He works at the Hospital, with people like Norman. How would it be if she persuaded him to come back and share the Priest's House with her in Ashbury? She can see the looks on those feminist faces. 'Have you heard about Molly and her new live-in lover?'

166

'No!'

'I never would have thought she had it in her.'

'You never can tell with people.'

'He's a magnificent-looking man.'

'Well, Molly's not bad herself.'

'I never thought she would get over Crispin.'

'Perhaps she never cared for Crispin at all. Perhaps she was always wanting somebody else.'

'I've heard loud music lately, coming from that house at night.'

'She's a dark horse, Molly, always was.'

'But you have to hand it to her . . .'

'You certainly do . . .'

Molly and Julian. Julian and Molly. How bright are his eyes. How strong are his teeth. How tall and how strong he is. How intelligent and witty and interesting.

And Crispin? Molly breathes in and stares at herself in the window. What would Crispin say if he knew?

She looks at the telephone. Should she ring Crispin? Should she ring and commiserate with Crispin, pass on her very best wishes? Tell him that she understands how frightening it is when someone you love goes away. Molly smiles to herself in the window.

Hah! Poor Rose. Poor, pathetic Rose.

Where has everybody gone? The speeches are finished and now people sit around tables, talking over old times, recalling old memories. Even the sprays of flowers that trail from the walls look gorged with gossip. Too close to each other, suddenly. Gorged with colour, satiated, tired.

Jayne and Dierdre, Harriet, Minnie and Marian are sitting together with empty wine bottles between them. They gesture to Molly with limpid arms. She gestures back but her eyes are not on them. They scan the hall as, tipsily anxious, they search for Julian. Where, oh where, can her prince have gone?

As she goes searching she gets caught in conversations. People she hasn't seen for years pull her in by the arms and they all want something from her. Some sign that she remembers, too. That she remembers and likes them.

167

But Molly doesn't like them. They were not kind to her. She remembers that. They, apparently, after so long, do not. They made her do the dirty work. They had all the fun while she was despatched to carry out their orders, made to do things she didn't want to do.

When they stopped playing games and 'fixed' on people, choosing their victims with care, consulting the voice and 'feeding' the demon, Molly was the one who had to place the symbols. It was she who had pinned the feather to Amy Macey's blazer. She who had left the blood-filled eye-dropper at the local chemist's, wrapped in a bag with a message, '*To be collected*'. It was her voice Amy had heard on the telephone, telling her to go and pick it up.

Erica's orders. To be obeyed or else! Poor Molly. Poor, fat Molly. It was she who had wrapped up the bone and left it on the tennis court, with a map on Amy's pillow telling her where to look. On the pillow next to Amy's spaniel pyjama case with the white, studded collar and the long floppy ears. The pillow of a child.

Erica's orders. It was Molly who, just a few weeks later, had crept into Amy's dormitory, strictly against the rules of course, and pushed the stone right down, far down the bottom of Amy's bed so that her feet would touch it when she got in. And in that bed, between those soft, sleepy sheets she had been able to smell Amy's fear.

And it was Molly, alone of all of them, perhaps, who could understand the repercussions of what she was doing. She was a victim – Amy was a victim – and so her heart bled while she did these things, these terrible, awful things. But all the time a voice was saying to her, 'It's not you, Molly, thank God for that. At least it's not happening to you. But if you don't do them it might be you. There is always a next time. Always another victim.'

And then there was the Crow Biddy. Molly had walked up to Amy, pale, trembling Amy, Amy who hadn't been eating properly for weeks, goody goody Amy without any friends. She had walked a long, long walk all the way up the dormitory corridor. Amy was coming out of the bathroom at the end of the corridor. Amy saw her coming. Watched them come. Amy saw the Crow Biddy. Molly never tried to hide it. She had it, openly, there in her hand. Holding it out in what could have been a hand of friendship. Amy fled then. Having held out her hand to take it like a dancer in a dream. She didn't throw it down, or even refuse to take it. She took it, looked at it, and held it to her face before she fled, along the corridor, up the stairs and out of sight.

Molly never saw Amy after that. Nobody did.

Molly could have dropped the horrible thing and held out her hand instead. She could have. She could have. But she didn't. She was too afraid to do that. Too afraid of Erica and the others and her own weak, watery self. Big, fat, horrible, cowardly, wobbly Molly.

Who goes round wanting to give herself away to someone else.

They are not in the hall, Julian or Erica.

Perhaps Erica's gone to bed. After all, this sort of thing is not really her style. Molly wanders off along the corridors, crosses the quad and goes out the quick way, out through the cold and in the St Mary's House door to have a look.

How easily you can be made to feel just like a little girl again. But she's not a little girl, she's not a frightened, fat child searching for a secret place, her tuck-box in her hand, she is magic and powerful, one of the band, and Rose is ill and dying. Molly has dealt with Rose.

Molly goes in the dormitory she shares with Erica, Jayne and Marian. What a mess. Not at all as it used to be when they lived here. Bedrooms were checked then, every morning, by the frightful 'hydra' who delved with gleeful, rheumaticky hands into drawers and cupboards, into the pathetic little hanging cupboards with the strips of curtain across – as if they would be foolish enough to stash anything in those!

No one there. Molly shivers. The effects of all that drink are wearing off, wearing the magic away and leaving the fuzzy head and the confusion. Molly doesn't want to be the first to bed. She doesn't want it to look as if she's not enjoying herself. She wants to wear her new dress a little longer. And she knows that Julian will be expecting her. He probably thinks she knows where he is, and is waiting there for her to join him.

Out goes Molly, out into the starlit Farendon night. She's missed her liqueur. It sits waiting for her on the table – golden and hot like Erica's eyes – but she can't be bothered with that. It's Julian she's after.

But Julian sits on the grass with his back to the plinth below the Founder, his long legs sprawled out in front of him and Erica beside him on the jacket he has considerately laid out. His head is just inches below the Founder's hand. If Dame Elouise Clough-Ellis leaned forward just a fraction she could smack him on the head with her book and tell him to pull himself together, tell him to stop feeling Erica's breasts right there in front of the sightless eyes. Sacrilege, young man! What on earth do you think you are playing at? With one of my Old Girls, too.

Good heavens above, you've only just met her!

Thirty

Molly sees. Molly sees and passes on, unnoticed, into the darkness.

'Norman! Where are you going? What's that you've got in your hand?'

Norman automatically puts his hand behind his back, but he sees that Molly is no threat. She's not going to make him do anything. She can hardly make herself do anything.

'It's a present,' he tells her breathlessly. 'It's a present I've been keeping for Erica. I'm going to find her now. I'm going to give it to her now.'

They have met in the grounds, ill-met, between clumps of rhododendrons. Norman has taken a short cut to Underwood in order not to be long. Dennis messed him about a bit, told him he ought to wrap it up.

'You can't just plonk a special gift into somebody's hand like that. You've got to put some thought into it, wrap it so it looks nice. Here, use this green tissue paper I've been saving in the kitchen drawer.' Dennis was thrilled that his thrift had paid off. He was not so pleased to be told that the gift was for Erica.

'Oh, that one,' he called her disparagingly, making Norman cross. 'She's back then, is she?'

Norman fidgeted and wriggled while he waited. Dennis always took so long. Everything had to be perfect. And he's slow, so slow. Even turning round seems to take him an age.

Eventually the deed was done, the doll was wrapped and tied with thin green ribbon.

'Doesn't that look better?' Dennis asked him, standing back with his arms crossed.

Norman nodded. 'Yes, it does. Thank you Dennis. She's really going to like this.'

'Well, I wouldn't give it house room,' said Dennis, 'personally I wouldn't. Nasty-looking thing. There's nothing nice about it. Nothing nice at all.'

'You can't tell with girls and dolls,' said Norman looking serious. 'They don't need them to look pretty. And this was Erica's doll in the first place. I've only been looking after it. Now I'm sending it home where it belongs.'

And Dennis sighed like a worried parent as he closed the door behind him.

'I must hurry,' he tells Molly now. 'I must hurry up and find her.'

'Norman.' It is the quietness of the fat woman's voice that stops him, for there is no force behind it. 'Norman, wait a little while.'

'I can't wait. I have to do this, now.'

Molly knows exactly what he means. She had the same feeling this afternoon. She doesn't know what's in his parcel. She only wants to delay him, spare him. She knows very well how Norman feels about Erica. Molly has always known.

'I know that Erica is busy just now. And I also know that you're longing to show somebody what's in that parcel. I am Erica's best friend. Now why don't you wait here with me, just for a little while, and show me what you've got there. I'll know whether she's going to like it or not. I'll be able to tell you.'

It is kindness for Molly that stops Norman. She looks ill. She looks beaten, this fat woman in her fairy dress. He remembers her of old, never quite belonging, as he never had.

'All right,' says Norman reluctantly. 'If you really want to see it. I don't mind showing you.'

Molly backs against a tree trunk; her high-heeled shoes are muddy, she can feel wet bark coming off on her back. She doesn't know what effect Erica and Julian would have on Norman – probably none. No matter. Best to be safe than sorry. Poor bastard, he doesn't deserve any more shit than he's probably got in his life already. Molly is not interested in Norman's parcel, in what he's holding so gently in the palm of his hand, between the folds of green tissue. It is all she can do to lean forward to look. His eyes are shining, he licks his lips. There is a too-wide gap between his teeth. He looks very silly standing there. Don't they both?

Her breath leaves her body with a hiss.

172

'What is it?' Her face, till now slack, empty, comes together. Makes a hard, stern audience for Norman to speak to. 'What is this thing?'

'Just a Jennie doll.'

'I beg your pardon?'

'Just a Jennie doll that Erica left behind her.'

'Where did you find this, Norman?'

Norman isn't going to tell. Norman knows he must say nothing about that, knows what happens to the people he loves when he tells the truth. His lying face crosses his bland one. It is subtly different, only Molly would not notice. Norman's lying face is smoother, emptier, his eyes are night eyes that miss what goes on in the day. Electrocuted eyes.

Molly has to repeat herself. Sounds like Miss Radley. 'Where did you find this, Norman?'

'I've been keeping this for a long, long time,' says Norman, deliberately babyish. 'I've been keeping it for Erica.'

'How long, Norman? How long?' Molly steps forward. She grips Norman hard. She wants to shake the information out.

Norman is not to be hurried. He gets out his fingers. 'Well now, let's see.' He starts to count. Molly's face tenses, her eyes are bright, they glitter like the dew that sits on the grass, wetting Erica, in spite of Julian's jacket, wetting Julian's socks for he has, by now, taken his shoes off. You would think they would find a more secluded place, but they don't care. They're drunk. They're lusting. And they're not the sort of people to care what people think of them. They're not Molly, not Norman.

Norman brings up his head and puts his fingers away. The doll is still in the palm of his hand, sleeping, it seems, in its nest of tissue. 'Twenty-two years,' he tells her with pride. 'I have had it under my pillow for twenty-two years.'

Molly peers down at the one-eyed thing. It looks as if he has. Is it the same one? Is it? And after all this time would she know?

'Can I?' she asks him.

'You can hold it,' he says generously, 'but be careful. It's very precious.'

'Yes,' says Molly. 'Yes, it most certainly is. What were you

173

going to do with it, Norman? Tell me again,' says Molly most carefully.

'I was on my way to find Erica and give it back to her.'

Molly smiles. She smiles and she gives the Crow Biddy back. She sighs and rocks back against her tree. She looks up briefly at the moon, twinkling away there overhead.

'Let me give you some advice now, Norman.'

Norman is all alert. He likes it when people talk to him like this. He knows they are going to say something interesting. He puts his lips together and waits for it, his innocent eyes quite blank. Molly can't hold them.

'I have a much better idea,' she says.

Norman raises his eyebrows. He flicks his hair back from his face and begins to smile. It is good fun to share a plan, to share an idea with somebody else. Especially when it's to do with pleasing Erica.

'Do you remember, Norman, all those years ago, when we used to meet together and dance in the copse? You often watched us when you came in the early mornings. I know you do remember.'

Norman nods. He loves to remember.

'Well, I'll tell you a secret, just as long as you promise to tell no one else.'

Norman nods. 'I promise.'

'Well, tomorrow night some of us are meeting there again. It is going to be another of those magic nights that we had. We are going to be dancing and drinking together in the moonlight. And Erica is going to be there. It is Erica's idea. It is going to be Erica's own very special night. It's the reason why Erica has come back. And do you know something, Norman?'

Norman shakes his head.

'Well I know, without any shadow of a doubt, I know that Erica would appreciate this doll much more, it would be an even more wonderful present, if you could wait until then, if you could come into the copse and give it her then. Not tonight. She's already gone to bed tonight. Now, do you think you could wait and do that?'

Norman sighs. He is very disappointed. When you've been

174

waiting twenty-two years for something it's hard to be
stopped at the end, but he sees Molly's point. And if Erica is
in bed . . . He's hurt by that. He thinks she might have waited
for him. After all, he had told both her and Julian that he
wouldn't be long. He was just popping back to the flat . . .

'Well . . .'

'Good boy, Norman.'

'If you really think . . .'

'Oh I do, I do. I don't just think, I know.'

'And she'll definitely be there?'

'Oh yes, she'll be there?'

'You're sure?'

'I'm sure. Now why don't you take your doll away, back to
your flat, and go home to bed. Everyone else has gone home.
Everyone else is in bed. It's all over. Nothing more going on
tonight. Take it away, why don't you, Norman?'

'But I have to find Julian. He is my responsibility. Julian is
my guest. I can't go home without him.'

Great is Molly's relief when she sees, through the gaps in
the bushes, Julian's figure making its way towards her on its
own.

'Here he is now, and he's probably looking for you. I'll go
back this way. If you call him he'll hear you – you can walk
home together. But don't forget, Norman, don't forget
tomorrow night. And let it be our very own secret.'

'What about Julian? Can't I tell him?'

'I wouldn't,' rushes Molly, eager to be gone. 'You can tell
him about it afterwards, can't you?'

'All right. All right. And thank you for sharing your secret
with me, Molly.'

But Molly is gone.

Molly, in her ball gown, is gone.

Knowing full well how near she came . . . how very near
she is . . . and that the only thing that stops her being Erica
now, is Erica.

Thirty-One

Friday goes by long and slow. November rattles in at the end of it.

Long and slow for Norman, who by now is fired to a frenzy by thoughts of his little raffia offering and the presentation of it; long and slow for Molly who has to pretend she is just the same, when she's not.

Tonight, after dinner, there will be a debate, a sort of mental cricket match between the Old Girls and the present pupils: *'That this House supports the motion that there be separate education of the sexes.'* Some Old Girl called Higgs is proposing and the Head Girl, Kim Bunting, is opposing. Farendon has used this device before and knows it will herald, as it boasts on the programme, *'a lively and interesting evening'*.

Well, Erica isn't going for a start.

During the day there are various, and similar, diversions, and an informal lunch in the Houses. It would be better if the Farendon cooks didn't try for special food. Everyone is secretly yearning for mince and a slab from those huge, burnt jam tarts. But no. For lunch there will be half-empty vol-au-vents, the sludge-grey of chicken and mushroom, followed by fresh fruit salad. Not proper Farendon food at all.

Coffee at eleven and a talk and slides by a group of girls who have just returned from Belgium. Belgium? Bloody hell.

There is a display in the gym this afternoon or a poetry reading session in the library. And at tea-time, not to be outdone, the science department is running a quiz entitled, *'Good evening universe'*, which is to be televised on what everyone gathers is a kind of home-built broadcasting system.

'Christ,' says Erica to Molly, not knowing. 'Nothing changes, does it?'

So the day is long and slow. It meanders, floods every now and again into swampy patches of reminiscence when two or three gather together with cigarettes and gin. They quite like hiding. Listening for Miss Radley. Washing out their glasses surreptitiously in the bathroom and opening the windows to let out the smoke. There is something rather pleasant about being made to sit quietly on hard chairs and pay attention whether they're interested or not. They quite like the feeling of being little girls again.

Molly wonders about Rose. The urge to telephone Crispin is strong, so strong that it itches and she has to wipe it off her hands. But she resists. She smiles frequently. She smiles like Norman. She smiles at Erica. Her hair looks nice, nicer than usual, her face is flushed and her eyes are bright. She must not telephone. She must not doubt her powers, because on Monday at the latest Mrs Tarrent of Little Court, Godalming, hospitalised or not, will receive the Crow Biddy and tonight, to complete the curse, Erica will receive hers. Leaving Molly free to rise like a phoenix and become thin, beautiful, alluring, charismatic – anyone she wants to be.

'What have you been doing with yourself for the last twenty years?' asks Dierdre Bott, dull-eyed after last night's blow out. 'Tell me about yourself, Molly. Did you have children? You always vowed you never would.'

'I got pregnant the first time I did it,' says Molly, not in casual clothes, but in a rose-coloured jersey dress that she thinks would suit Erica. 'That's why we got married. We had to.'

Dierdre muses. 'At least you're on your own now. I'm still stuck with Alistair.'

'Don't you want to be?' Molly is astonished. 'I imagined you were happy in your country home with your horses.'

Dierdre's face is mottled and mournful as the pheasants she hunts, and she dresses in the autumnal colours of game birds. She even smells of bracken. Can you buy it – bracken – bottled? 'I wouldn't know what else to do,' she confesses. 'At least I'm busy. And I do like Alistair. We share the same interests, you see.' Dierdre smokes a cheroot in a cigarette-holder. The whole contraption is very long, and bends at the end so she has to rest a finger under it. Her trigger finger, thinks Molly, staring.

'It's not enough though, is it? We're all disappointed,' says

177

Molly. 'That's why we came back. The ones that didn't come, well I suspect they're all right.'

'Half and half,' says Dierdre heartily, pulling herself together as her nanny taught her. 'At least half of us, then, turned out successfully. But I'm surprised at Erica. You'd think, wouldn't you, that she could cope. That she could command the world if she wanted to. What's she doing coming back here like a dog with its tail between its legs?'

Molly knows what Erica is doing. She has come out of fear, with the rest of them, for a renewal, to bathe in the heady, life-giving waters of the fountain of her own creation before it's too late. Before she's too old and it all runs dry.

During the day Dierdre, Harriet, Moaning, Marian, Jayne, Molly and Erica meet frequently, apart from others of their class, for they are apart. They might be sitting in the library listening, closed-eyed, to Yeats, but their thoughts are not there, the poet's magic is not their magic. It can't give them what they want. They stare at each other covertly, if eyes meet they are lowered. If hands brush they flinch. They talk too quickly and too often. Looked at starkly in the light of day their plans for tonight are disgraceful. The library light is a cruel light, the woodpanelled walls too respectable. They want to talk about tonight but they daren't.

The day moves slow and long for poor Norman, but he has last night's bliss to dwell on and promise of more at midnight. Having a secret upsets him. He loves it but it upsets him. He longs to tell someone, Julian or Dennis, but he's promised so he won't.

Julian asked him about the parcel as they wandered happily home together. Norman was strong. Norman said, 'It's a surprise. I'll tell you tomorrow. Don't ask me any more, I mustn't say anything.'

Julian, his mind on other things, didn't press him. Julian enjoyed the night immensely. You often do when you expect not to. It is his first sortie into sex since Sylvie left and he has enjoyed himself. He didn't think he'd ever find anyone else to attract him: he can put that worry firmly behind him now.

He's not going to live life as a hermit just because Sylvie's upped and gone.

Julian has no idea, absolutely no idea, how Norman feels about Erica. He knows that he liked her, once, but a man like Norman cannot experience the intenser feelings. Hell, he is an innocent man. Unsullied. Julian has no idea, absolutely none, about how Norman feels about him. Oh, he knows he admires him and sometimes tries to copy him. He believes that his charge sees him as a mentor through whom he can find his way out of his prison, his hell-hole life of bars and drugs. That's it, as far as Julian's concerned.

And as for Molly – Who is Molly? Julian would answer if you asked him. Oh, the chatty, rather plump one in the extraordinary dress who sat on my left-hand side? Quite pleasant, a little hysterical perhaps, but a nice enough person to chat with for twenty minutes or so.

'Skip to my lou my golden one, skip to my lou my golden one, skip to my lou my golden one, skip to my lou, my darling.' Norman weeds the front path and keeps an eye out for Erica. He wears his cravat and his bobble hat sticks out of his pocket. When he's pulled the weeds out he gives the path a sprinkle of weedkiller and rakes it over. He takes a break and rests his back against the Founder's plinth. Not quite such a depressing place, this part of the garden, not this morning. He kicks at the couch grass which pokes from the concrete base of the plinth, where the concrete meets the shingle drive. He's often wondered why they bothered with a plinth, why they didn't just put the bronze on the ground so that people could stroll up to it and look Dame Elouise Clough-Ellis straight in the eye. It is the looking up at her that does it, that creates that strange, and to Norman, after his early, quite distressing experience, that rather shocking effect.

He had planted sweet peas – made an inch-wide bed round the base of the square and planted the seeds with his dibber – but Miss Potts had come out and said, 'Appleyard, what do you think you are doing?'

'I thought it would look nicer with a bit of colour round it.

179

The base is an ugly thing, and hard to keep the moss off. A few sweet peas would soften the effect, I thought.'

But Miss Potts had not been pleased. She had risen up, in the way she had, lifting her eyes, her chin, her shoulders, her chest and stomach. The dumpy headmistress had risen up and said to him, 'Certainly not, Appleyard. Sweet peas are quite out of keeping with the Founder's statue. They would not be right, they would not be right at all.'

'But I've put them in now. I've patted them down and trimmed the border. It looks nicer already.'

'Norman, I don't intend to stand here and argue. I want those sweet peas out and that shingle put back exactly as it was. Roses I might tolerate, but sweet peas, no. The statue needs to be stark. That's how it stands out. By being stark.' And back inside she had gone again, leaving a screwed shoe mark on the grass behind her.

Norman had obeyed. Miss Potts was a woman without a soul, not like Miss Blennerhassett. She might approve of sweet peas. She, in her lace dress with all that pink underneath it, she might feel like Norman does about sweet peas.

Norman wonders whether she would or whether she wouldn't as he lifts the jam jar of freesia and sniffs it. It'll do another few days. It is so small, as it sits there on the Founder's plinth, that no one can see it. Never mind. Norman can see it. Norman tends it. Norman knows it's there.

Thirty-Two

They do not go with blankets, naked. Well, look – how can they possibly, at their age? After all, it is November.

The very fact that they go is absurd enough, and the terror is there, that same sweet terror that tastes of school ink, but of Blennerhassett this time, of Radley and Butler and others of their ilk. What would they say they were doing? How ignominiously shameful it would be to be caught.

The daylight gold has turned blue. Just as bright. But starker. Blue. They go along the track behind St Mary's House, single file, in shadow. Shuffling.

'We should have worn trousers,' Moaning turns to whisper. 'Remember? We've got to climb through that old drain.'

Molly doesn't tell her the wall has fallen down. Molly doesn't tell her she's been there.

'We're starting in the Chapel,' Erica says, turning to go that way. 'Like we always used to.'

There's something reassuring in hearing Erica say this. They can remind themselves that this is not the first time, that they are not breaking new ground. They try to remember how they were then to give themselves role models, something to copy. Were they as frightened then, as apprehensive? Did they feel foolish, going out into the night with evil intent? And were their eyes burning?

Dierdre looks as if she's going hunting. She wears a hunting look on her face. And she lifts her hands up naturally to part the leafless branches. She places her feet quietly, with care. Jayne, grey, ghostly, moves twitchily and with fear. She has goose bumps on her arms, she is already cold. Moaning is small and golden-haired, she always said she wanted to be a hairdresser and now she owns a string of them. She has hairdresser's hands, hard and red-knuckled with short nails, although she's never scrubbed a head over a basin in her life.

The hairdressing chain belongs to her husband Francis. Marian and Harriet bring up the rear, together. They were always together like that at school, clutching each other, leaning, hanging. Erica turns to make sure they are following. They remind her of black-headed gulls, beaky and inquisitive, always cawing.

They reach the Chapel and creep inside. The light burns red and steady. Erica marches straight to the front and picks up the candles in their heavy silver sticks. She takes them behind the reredos. She lights the incense she's brought. Jayne makes a circle on the floor. Moaning makes the pentacle. Dierdre lifts the Cross from the altar and balances it, on its end, outside the circle, to the north of the circle, while Molly creaks open the vestry door and fetches the chalice, the clean altar cloths and the surplice.

Remembering, exactly, how it was.

Erica pulls on the white robe, the one the Chaplain wears at Christmas. Its high collar tugs at her hair. She lifts her hair and moves it inside. The collar comes up to a triangle behind her head. She bangs the gavel eleven times.

Effusus labor. Defuncta vita. Fiat nunc voluntas mea.

Dierdre, Molly, Harriet, Marian, Jayne and Minnie hold hands, wet, sticky hands like the hands of children after running. There is a frantic beating in every chest, a difficulty in breathing, their eyes are sharp and their bodies are taut. Taut and waiting. For Erica.

The moonlight streams in through the north window of the Chapel. It casts a pool on the floor within the circle, striking the stone with its light, sparking on an anvil. The red light breaks it as it comes, breaks it and the moonlight bends, taking on a purple shard. Like a spear.

Erica turns. 'Let's see if Amy can tell us what we want to know. Let's see if Amy can tell us about the curse. Who better to ask?' The scar in her eyes cuts sharp. Her face is white, her lips look black when out of them comes the mantra – AMY AMY AMY

They take up the chant.

They are as they were.

Nothing is changed except Molly.

182

*

Norman waits for the correct time. Molly said half an hour after midnight. Molly knows best. Norman will not break his promise. He will not let Molly down. His doll is ready, rewrapped with a tut by Dennis, who says, 'I don't know, I don't know. Think I've got nothing better to do all day than stand here wrapping things for you.'

'You really don't have to, Dennis.'

'No, I will, it's better wrapped. If it's a present it has to be wrapped. Really.' And his tongue comes out between his lips in an extra effort of concentration. Eager to get it just right.

Before midnight Norman brings his Mickey Mouse clock into the little sitting room. He puts it on the driftwood table and sits staring at it. Tick tick tick. He smiles as he remembers his robin friend. He frowns when he thinks how slowly time goes when you wait for it to pass. Norman has always liked to keep his eye on the time. It can so easily be taken away from you. Julian is working tonight. Norman doesn't mind – now he understands that Julian goes out to work, not to meet with other people rather than Norman, Harold and Dennis. It is not from choice that he goes, but from necessity.

Harold is in bed. He goes to bed every night after the ten o'clock news. He likes to hear the weather and the local news at the end. Sometimes he sees places he knows. That is often, for Harold, dangerous. The Cathedral clock-tower, the last point he recognised sometime last week, proved disastrous for him. He wore himself out and went to bed looking grey and punished.

'This is all very peculiar,' says Dennis, testily.

'You don't have to stay up. You can go to bed if you like. I'm quite happy sitting here on my own.'

'I can't understand why you didn't give it to her yesterday like you said you were going to.'

'I can change my mind if I like. I don't have to do what I say. Everyone changes their minds sometime. Even Julian.' Norman resents Dennis's presence. An interfering, rather shrewish presence, Norman thinks to himself. He would rather be alone. He wants to be alone with his thoughts which

183

are pleasant thoughts, full of love. He has lots of memories now and he wants to take them out and polish them. Everything Erica said to him last night, smiling. Everything Julian said. He's thought a lot during the day, but he hasn't finished yet. And he doesn't want to forget them. They are going to have to last him.

Eventually the big hand and the little hand together point to the twelve.

'I must be going,' says Norman, at last. 'I don't want to be late.'

'Well, I just don't know . . .' says Dennis, scratching his frantic hair.

'Don't worry,' says Norman, opening the door and feeling the cold ache his teeth. 'Don't you worry about me, Dennis, that would be silly.'

'What time will you be back?'

'I won't be long, I won't be long. I'm only going to give her this.' And he shakes the parcel crossly at Dennis before he closes the door.

Off goes Norman Appleyard, taking the short cut again, over the bridge, no traffic at this time, and he doesn't pause to watch the Hospital waver in the water. He keeps his eyes ahead of him. The mess in the gutters doesn't worry him – let the council deal with it. When he reaches the Farendon entrance he goes between the saplings, climbs the bank, and heads across the blue-grass, straight to the Chapel, the woods and the copse.

Quiet. So quiet you wouldn't think anyone was out. His footsteps throb in his head. His breath comes quickly. He mustn't hold the parcel too tight because he might crease the paper, but he wants to hold it tight. He wants to feel it and crush it in his hand, because of the pleasure it's going to bring. Pleasure to him. And pleasure to Erica. His will come from the look of love he sees in her orchid eyes. She might even kiss him. She never meant those things she said – he could tell that last night. She must have been upset, over something else. It's easy to say things you don't mean when you're upset. Norman knows that himself.

Down the Chapel path he goes, down deeper into the

woods. He climbs on the pile of Abbey stones to see if *they* are there. Not that he doubts Molly, not that he doubts her for a moment. He doesn't know what he'll do if they're not there. He can't bear to think about that.

Norman needn't worry, for there they are. He smiles. He can see better this time because the wall is down and he doesn't have to climb so high for a view. Also, the moon is out. It is kinder, milkier, than the misted dawn light he used in the past. They dance like blue flames, like blue gas flames, whitely blue and flickering, their arms and their legs, their wild faces and their hair, part of the shadowy firelight. Norman wants to warm his hands. The air carries frost, his ears burn, but down there in the copse is all the warmth Norman needs. He could stand and watch for the rest of his life, stand and watch till he died and Norman would not be cold. He holds out his hands as if to a fire, as if to a train, as if to love.

But my goodness Norman can't just stand there doing nothing, vacant-eyed and stupid. He reminds himself that he has an important job to do. Clutching his offering, he climbs off the stones and walks, like a man in a trance, to the break in the wall. He stands for a while before he's noticed, stands there for what – five, six seconds? Then he holds out the green paper parcel. Clears his throat and says, 'This is for you, Erica. I kept it, specially.'

Stopping the dance is like stopping time; the air is flaccid, impotent. And through the V in the stones they see Norman Appleyard, dressed in a shiny brown suit with a cravat round his stumpy neck. He comes on a wind from the west, he comes from the devil place, and Molly Tarrent smiles.

Erica's hair is wet. It sticks to her face in sworls. Her eyes are quite blank, unlike Norman's. Her face has marks like bruises on it, marks that follow and highlight the bones. A bruised, abused child in a charity advertisement. There are gems on the white of her robe, like the gems on the collar of Amy Macey's pyjama case spaniel.

'What?'

No one else speaks. The spell has been broken. They have drunk far too much and are out in the cold, freezing where the sweat sticks, where it runs down their backs and their arms. Their feet are bare, wet and bare, and they realise they stand on mould. The smell of decay is noxious. It smells like the old woman's voice – sinister, rotten and of time long gone. The time has gone. It has all gone. There is no elixir. One day they, too, will be earth, and ivy will claw a roof over their bones.

'*What?*' Flames come back into Erica's eyes.

Norman steps forward. 'This. For you.'

Erica throws back her head and laughs. 'Take it away, Norman. Go away, Norman.' And then she screams, 'Go away, Norman!'

Molly thinks her voice sounds fat and squeaky. It doesn't. It is surprisingly soft and smooth. She is giving the Crow Biddy to Amy again, destroying someone again. She doesn't care. 'See what he's got for you, Erica. It's something very special, isn't it, Norman?'

Norman nods, feels uneasy, not ready for this.

Erica's feet make no sound as she steps forward. The others fall back to let her pass. She takes the parcel from Norman's hand. The moon on the green turns the paper red. Blood red. She unwraps the parcel, tugging at the string. Norman steps forwards, says, 'Be careful,' as he thinks of the care with which Dennis wrapped it, but Erica hisses at him between tight teeth.

Erica brings out the Crow Biddy and holds it high. Harriet cries out. Moaning weeps. Marian hides her face in her hands. Jayne Cromwell stands very still. Still like the stone she stands on. And Molly, she smiles.

Erica smiles, too. At Norman. She steps forward once more. She holds out her arms and her sleeves touch the ground between them. Her eyes scorch like burnt earth. Norman goes towards her. She kisses him, softly on each cheek with cold, cold lips, and he can feel her eyelashes as she moves back. In a stream of cold the words come: 'Cretin, idiot man, what is this? What is this? Is it revenge? Were you watching us then, last night, when I shagged your special man? What is he to you, Norman? What is Julian? Your lover? Your *amour*? Are you in love again, Norman, with the man that I had last night? He touched me, Norman – my breasts, my thighs, my hair, he stroked me all over my body with his long cool fingers and his magic hands. His fingers, Norman, magic fingers, went *everywhere, right inside me, Norman, everywhere.* Fool! Imbecile! Idiot!' Erica's laugh is cold and tight as hoar frost on a fern.

'It wasn't my idea.' Norman steps back. 'It was Molly's! It was hers! She told me to come here and give it to you tonight. I wanted to give it to you last night but she said no, she said she had a better idea. She told me to come. I wouldn't have, I didn't know, how could I have known . . .'

'Get out of here.'

And Norman, stumbling, broken, goes.

Silence. Terrible silence.

Into it Molly laughs. The sound comes barking from a parched throat.

'And so . . .' Erica turns to face her. She smiles, a warm, endearing smile for which you could forgive her anything. But her voice crackles hoarsely, an old woman's voice, softly savage, when she says, 'And so you thought that by doing this you would make the curse complete!'

'Yes.' Molly laughs again. A fat, foolish laugh. 'I knew I would! Yes, yes. You can do nothing now, Erica. You have the Crow Biddy. It is done! You are dead and I am free. I am the one . . . the one I should always have been! And there is nothing – nothing more that you can do!'

But Erica's smile follows Molly as she goes, back up the track, cold to the heart, back past the Chapel to an uncertain safety.

Thirty-Three

'I knew it, I knew it,' says Dennis. 'What have I been saying all along?' But no one knew what he had been saying because he hadn't told anyone.

It was Molly who, unable to stand the weight or the sleeplessness of it, eventually came to tell them. Bravely and determinedly made her way into the bleak dawn of Underwood Hospital, asked at reception and was told by a sleepy watchman where to go.

Immediately Harold and Dennis set out, Harold fearful, terrified of the dark, yet determined to go and find Julian. They searched Bushy Grove for number twenty-nine, had to keep ringing to get someone up. Julian finally came to the door in a silk dressing gown – his last birthday present from Sylvie – and leather slippers.

Alarmed, he listened to their story while he dressed. He listened to Dennis's story, which told him much that he didn't know, much that he hadn't understood. Much that made him ashamed. But not all.

'Where?' he shouted, enraged, beside himself. 'Where shall we look?'

'I know where he'll be,' said Harold dully.

'Where?' Julian's eyes opened wide. He stood before Harold with outstretched arms, imploring. 'If you know where he is, why are we still here?'

So he followed them. The first of the morning traffic was just starting, touching the air with puffs of cloudy-white exhaust. They took him back to the Hospital, but not to the flat. They marched through the Hospital entrance where the night porter was just handing over.

'No visiting yet,' the new man groaned, already bored.

'We're not visiting,' said Julian grimly. 'We're here on official business.'

'Please yourself,' came the muttered reply, as he picked up a full flask and unfolded the morning paper.

Julian followed them through the still-unfamiliar corridors, along the pipe-ways and up the steps. The Hospital was full of Dettoled sleep. It settled on it like a shroud; the lights seemed uncertain, pale lights, night-lights, about to make way for the bright ones, the lights that missed nothing.

A few nurses passed them. Alarmingly chirpy at this late hour, they all carried shoulder bags, all wore cloaks, and their voices were corridor voices, tinkling cold. Julian's anxiety clutched him like a corset, he hadn't the will to hurry. He creaked under it and his limbs hurt. He couldn't expand his lungs enough to breathe properly. He didn't want to arrive. He didn't want Dennis or Harold to see what he'd done.

Through the night-tube that was the approach to Pitt . . . just like the Underground without the posters. Posters would have helped, so would the sounds of trains. Any sound. Any shushing sound to take away the awful, grim silence of the place. All Julian could hear was the steaming pipes and a distant sound of metal trays.

'Will you trust me?' Julian asks them. 'Please, just one more time?'

Dennis nods and Harold pulls his lip. Neither wants to leave.

'Please, will you leave me with him?'

They slouch unhappily off, glances of accusation slung over their shoulders. Julian watches them turn the far corridor, under the EXIT arrow, following the blue painted line. Even when they are very small and far away he can hear them. The circular ceiling causes that baggy sound.

Norman is kneeling facing the door. Slumped pleading at the door. His raw hands cling to it. His head hangs down. Julian sits on the floor beside him, his arm on his back, saying nothing. Nothing at all. They sit and they wait. A man passes by on his way to nowhere. He never even glances down. He wears new slippers with bright orange tongues. His slippers take him and he follows.

Suddenly the gingham curtains shake, the ward door opens fiercely, and laughter, like a jack-in-the box, bursts out.

'What's this?' says a uniform that looks like Nurse MacNelly, but it isn't her. Another one is beside her. There are keys at their waists. Julian doesn't answer. Just sits and doesn't answer. Neither does Norman.

'Norman!' There is great surprise in the exclamation. 'What on earth are you doing here?' But she doesn't look at Norman, she looks into the face of her companion.

Who bends down to look at Norman kneeling there with nothing to hang on to now the door is open. But he still holds out his arms. Seeking something.

'Aren't we being a silly billy this morning? What on earth are we doing here on the floor at this hour?' And the Nurse thrusts a finger under Norman's chin. 'Anyone would think he was eager to get back.' She looks at Julian. 'Do you work here? Do I know you? Are you with him?'

'Which of those questions should I answer first?' Julian hasn't shaved. His chin is stubbly and he brings his hand down it and towards his mouth, tiredly towards his mouth.

Immediately the Nurse's eyes look shrewd. 'Are you with him?'

'Yes, I am with him.'

'Well, what is he doing here, out at this hour? It's six o'clock in the morning. He shouldn't be out.'

'We're just waiting here, having a rest. We're on our way home.'

'Home?' Then she smiles understanding. 'Oh, back to the path lab.' She puts back her head and her starched bonnet bobs. 'Well, I don't think it's a very good idea to keep him out this late – this early, should I say.' She laughs. 'He needs his sleep, does our Norman. Don't you, Norman? You like your sleep?' She shouts with a big wide mouth when she bends to talk to Norman.

Julian breathes out. He breathes out three times. He tries to ease the knot from his shoulders. It won't go.

'My goodness,' says the second Nurse, locking the ward door behind her. 'Out on the tiles! Whatever next? I don't know.'

Julian sits back on the floor to watch the nurses walk away. They, too, follow the arrow. They make for the EXIT sign. It flashes a dull red, away there in the distance. Down the tube. In the distance. To where the trains ought to be.

They are so long there together that they breathe together. A smell of greasy bacon comes up from what must be the ground. There is little sensation, here, of high, of low, of right or of left. They are in the middle of something. They are in the heart of the monster.

Time, slow and silent, time passes.

'Will you lend me your jacket?'

Surprised, Julian takes it off. 'Are you cold?'

'No, I just want to put it over my head.'

'Ah! I feel as if I would like to do that. I didn't know, Norman. If I knew how much you loved Erica then I would not have made love to her.'

More time goes but they don't speak. Norman might even be asleep because he is very still. This is going to take a very long time for Norman to say. Eventually he tries it . . .

'I tried to feed her,' says Norman, muffled, from under the jacket.

'Who?' Julian is weary. He sounds weary. Sensing something . . .

'She wouldn't eat it. I brought her cake and milk. I tried to put it in her mouth but she just didn't want it.'

Now there is a longer pause while Julian, so clever at thinking, thinks. What, actually, is Norman talking about here? Julian evades the issue, still playing his games. 'People don't always want what you give them. Often, sometimes, you are trying to give them the wrong thing.'

'She was in the cage on the roof and I found her there, holding her Jennie doll. She was there for seven days. She wouldn't eat. She couldn't get out. She was too small and the trapdoor stuck shut behind her.'

'What trapdoor?'

'It was the old fire escape before they blocked it up and changed it. They should have blocked off the trapdoor, but

191

they didn't. She must have found it. They put up the cage to stop people falling off.'

They breathe together. Julian tries to speak. Julian tries to understand what he hears. He doesn't want to hear or believe but he has to. 'Couldn't you have told somebody where Amy was, Norman? They might have been able to get her down.'

Silence. No answer. Just the jacket moves. So Julian knows that Norman has heard him. Julian doesn't press for an answer. He waits, humbled, on the floor. His head sags on his chest. An expert at life, but hell, what does he know of it? What does anyone, really, know of it? Norman says, 'When I told the men that Jennie was dead they took me away. They took *her* away. They told me she was never coming back. That she couldn't look after children. It wouldn't be right to let her. They said *she* let Jennie die.'

'And did your mother do that? Did she let Jennie die?' Julian has to whisper. He doesn't have a voice.

Norman moves just a little, once more, underneath the jacket. 'It's hard to remember. I've tried to think so hard about it. We were all the time in the play-pen. Only *she* didn't like feeding Jennie. She used to hit her. She never hit me. Only when she found me climbing out to get food from the kitchen for Jennie. Then she used to hit me. She used to scream, "I can't . . . for the love of bloody Christ I can't I just can't cope".'

Little fingers patting, all cake and milk, and that thin, sharp scream must be his as he slips like ice into uniformed hands and his five-year-old heart burns like a wound. Two big tears roll from his eyes as he cries . . . But Jennie is already dead because they say . . .

' "Sweet Jesus. This one's been dead a week and the other's nearly had it", that's what they said,' says Norman. 'I didn't tell anyone. I didn't know what they'd do to me if I told them. And I didn't want anyone blamed for it, punished and taken away.'

Julian nods. Limply. Hopelessly.

'I didn't want Erica taken away,' says Norman. 'I wanted to give her the doll, to show her that she was safe.'

'It was Erica's doll then, was it? She gave the doll to Amy?'

192

'They all did. They all gave Amy the doll.'

Julian straightens himself. Outside. He cannot straighten the in. He will never be able to straighten that now. Norman has mixed them together – the play-pen and the cage. Amy with Jennie.

'Where did you put her, Norman? You must have carried her down.'

'In a waste bag with the leaves,' he says. 'Out through the front door. It's the only way to get those leaves out. It's the only way that's wide enough.'

'Will you show me?'

Later, after walking and talking, in the light of morning Julian looks at the vase of freesia. He looks up into the Founder's dead eyes. He puts his hand on the cold stone plinth, hollow inside, says Norman, who knows.

'Let's go home,' says Julian, kicking the leaves. 'Do you want to hold my hand?'

'No,' says Norman, looking up, awareness, intelligence waiting there frightened, behind his eyes. 'No, that's silly. People, men like us, don't do that.'

So Julian smiles. His work will take him a lifetime to do. And that's okay. That's just fine.

Thirty-Four

Inevitable. Sadly, it is all so inevitable. Molly is a fool. She puts herself at risk. Molly has lost herself but Norman was always there, only pretending he wasn't.

Molly is a fool. She should never have given Erica a key, she should never have taken her in, she should never have thought she could outdo Erica, but her fatal mistake, her really fatal mistake was to show Erica her soul.

There is a black-rimmed card on the *Welcome Home* mat. The white within the border looks very white indeed. It shines down there on the mat as if it is made of plastic. Rose Tarrent is dead. Crispin's Rose, Molly's Rose, is dead.

Molly will be pleased. Molly will be thrilled.

Erica picks it up and looks at it, taps it with a scarlet nail as she crosses to the window. Now she thinks what a quaint idea it is to draw the curtains when you go away. The card looks right in here, as if it should be propped beside a body, in a coffin, on a trestle making wheel-marks on Molly's carpet. She draws them back, sheeny, chintzy curtains on a string above the windows, so that the morning comes in and settles upon that hopeless rug. But it is always dark in here without the lights on, here in the Priest's House behind the Black Death door.

Erica is first home. Not to stay, but to pick up her things and leave this dismal place as fast as she possibly can. Molly has to spend another whole day at Farendon, has to wait for the Monday evening train. Most of the others decided to leave after that Friday night. Well, how could they stay? How could they stay and face each other after that? It was embarrassing. But Molly stayed. She stayed in bed the whole time, talking to no one, seeing nothing, a woman in a trance with a stupid smile on her face. Erica stayed. Erica stayed for the laugh. Erica offered Molly a lift under one of those endearing smiles. 'Come on, no hard feelings. These things happen, we all get carried away sometimes,' but Molly turned it down. Molly waved Erica off, unseen, behind the curtains, believing that she would never arrive, believing the Crow Biddy would do her work on the hurtling black tarmac between the services. Molly wouldn't risk a journey with Erica. Not now. She's terrified of her.

Erica has driven down the motorway at one hundred and twenty miles an hour with her loud music blaring, laughing. For Erica is safe as she will always be safe. No one-eyed raffia doll can touch Erica, who hasn't been sent the feather, the blood, the bone or the stone. Molly is a fool. She always was. A fool and a natural victim. She should not have believed Erica.

If Erica gives a thought to Norman it is a fleeting one and it is this – that the creepy cretin had clearly picked up the Crow Biddy all those years ago, the Crow Biddy dropped by Amy Macey on her way to annihilation. Too imbecilic to show it to the police, he picked it up somewhere in the grounds and kept it, thinking that Erica wanted it back. God! And this is the conclusion of all of them. It is not important now. It never was.

Erica moves like a leopard. She can't help it. She doesn't know she moves like that but she does. She places the card on the hall table so it will be the first thing Molly sees when she gets home. It glints against the walnut like the white of a dark-brown eye. She moves up the quaint little stairs, goes to her room and looks out at the view of the dismal duckpond. Rain makes pools on the surface but the ducks love it. They shine in rain, it is their element. As moonlight is Erica's.

But it didn't work. It was interesting, it broke the boredom for a little while but was it worth it? Erica is going to have to search for something else now, something else to charge her brain and fire her emotions. Molly is luckier than she is in this – Molly is constantly charged. No wonder she has been able to withstand this grubby wellington-booted life in the stagnant waters of Ashbury. Nothing really touches Molly. She isn't here. She's never been here. She's rushing the waves with Crispin, banking and whirling on hot streams of yearning . . . yearning for what she can never have in her silly make-believe world. But Molly has given Erica the key . . .

Poor Molly. Erica boldly goes into Molly's room. There by the bed is a picture of Crispin in a silver frame, a cherished picture, much handled. Much handled and wept over, probably, fondled and kissed. Nice . . . sexy . . . a cruel mouth, you might call it. His gold tooth shines just where his smile begins and his hair is crinkly black to the shape of his head. His eyes have power behind them. Steel blue power, it jets from the picture, looks on the room with a cynical air. Looked back at Molly, Erica thinks, stared back at her and her yearning with a fascinated, cynical air. Poor Molly. Erica sits and coolly regards the only thing in the world that Molly really wants. The only thing she's ever wanted.

Erica is in here now, she'll take a look. She goes to Molly's wardrobe and opens the drawers. She finds the purple envelopes. She frowns. She looks further – under Molly's shoes she finds the crumpled sheets of paper, page one headed, 'Jesus'.

Molly's writing has not improved. No wonder Miss Butler stabbed at it. *'Jesus/Crispin/Jesus. If I could not love you I could not live. You are my life, my soul, through you I have my being . . .'*

Erica can't stand it. She skips a page, but it goes on in the same vein . . . *'I chase you through the wilderness places of my heart, the wild, bleak places where only you can strike the rock and work the miracle, change sour water into wine . . .'* Ugh. Erica reads on, embarrassed to be doing so. She feels for the writing group, that they had to sit and listen to this garbage, week after week after week . . .

'I knelt before you then and I kneel now, in worship, and in my dreams we come together, fragile like the gossamer threads of a broken cobweb . . .' Erica screws the paper up again, wincing. Good God, how can Molly expose herself like this?

Writing . . . writing – *that* handwriting. The writing of the name *Mrs Tarrent* on the envelopes that came back.

Erica sits on the end of Molly's bed. Soft, squidgy mattress, soft, squidgy Molly. So predictable. Erica understands, now, about the re-direction labels. About the London postmark and Molly's oddly regular excursions to Exeter. Molly has been sending things to Rose. Rose has been sending them back. Each action motivated by malice, for Rose's thoughts could not have been kind ones. There. It is enough.

Except that Rose is dead. Molly has certainly sent the Crow Biddy, but the Crow Biddy will not return to Molly. Crispin is unlikely to re-direct the post, as Rose did. Especially in the sad circumstances in which he now finds himself. Alone. Lonely? Aching for comfort. No, muses Erica, the Crow Biddy will never be sent back to Molly unless . . . unless . . .

A most fascinating man . . . As she stares at the photograph the sides of his mouth seem to move. Most appealingly.

Erica's face is set. Molly must learn the hard way. Molly must learn in the only way there is left to teach her.

Erica sees exactly how it will be. For Erica is powerful and can make anything happen. Next week Molly, home again and making her jams, will open a parcel, her eyes wet bright as she sees the postmark. All that hope in her eyes . . . hah! Brown paper round a pretty, pretty box, a presentation box with red flowers on it and maybe green tissue inside. Oh yes, Erica will make it nice. She always likes to do things nicely, kindly if she can. Molly might be singing, she might be singing by the sink when the postman rings the bell, happy because Rose is dead, happy because she expects to hear from Crispin, happy because she expects to hear, any day now, that she has inherited Erica's power and is not under her spell any longer!

Ah, but this won't just be a letter from Crispin, oh no, much more than a letter – a parcel, with something tiny and hard inside. Just two fingers high and a bead for an eye.

Erica's smile is deep and soft (Molly has always wished she had a mouth like that) – an endearing smile for which you could forgive her anything. Almost anything.

Poor Crispin, it's time he had a real woman and stopped messing about with tarty little pieces like Rose and great big softies like Molly! Erica moves to the telephone. She sits on Molly's bed, slides up the eiderdown and stares into the eyes of a photograph as she dials.

And Erica has the knack of doing this sort of thing very nicely. She has the perfect touch.